TROPICAL SNOW

A LENNY AND LUCAS ADVENTURE
BOOK 1

AJ STEWART

JACARANDA *Drive*

Jacaranda Drive Publishing

Los Angeles, California

www.jacarandadrive.com

Cover artwork by David Berens

ISBN-13: 978-1-945741-69-2

*To all those—young and old—seeking their next adventure.
Today is the day.*

And Heather, always.

CHAPTER ONE

SEPT. 6, 1983 UPDATED 6:43 A.M. EDST

NEW YORK (INTERNATIONAL PRESS AGENCY)—DRUG smugglers have paid bribes totaling millions of dollars to facilitate the smuggling of cocaine into the Unites States, according to an NBC News report by Brian Ross that aired Sept. 5. *The Bahamas: A Nation for Sale* alleged that bribes were paid to officials at all levels of the Bahamian government, including the prime minister, Sir Lynden O. Pindling.

It also claimed that Carlos Lehder, a founder of the Colombian-based Medellín cartel, made payments in exchange for using the Bahamas as a transshipment point for moving narcotics from Colombia to the United States.

Through a campaign of coercion and murder, Lehder had gained full control of the Bahamian island of Norman's Cay, including its private airstrip, which he used as both his residence and a logistics hub for the transport of narcotics under alleged protection of Bahamian law enforcement.

A spokesman for the White House said President Ronald

Reagan was aware of the report and that "the war on drugs is an ongoing priority of my administration." He also said dialogue with Bahamian officials would continue.

Carlos Lehder and other senior members of the Medellín cartel remain at large.

CHAPTER TWO

WASHINGTON, D.C.

Skipper Tomlinson shared a look with his boss as they strode out of the Oval Office. Tomlinson had said nothing during the meeting; he wasn't there to offer opinions. More often than not, he wasn't there at all. The normal information flow went from the president to his chief of staff, James Baker, then to Baker's deputy, and then onto Tomlinson. In fact, his information was usually third hand.

But today was different.

Today POTUS wanted everyone's ear. He was on a rant, as worked up as Tomlinson had ever seen him. Normally POTUS possessed a measured calm, more prone to smile than to scowl, despite the demands on the job. President Reagan knew the value of winning people over and had the charm to do it. But today he had a bug up his butt about one thing.

Drugs.

Well, drugs and the prime minister of the Bahamas. The NBC report from the previous evening had pointed the finger at the Bahamian government for taking bribes from the Colombian cartels to facilitate the onward passage of massive quantities of drugs into the United States. This was not news, at least not inside the West Wing. It was President Nixon who had coined the phrase *war on drugs*, and it had been a minor focus of the White House ever since. It was a poorly held secret that Bahamian officials had been on the take.

But now it was on every television in America, and in every morning newspaper. The drugs kept coming, and America's friends in the Caribbean were outed as helping move them through.

"James is clear on this," said Michael Deaver, deputy chief of staff. "POTUS needs to be focused on domestic issues. That's what's going to win the next election. The Cold War is enough foreign policy for us to handle. This is a distraction."

"Yes, sir."

"But it's on the front page of the *Post* and the *Times*."

"Yes, sir."

They walked into Deaver's office, and Tomlinson closed the door.

"Thoughts?" asked Deaver.

"We need to get the president's mind off it."

"That's my point. How?"

"Get him a win."

"What kind of a win?"

"There are two kinds, sir: one for public consumption and one that's not. I think maybe we need one of each."

"This is your area, Skip, not mine."

"Let me make a call, and I'll circle back around."

"Do it."

———

THAT NIGHT SKIPPER TOMLINSON DROVE OUT OF THE district and into Virginia on Interstate 395 until he reached the

Springfield Interchange, where he headed west onto the beltway before pulling off at North Springfield. He parked outside the sports bar, loosened his tie, and wandered inside.

The bar was pretty full for a weekday. The crowd was mixed— enough suits to make Tomlinson fit in but more denim jackets and dirty jeans. Most patrons were glued to a taped replay of the Colts-Broncos game on a large, rear-projection television. Tomlinson eyed the space and found his contact at a tucked-away table near the back of the room.

"Not interested in football?" he asked as he sat.

"Baltimore stinks," said the man in the brown leather jacket.

"Maybe Elway was right not to come."

"Of course he was right. Even if he did get dragged from this game. DeBerg saved his bacon."

A server stopped by, and Skipper ordered a beer.

"So what's up?" asked the contact.

"You see that thing on NBC?" asked Tomlinson.

"Old news."

"Maybe to you and me. Not to the public."

"Let me guess, you've got a PR issue."

"That, and a little more. The boss is taking it personally. It's distracting him. Baker wants him focused."

"Baker's days are numbered."

"I know there are factions in the party that want him out, but Reagan likes him. He trusts him."

"I heard he wanted to head up the NSA."

"Not happening. He used to be a Democrat. No way Reagan puts a former Dem in the NSA."

"Also heard he was looking at the commissioner of the NBA job."

"More likely, but no. Look, Baker's a domestic policy guy. He thinks when people vote next year they won't care about drug cartels or even the Soviets. They'll care about the economy, about having a job."

"Probably right."

The server dropped off the beer, but Tomlinson didn't pick it up. "It is right. So we need POTUS focused on that."

"Fair enough. So why are you talking to me?"

"We need a win."

"On the drugs thing?"

"Yes. Something for the PR wonks and something for the boss."

"I take it those two things aren't the same."

"Not today. The boss is feeling personally betrayed on this one, and he's ready to crack skulls. But the public doesn't care about the politics. They want to see that he's doing something about the drugs. Now, we've got law enforcement to take care of the PR side. Some big hauls and people will forget about it all soon enough."

"But your boss..."

"He's your boss too."

"I don't pay a lot of attention to the color of the head cheese's tie."

"Still."

"Still. You want something that you can point to and say, 'We did that,' but at the same time no one else can say that we did it."

"Something like that."

The contact sipped his beer.

Tomlinson still didn't touch his. "We have to do the diplomatic dance with the Bahamians and whoever else, so we can't go in all gung-ho."

"The CIA have people for this, you know."

"Of course I know. The veep was all over that. He's pimping the CIA for the job. It's like he's got them on speed dial."

"He does—he ran the damn place, remember?"

"Hard to forget," said Tomlinson. "But there's a feeling in parts of the administration that the CIA might be as much a part of the problem as the solution, so we're looking at other options."

"A win, not CIA, not public. You want small, fast, invisible."

"In a nutshell. The DEA can get the public wins, but this is something else. This is under-the-radar mayhem."

"If it's under-the-radar mayhem you want, then yeah, I know just the guy."

Tomlinson pushed his chair back and stood. "Let me know."

"You didn't touch your beer."

"Not thirsty."

The contact pulled the beer over to his side of the table. Tomlinson walked out of the bar without looking at the television. He didn't need to.

The Baltimore Colts stunk.

CHAPTER THREE

LENNY COX WAITED BY THE BUS STOP. HE HAD BEEN stationed on a good number of bases during his time, but Marine Corps Base Quantico was not one of his favorites. It was JAFB—Just Another F'ing Base—but its proximity to the capital gave it a bigwig-to-grunt ratio that was too high. He liked Lejeune well enough—Jacksonville was a neat little town on the New River and the locale lent itself to getting away from humanity and out into the wilderness or onto the water—and he missed the waves out near Pendleton.

But there was one benefit of Quantico's proximity to DC.

The bus arrived, and he stood aside as a kid stepped up into it, bopping to the beat of his Walkman. Lenny offered the driver a shrug and dropped his money in the slot, then he found a seat and watched the little town disappear.

The town of Quantico had the distinction of being the only town completely surrounded by a Marine Corps base, although Lenny noted that it was technically hemmed in by the Potomac River and Quantico Creek on either side. To reach it, the bus had to pass through the main gates of the base. It pulled away in that direction, heading for the capital.

Lenny did what he always did when he wasn't driving: he slept. A Marine always needed more sleep. The bus gave a hydraulic hiss when it reached the end station in Rosslyn, and Lenny opened his eyes. He stepped off and started walking. He had time to kill, and the afternoon was fine.

He ambled across the Key Bridge into the District of Columbia, then into the streets of Georgetown. He stopped off at a newsstand to check a Rand McNally map of the city then continued on his way.

It was nearing six when he reached the apartment a handful of streets east of the university. The brick building had a slight bow to it, testimony to its age in the part of town that predated the capital. It had clearly been a single residence years ago.

Lenny hit the buzzer and waited.

"Hello?" said a voice.

"Sergeant Cox, reporting for duty, ma'am."

There was no reply, but the door buzzed. Lenny let himself in and climbed the stairs to the second floor. The door to the apartment opened before he could knock, and a woman leaned against the jamb and looked him over.

"Sergeant," she said.

"Miss Brooks."

"You cut your hair," she said, tucking a loose blond strand of her own hair behind an ear.

"I'm back in uniform."

"I liked the other way better."

"I'll mention it to the commandant."

"Do." She invited him across the threshold with a wiggle of her finger but didn't move out of the way, instead planting a kiss on his lips.

"It's been a while, Marine."

"Yes, ma'am."

"Come in."

Finally she stepped aside. He walked in, and she closed the door behind him.

"Nice place, Ally," he said.

"You haven't been here before, have you?"

"You're not usually in DC."

"You either."

"Serendipity."

"Or fate."

"I'm okay either way."

"Me too. I just got home. You want a drink?" She took off a blazer with shoulder pads like a linebacker and hung it on a hat rack.

"A drink would be good."

She poured two glasses of scotch. "How's Quantico?"

"Fun and games."

"What have you been doing since Thailand?"

"Training. Hence Quantico."

"No deployments?"

"Nup. How about you?"

"As I told you on the phone, I was in Europe for a month but now back here."

"For good?"

"At the attorney general's pleasure."

They clinked glasses and sipped the single malt.

"I'm going to slip into something that doesn't scream *work*," Alice said to her white blouse and pearls.

"You want some help with that?"

"Easy, tiger. Let's get some dinner first."

———

ALICE HAD MADE RESERVATIONS AT AN ITALIAN PLACE on M Street. They ate pasta, drank Chianti, and had a superficial chat about what they had been doing since the last time they met.

"So what's your job in DC, then?" he asked, and took a sip of wine.

"Same, really. I'm there to advise on the legality of US foreign policy implementation."

"You mean, how they use people like me."

"Up to and including, yes."

"Doesn't the Corps have their own lawyers?"

"They do, but their job is to advise the Marine Corps. My job, through the AG, is to advise the president."

"You'd think those two things were one and the same."

She smiled. "You'd like to think so, but..."

He observed her easy smile. She was a good five years older than him but looked like she was hitting her prime—her vitality shone through her otherwise serious demeanor. At twenty-three, he already felt an ache in every joint.

After dinner they strolled for a while in the cool night. He offered her his tan leather jacket, then she took his hand. Hers felt soft, and small to him despite her being only an inch less than his five ten.

Lenny knew they had walked west along the river and then cut through the college to the north, but he was surprised when they arrived back at her apartment building.

"You look confused, Sergeant."

"I guess I got turned around."

"I thought you had an innate sense of direction."

"I was distracted."

He leaned in and kissed her, then she unlocked the building door and led him in by the hand. She was on the stairs to the second floor when he tugged her to a stop.

"What's up?" she asked.

Lenny nodded at the first-floor apartment. "You know your neighbor here?"

"Sure. Melodie. She works for an environmental lobbyist. Why?"

"Does she normally leave her door open?"

Alice stepped down and examined the door that was slightly ajar. "Maybe she forgot to close it."

"She single?"

"Yes, I think so. Dating maybe."

"You ever forget to close your door when you get home?"

"Maybe she was going out and was distracted. Like you."

Lenny pushed the door open with his boot. The place was dark, except for dull lamplight near the window at the other end of the apartment.

"Call her name," he said.

Alice moved into the doorway. "Melodie? It's Alice." She glanced at Lenny then back inside. "Hey, Mel? It's me, Alice. You home?"

There was no answer.

"Like I said, she went out and forgot to lock the door."

"She didn't forget to lock it, she forgot to close it. That's a whole other level of forgetting."

"You can't go in," Alice said as he began to step inside.

"It's not a B and E, Alice."

"You're not the police, Len."

"I know that. But let's make sure there's no reason to call them."

Lenny walked through the short hallway and into the living room. He stepped past an efficiency kitchen that opened up to a round dining table, and a living room with a sofa facing a portable television on a cart.

"No one's home," said Alice, placing her hand against his back.

"No." But he went to make sure. He pushed the bathroom door open with his foot and found it empty. He continued to the bedroom door. It too was ajar, but the room was dark.

"Okay, can we go now?" asked Alice. "I feel like we're intruding on her privacy."

Lenny didn't speak. Instead, he used his knuckle to flick the light on.

The woman was sprawled out on the bed in business attire not dissimilar from Alice's, only her blouse was blue and there were no pearls. Her red hair was splayed across the pillows and her arms were stretched out like she was making a snow angel.

"Is she asleep?" Alice asked, but her tone suggested she knew otherwise.

Lenny knew for sure. He saw the white powder cut on the bedside table and swept around the bed to put his finger on her pulse.

"Lenny?"

"Nothing. Call the paramedics."

Alice ran from the room as Lenny checked Melodie's airway. He began CPR, pushing hard against her chest, unconcerned about breaking bones. That was the least of her worries.

Alice called from the living room: "They're asking what the substance is."

"Cocaine," shouted Lenny, continuing his work.

"They asked if you're performing CPR."

He didn't bother responding. He just kept at it until, ten minutes later, two paramedics rushed into the room.

"How long?" one of them asked.

"Ten or fifteen," said Lenny. "But she was unresponsive when we got here."

"Sure it's coke?"

"Look at the table."

The paramedic glanced at the white powder. "Yep." They yanked the woman off the bed and onto a gurney. One paramedic continued CPR as the other rolled her out of the apartment. They didn't stop to talk about it or say where they were going. As quickly as they came, they were gone.

Lenny ushered Alice back into the living room.

"Is she going to be okay?" Alice asked.

Lenny was sure she knew the answer. "They'll do their best. Come on." He led Alice up the stairs to her apartment, then found her key in her handbag and opened the door. He sat her on the sofa and poured her a scotch. She was a tough one. She'd worked in some rough places and had seen some of the same things that kept Lenny awake at night. But witnessing a neighbor getting wheeled away after OD'ing was tough on anyone, and he could see the shock in her eyes.

She sat with the scotch in her hand but didn't make any effort to drink it.

"She'll be okay," she said to no one in particular.

"I'm going to go back down, okay?"

"Why?"

"The police will come. I need to let them in. I'll leave the door open up here. Just yell if you need me."

Lenny stepped away and then turned at the door. Alice hadn't moved and maybe she wouldn't for a while. He walked down to the first floor and was sitting on the interior stairs when he saw the flashing lights appear in the street. He opened the building door and then sat again.

The first officer appeared. "Sir," he said in the vestibule.

"Overdose," Lenny said. "Cocaine." He pointed at the doorway to the apartment.

"Are you okay, sir?"

"I'm fine. I'm not on anything. We just found her."

The officer stepped in farther as his partner arrived behind him. "You live here?"

"No. I'm visiting a friend. She's upstairs. In a bit of shock."

"And you found the victim?"

"Yes."

"She was inside her apartment?"

"Yes. The door was ajar when we got home from dinner, so we called out to her and got no response. I did a welfare check and found her in the bedroom."

"A welfare check? You in law enforcement, sir?"

"No. I'm in the Marine Corps."

"I see. Well, my partner will secure the apartment. You say you're upstairs?"

"Yeah." Lenny stood. "Let me take you up."

They walked up to Alice's apartment. She was still on the sofa, but the scotch glass was empty. She looked up as Lenny and the cop came in.

"Is she okay?" Alice asked.

"On her way to the hospital," said the cop. "I just need to get statements from you folks." To Lenny: "You say you were out for dinner?"

"Yes," he answered. "On M Street. We had a reservation, so you can verify it, and Alice paid with American Express."

"Is there a reason why I would need to verify it?"

"Procedure. It's a suspicious death, officer. I'm not a cop, but I know how it works. You need to eliminate us."

"Okay. Can you tell me the name of the restaurant?"

Alice told him, and as he wrote it down his partner appeared. "All clear. I grabbed the keys from the kitchen counter and locked up."

"Good," said the first cop. "Now, can you tell me exactly what happened?"

Lenny explained how they had come in, found the door open, checked for Alice's neighbor, and found her in the bedroom.

"How well did you know—what was her last name?"

"Masters," said Alice. "Melodie Masters. And she's lived there for about two years. But I work overseas a lot, so I never knew her that well. Only that she was a lobbyist and that she did baked brownies for fun."

"Were you aware of anything out of the ordinary? Financial or otherwise? Relationships?"

"She dated, but I wasn't aware of anyone special. And no, I didn't know anything about her finances, but word around town was that she was good at her job, so I'm guessing she was well paid."

The cop finished up their statements and took down Lenny's rank and contact details at Quantico, while his partner moved into the corridor to use his radio.

When they were done, Alice stood. She seemed to be brushing off the shock. "What about Melodie?"

The second cop shook her head. "I'm sorry, ma'am, she was pronounced dead on arrival at the hospital."

Alice sat again. "But how? She's successful, she's happy—at least she seemed to be."

"There's a lot going on with people that we don't always know," said the first cop. "And coke, it's everywhere. There's even this new version hitting the streets—crack, they're calling it. It's even more potent and more deadly."

"Where would she get it?" asked Lenny.

"Any number of places. She might have had a regular dealer, or there are nooks all over the city where it's sold on the street. We find them and arrest them, and if they don't get bail, there's a replacement out there five minutes later."

Lenny sighed. "The war on drugs."

"Yeah, well, the drugs are winning. But we keep fighting the fight, right Sergeant?"

"Yes, officer. We do."

"I hope you folks are okay. Just so you know, the drug squad may have some questions. They'll call if they do."

"Anything we can do to help," said Lenny. He walked the police back downstairs and saw them out. When he got back, Alice was still on the sofa, frowning as if thinking things through.

"How does this happen?" she said again.

"Sometimes it's because the person's trying to fill a void, or soothe a sadness. Maybe things *weren't* going well for her. But maybe they were and she was looking for a high she couldn't find any other way. I've seen it before. There are a thousand reasons, but they all come down to one thing: escape."

Lenny offered his hand and helped her stand. "Time for bed," he said.

"I'm not really in the mood."

"Sleep, Ally. You need sleep."

CHAPTER FOUR

IN THE MORNING, AFTER LENNY MADE COFFEE, THEY SAT with the early sun casting a glow through the dust in the air. Alice then took a shower while Lenny collected *The Washington Post* off the doorstep, and he read the back page while he ate toast. When Alice appeared, he passed her the paper, but she didn't devour it as usual.

"I can't stop thinking about her, Len."

"I know. I get it."

"Was she already dead when we found her?"

"Yes."

"But you tried to save her anyway?"

"Of course. I might have been wrong."

Alice sipped her coffee. "I don't get it. She was a young woman with a future. She had a good job, and I wasn't kidding when I told the police officer that she was well paid. Those lobbyists do rather well. She always had a smile, you know? How does a person like that overdose on drugs?"

"Like the cop said, a thousand reasons. This isn't a working-class versus professional-class thing, Ally. The drug of choice might change, but people everywhere have reasons. Some are running from something and others are running toward something. People like her might feel pressure to perform, and not everyone can deal with it. I've seen them in the Corps, in all the branches of the military. People have coping mechanisms. Some people smoke weed, and some drink too much, and some lose themselves in higher highs and lower lows. And stuff like coke or heroin, there's just not much margin for error."

"You don't think she was trying to kill herself?"

"I don't know. Not sure we ever will. If it all felt like too much, maybe she did. But just as likely she got the dose wrong. You want a higher high, you take a little more. But a little more might be deadly. And with stuff like coke you never really know what else is mixed in with it. That's why this stuff is so dangerous."

Alice frowned. "Len, why do you think her door was open? Did someone do this to her?"

"That's for the cops to decide. I don't think so, but I'm no detective. I didn't see anything amiss, and now knowing what we know, the door makes a bit more sense. If she had taken something before, then she could have been absent-minded about it. Same if she was desperate for a hit, I suppose. Distracted."

"I wish we hadn't gone for that walk now."

"It does take the shine off it, but you can't do that. This isn't your fault. People have to take responsibility for themselves."

"Do you really think? If that's true, why do what you do? Why can't everyone fend for themselves?"

Lenny nodded but said nothing.

"Everybody needs help sometimes, Len. We can't wipe our hands of them. That's not how society works, at least not any society I want to be part of. We're supposed to look after each other."

"You're right."

Alice leaned on her elbows and looked at Lenny. "You're a candidate, you know that?"

"For what?"

"For this. For drugs and overdoses and so on."

Lenny laughed but it didn't come from the belly. "How do you figure that?"

"You see things—hell, you do things—that no human should. You said it yourself: you've seen it happen in the Marines. The brain can only take so much, only hold so much bad inside. I worry about you."

"Don't worry about me."

"Why not? I care about you, so why wouldn't I worry? I remember when GIs came home from the war. Heroin was a huge problem because they got hooked on it in Vietnam, where they grow the opium poppies. And why did they get into it over there?"

"I don't know."

"Yeah, you do. You already said it. To escape—the horror of what they were seeing and doing, and the tedium of sitting around doing nothing in between battles. You weren't in Vietnam, at least not during the war, but you're in the same boat. You've witnessed things, done things."

"Ally—"

"No, Lenny. Just promise me. If you find yourself at that crossroads, promise your first call is to me."

He reached across the table and put his hand on hers. "I promise."

She smiled. "I need to get to work."

"Do you think maybe a sick day is in order?"

"No, I'm okay. In fact, I'll be better if I don't sit around stewing. What will you do today?"

"I'm not due back on base until tomorrow, and if you're working, the paper says the Orioles are home at Memorial Stadium."

"You becoming a Baltimore fan now?"

"I'll stick with the Padres, thanks. But I haven't seen a game in a good while, so beggars can't be choosers."

"You want to borrow my car?"

"Nah, I'll take the train up. I'll be back for dinner, if you like."

"Let's do something in. That would be nice."

Alice got ready for work then headed out the door. Lenny took his time over another cup of coffee, but he could already smell the hot dogs wafting across the bleachers.

After a shower, he picked the phone up off the cradle on the wall to check in with the colonel. Alice had one of the new touch-tone phones, but the lack of a rotary dial messed with his muscle memory, so he had to repeat the number to himself as he punched the buttons.

"Having a nice time, Sergeant?" said Lieutenant Colonel Yardley.

"It's a fine day for baseball, sir."

"Nice for some. Listen, don't come back to Quantico tomorrow."

"Sir? Something I should know?"

"Your little sojourns with the CIA have gotten you a fan club."

Lenny thought about his previous mission on assignment with the CIA. It hadn't gone according to plan as far as the spooks were concerned.

"Problem, sir?"

"I don't know. But it seems your skills are in demand."

"The CIA?"

"Oh, this one's a cast of thousands—every three-letter acronym I can think of. I'll be driving up tomorrow."

"Driving, sir? Where?"

"You've been invited to visit the National Security Council, Sergeant."

"The White House, sir?"

"Not quite. The NSC's admin office is in the OEOB. I'll come get you on the way."

"I don't have my uniform with me, sir."

"Call the barracks, have them send it over to me. I'll see you at ten."

CHAPTER FIVE

LIEUTENANT COLONEL YARDLEY ARRIVED AT ALICE'S apartment the next morning like a delivery service from a dry cleaners. He gave Lenny five minutes to get into uniform, and Lenny gave the colonel a coffee that was vastly better than the stuff on base, which earned him an extra minute.

The Old Executive Office Building—OEOB—was a massive structure built to look like a French chateau. It was part of the White House compound but was generally accessed from 17th Street.

"Lieutenant Colonel Yardley and Sergeant Cox for Ray Caan," announced the colonel at the front desk.

They were asked to wait in the ornate lobby. After about five minutes, a man in an immaculate suit approached them. His shaven head was glistening like a jewel as he offered them a genuine smile. Lenny pegged him for some kind of bureaucrat.

"Ray Caan," he said. "Colonel, Sergeant, please come this way."

"This place is impressive," said Lenny.

"It is. Some of the rooms look like they've been pulled from the Palace of Versailles."

Caan led them through a series of rooms before they walked down a flight of stairs and beyond a locked door into a bland corridor. Caan used a key to unlock a door then held it open.

Lenny stepped into a windowless meeting room. The round table was scratched up from decades of use, and the frayed fabric on the chairs had been worn threadbare by a thousand backsides. The walls were a sickly taupe, and the carpet was where color went to die.

"So much for Versailles."

"You know how it is," said Caan. "There's the public face and then there's where the work gets done. Can I get you guys coffee?"

"Thanks," said Yardley.

Caan disappeared and the two Marines took their seats. Neither man spoke. Lenny knew his CO was thinking exactly what he was: *These walls have ears.*

When Caan returned, he had two men with him. He introduced them as Brian Purchase from the Drug Enforcement Agency and Skipper Tomlinson from the White House. After the three sat down, Caan passed around coffees in paper cups.

Lenny sipped his. Military coffee might not have been as good as Alice's, but it was better than this. No one was fighting a war on this dishwater.

"How can we help you, gentlemen?" asked Yardley.

"Colonel, are you aware of the war on drugs?" asked Skipper Tomlinson.

"I've heard the phrase."

"We are fighting a battle against forces to the south that wish to flood our streets with drugs. Cannabis, cocaine, heroin. It's an epidemic."

"I'm sure."

"You must be familiar with these issues in the military."

"Marines might be a cut above, sir, but we are still human."

"Indeed. And you, Sergeant? Have you lost friends and colleagues to this scourge?"

Lenny thought about Melodie Masters. Not a friend or colleague to him but certainly lost.

"I've seen what coke can do," he said.

"Well, the president has had enough. He wants our streets cleaned up, and he wants these cartels shut down."

"That's fine with me," said Yardley. "But surely a matter for our friends here from the DEA."

"And I assure you they are on it. But... think of this problem as a pipeline: the drug cartels at one end who manufacture narcotics, and at the other end the users here in the United States. Now, the DEA can work with local police on rounding up the local dealers and distribution points but, as I'm sure you can imagine, there's a lot of money involved. That means numerous people willing to do the dirty work. As soon as we bring in one dealer, another takes their place. If the DEA intercepts a shipment at the Port of Miami, then another makes it through New Orleans. It's an ongoing battle, and not one we are winning."

Tomlinson steepled his hands as if to emphasize his point. "To give our law enforcement agencies a chance, we need to affect the other end of the pipeline as well. We need to disrupt production and transportation. But these things happen outside US jurisdiction. So you see the problem."

"I do," said Yardley. "Don't we have agencies for things like that? Langley, for example?"

"Yes, yes we do," said Tomlinson. "And they have problems they're working on, for sure. But this time, the administration wants to—how can I put this?" He paused for a beat. "Use a sharper spear."

"Why don't you tell us what you want?" asked Lenny.

Tomlinson looked at Caan. The bald man continued.

"The United States provides a significant amount of aid to countries in the Caribbean, and South and Central America. Part of this aid is earmarked for fighting the war on drugs. Unfortunately, our friends have not always held up their end of the bargain."

"So withdraw the funds," said Lenny.

"That's a consideration for politicians," said Caan, who sounded like a politician to Lenny's ear. "Did you guys see the report on NBC the other night?"

"We don't watch a lot of TV in the Marine Corps," said Yardley.

"Fair point," said Caan. "It seems that our friends in the Bahamas have been taking our aid as well as taking bribes from the Medellín cartel to move narcotics through the Bahamas. The administration would like to get a little more proactive in hobbling this activity."

"Sounds like a good idea to me," said Lenny. "But as the colonel said, isn't that a job for the CIA?"

"The CIA is working on it in Central America, but we want something different in the Bahamas."

"Different how?"

Tomlinson leaned into the table. "Small, fast, surgical. Preferably invisible. We're not looking to make headlines here, just to get a job done."

"Sounds fine," said Lenny. "But again, CIA?"

"Let's just say there are certain political considerations that make the CIA the wrong choice for this particular job. And you come highly recommended, Sergeant Cox."

"By who?"

"People who the White House listens to. The president would consider it a personal favor if you would take this on. You'll be saving American lives, and I don't think I'm speaking out of turn in saying, I'm sure that's why you became a Marine."

"Do you have targets?"

Tomlinson and Caan both looked at the DEA man, Brian Purchase.

"There are distribution points in the Exumas and Grand Bahama. We can provide the points of interest that we know."

"And you want what, exactly?" asked Lenny.

"A little bit of mayhem," said Tomlinson. "Take out facilities, destroy property and merchandise, but keep the civilian casualties low."

"How low?"

"Zero would be best."

"And the bad guys?"

"Are bad guys. Fair game, I'd say. So, what do you need?"

"Need?"

"What kind of a team?"

"Right now, just me."

"You're sure?"

"Until I see what's on the ground. But if I need more, I'm not the only Marine in the Corps."

"Any other resources?"

"It's not really my area, but I take it this isn't a line item on the Marine Corps budget?"

Tomlinson looked at Caan.

"I've spoken with my boss," Caan said. "We have certain funds available for operations like this."

"Who's your boss?" asked Lenny.

"Lieutenant Colonel North."

"What branch?"

"Marine Corps."

"Well, okay, then."

Tomlinson said, "Colonel Yardley, I believe you should be receiving your man's orders shortly."

"I have a cooperation request from HQMC already."

"Then I guess we're good to go. Sergeant Cox, I have it on good authority that you know how to handle an operation with discretion. We're depending on it."

"No parades, roger that."

"Good, because I can't emphasize enough the delicate nature of this operation. You'll be working in-country on the soil of our allies. This can't get back to DC."

"Understood."

"I hope so. The administration will be limited in what we can do if you get caught. So don't get caught."

"Roger that. Cause mayhem, don't get caught. Sounds like high school."

Tomlinson smiled as he stood. "Brian can provide you with operational details, and liaise with Ray on resources and supply. Anything else?"

There was mutual headshaking as the rest of the men rose out of their seats.

Ray Caan led them out of the basement room and back up toward the entrance. Tomlinson headed east to the White House, and Caan walked into the interior of the building.

As the other three reached the street, the DEA man stopped them.

"Are you gentlemen headed back to Quantico?" asked Purchase.

"We are," said Yardley.

"I wonder if you wouldn't mind giving me a ride back to my office in Arlington. We're near the Pentagon."

"No trouble at all."

The trio walked back to Yardley's pool vehicle. Once they were on the road, Purchase spoke.

"Cox, you should know something. I'm not sure what this whole thing is about, but our intelligence suggests that the Bahamas is largely shut down as a source of narcotics."

"What about the bribe story on TV?"

"That's true. Plenty of officials are on the take there, but the White House demanded action last year about some of it. What's going through there is a fraction of what it was. Now, I have to temper that by saying our intel may not be as good as the CIA's, and honestly, I have no clue what the NSC or the director of intelligence might know. But the pipeline analogy is sound. We fight this end. CIA, NSA, and other friends fight the other, so they know more. But our people are saying the stuff isn't moving the way it was last year."

"How's it moving?"

"I wish I knew. I'm just telling you to keep your eyes open, okay?"

"That's rule number two, always."

"What's rule number one?"

"Breathe."

After crossing the Potomac, Yardley drove into the parking lot of the utilitarian building that housed the DEA.

"Thanks for the ride," said Purchase.

"Stay in touch," said Lenny.

Yardley pulled back out toward I-395 and headed for home. They drove in silence for a few minutes, each man processing the meeting, before Yardley spoke.

"I don't like it when spooks don't do their own dirty work," he said. "They have people for this sort of thing."

"I've done jobs for the CIA before," said Lenny.

"As a sniper. That's your job for the Corps. This is something else. They're distancing themselves from something they either don't want to get associated with or expect to fail."

"I'll go take a look and see what's what. Like you said, I'm a sniper. I can see things from afar."

"Do. And this crap about not backing you up if you get caught? Forget that. These intelligence guys might leave their people behind, but we don't work like that in the Marine Corps. You get into any kind of fix, your first call is to me. Got it?"

"Aye, aye, sir."

Once through the gate, Yardley returned the car to the motor pool and they walked back together. The lieutenant colonel then strode toward his office, and Lenny headed for his billet.

When he got to his door he found a note stuck to it, written with typical Corps brevity.

Phone call. Sergeant Burnside, Aust. Army. In country. Call to meet.

There was a number scrawled at the bottom. Lenny didn't have a phone in his billet, but he'd return the call from the commissary after he'd gone for a run.

CHAPTER SIX

LENNY SAT IN THE BLEACHERS WATCHING THE BOYS running drills in full pads. It was a beautiful fall afternoon, cool but bright. The trees on the far side of the high school football field were turning a blaze of yellow and brown and copper. Coaches yelled and whistles blew. Then Lenny felt the thunk of feet on metal and saw Ventura striding up toward him.

He hadn't seen the CIA man since leaving Thailand and had no real desire to see him now. But ever since the meeting at the NSC, Lenny had thought about the words of the DEA agent, Brian Purchase, that the Bahamas wasn't the trafficking route it once was. Before he went causing mayhem, he wanted a better understanding of the lay of the land.

Ventura sat beside Lenny and glanced around like they were meeting in Gorky Park. He leaned forward, elbows on knees, and rubbed his hands together against the cold.

"You don't have an office?" asked Lenny.

"You think I want to be seen with you at Langley?"

"And two men sitting in the bleachers at a high school isn't suspicious."

"People watch football, Cox."

"Those people are called parents."

"So we're just two dads watching our boys."

"You wanna give little Ventura Junior a wave?"

"You're hilarious, Cox." He glanced around again.

"So, you're back at Langley?" asked Lenny.

"For the moment."

"You don't grab me as an office kind of guy."

"If you want to know, it stinks. I should be in the field, but the last op didn't go so well, so I'm biding my time."

He sounded bitter, and Lenny knew why. He had been there for Ventura's last field operation, and it most definitely had not followed the script.

"So what is it you want, Cox?"

"What do you know about the movement of narcotics in the Bahamas?"

"Narcotics? What the hell are you talking about?"

"I've been told the DEA knows all about the US end, but the CIA has eyes on what's happening overseas."

"I'm sure that's true, but what does it have to do with you?"

"I can't go too much into it," Lenny said, holding back a smile. He knew it would drive Ventura crazy for Lenny to be on an op while he was stuck pushing paper.

"What are you into, Cox?"

"Did you see that report on NBC about the cartels bribing officials in the Bahamas?"

"The Ross thing. Yeah, I saw it."

"Let's just say questions are being asked at the highest levels about those allegations. People are wondering if enough is being done to stop the flow of narcotics into the US."

"That would be the DEA."

"Not in the Bahamas, it wouldn't. There are people who want some action. They want to slow things down from the other end."

Ventura nodded but didn't take his eyes off the football field.

"So you've been tasked with what? Shooting some drug dealers with your little sniper rifle?"

"Making them hurt a little. Let's just say there are people who want a win or two for the good guys."

"This doesn't feel like a Marine Corps gig."

"I don't make the decisions, Ventura. I just follow orders."

"I don't seem to recall you being an order follower."

"From my chain of command, always. So what do you know?"

"Not much. I don't work the Caribbean desk. But I can find out."

"Can you?"

"What's in it for me?"

"Maybe they'll give you a gold star?"

"You're hilarious."

"Or maybe I'll just go around the Caribbean bumbling into CIA ops and blowing them to hell."

"All right, hotshot. I'll check it out. Don't do anything until I give you the go-ahead."

"Sir, yes, sir." Lenny shot him a salute.

"I thought you guys didn't *sir* if you weren't in uniform."

"You're an irony-free zone, my friend."

Lenny stood and eased past Ventura. "I'll be at Quantico for another day or two."

"Don't worry, I'll find you."

Lenny walked down the bleachers then turned away from the scrimmage and set off toward the Metro station.

———

VENTURA DROVE BACK TO LANGLEY AND SAT IN HIS cubicle. Cox was right about one thing: Ventura was not a desk guy. He had been trained to be out in the field, and in a time of high alert—with Soviet threats everywhere—wasting his days in a cubicle in McLean, Virginia, was not his idea of a good time.

He had been put on ice after the failure of his last mission, but that was a series of events outside of his control. Now his boss was telling him to keep his head down and do his penance, but six months rotting away under fluorescent lighting was too much.

He was going to make a call but decided against it. This was a thing best done in person. He rode the elevator up a couple of floors, then walked through more cubicles until he reached the offices at the far end.

A secretary sat at a desk outside and watched Ventura approach.

"I need to see him."

"Do you have an appointment?"

"You know I don't, Erica. But I have some intel he's going to want."

"He's very busy today. Why don't you put it in a briefing document?"

"Because by the time it gets to his desk, the intel will be useless and the agency will have lost valuable assets."

She looked at him dispassionately then picked up the phone. She spoke at a volume that ensured Ventura couldn't eavesdrop. He was surprised that the person on the other end could hear her. When she put the phone down, she looked at him.

"Five minutes. I hope it's worth your while."

"Thank you, Erica."

Ventura stepped into the office. It wasn't large and it had a view of the expansive Langley parking lot, but it was a private office, which meant something in the agency.

"Sir," he said as he entered.

The man behind the desk kept reading. "I've got a briefing with the deputy director in ten."

"Yes, sir. I just had a meeting with a Marine that we've used on previous ops. He mentioned that he's been tasked with a covert operation in the Bahamas."

The man looked up, wearing a permanent frown. "What kind of op?"

"One intended to cause harm to the narcotic supplies heading into the United States."

"Right. The deputy director mentioned that POTUS was on the warpath after that NBC story."

"Yes, sir."

"Is this guy one of ours?"

"He's done sniper duty for us, but if you mean is he on board with the agency, the answer is no."

"Bahamas, you say?"

"Yes, sir. But this particular guy has a habit of going off reservation."

"Meaning?"

"Meaning he might stumble into assets we have in place. And not just in the Bahamas."

"That's not good. Can you keep him on a leash?"

"I can try, sir, but I'm not read into any operations down there."

"No."

"And I'll need to give him a direction to head in."

"But he's been told Bahamas?"

"That's what he said."

"All right, I'll mention it to the DD, see who's running this thing. Come back tonight and we'll figure out what you can tell him."

"Yes, sir."

The man stood and shuffled his papers into a manila folder. "And cancel your dinner plans, Ventura. We might need to get you up to speed on a few things."

"Yes, sir."

Ventura didn't wait to be dismissed. He stepped out of the office, thanked Erica, and walked away, trying hard to hide the smile breaking through.

CHAPTER SEVEN

When Lenny arrived at Alice's apartment, she had visitors: Melodie Masters' parents were sitting on the sofa. Alice introduced Lenny to her mother, whose eyes were red and puffy, and her father, who looked stoic, as if letting his emotions out might see him unable to control them.

"Did you know Melodie too?" asked her mother.

"I'm afraid I never had the pleasure," said Lenny. He withheld that he had tried to resuscitate their daughter and failed.

"Well, you have company," Melodie's father said to Alice. "We shouldn't keep you any longer."

"It's fine, really."

Her father stood and, with a gentle hand on the small of her back, encouraged his wife to do the same. "Thank you for your time. We're sorry to have intruded, but we just wanted to meet some of her friends. Try to understand, why..."

"I'm sorry we had to meet under these circumstances," said Alice. "Melodie was a beautiful person."

They moved toward the door.

"Hopefully we'll see you again when we're able to collect her things," her father said.

Alice walked them down to the street, and Lenny followed but stayed back. Melodie's mother gave Alice a hug like she might collapse if left to stand on her own, and her father turned to Lenny.

"If I could get my hands on the people who gave her that damn poison." He shook his head, his hollowed-out eyes glazed over.

Lenny put his hand on the man's shoulder and felt the air leave him like a deflating balloon.

Then they climbed into their car and drove away, leaving Alice and Lenny standing on the street.

"They just drove from Pittsburgh," Alice said. "Looking for answers." She turned to Lenny and hugged him. "I didn't have any."

"I know."

"They can't even get into her apartment. They said the police will be done in a few days. Nothing suspicious about Melodie's death, just the bureaucratic process."

Lenny held Alice and looked down the street, where the car had driven away.

"Geez, you two, get a room."

Lenny spun around to see Lucas Burnside walking down the sidewalk. He wore a denim jacket that he might have stolen from a hippie, but his haircut was all military.

"Lucas!" said Alice, breaking from Lenny and giving the wiry Australian a hug. "It's been too long."

"Tell me about it." He reached out a hand to Lenny. "How are ya, mate?"

"We live in interesting times."

"I've said it before and I'll say it again: you're a poet and a scholar."

"What brings you to the United States, Lucas?" asked Alice.

"Here for a spot of sailing. Headed up to Rhode Island shortly."

"I thought you were in the army."

"That's what they tell me."

"Well, it's good to see you. I'm sure you boys are going for a few beers, but I'd love to see you before you go."

"Why don't you come with us, darl?"

"Not tonight. But you boys have fun."

"Always."

Alice turned to Lenny. "Just do me a favor. If you come home with beer breath, crash on the sofa."

"Roger that," he said.

Alice kissed him and gave Lucas another hug, then she went back inside.

"Any good watering holes around here?" Lucas asked.

"This is a college town. I'm sure we'll find something."

———

THEY FOUND A BAR WITH RED-AND-WHITE CHECKED tablecloths and a jukebox playing "Every Breath You Take," by The Police. Lenny ordered two beers and the server dropped off a bowl of nuts.

"So sailing, huh?"

"Yeah. I'm not doing the sailing, mind you."

"The America's Cup?"

"That's it."

"What's an SAS guy doing at the America's Cup?"

"Enjoying the hospitality, I hope."

Their beers arrived, and they touched mugs and drank.

"I hope I didn't break up anything," said Lucas. "With the missus."

"No."

"But you're still on with her?"

"Hard to say what it is. I hadn't seen her since Thailand until a week back, so six months?"

"She's a good one. That's all I'm gonna say on the matter."

"I agree with you on that."

"As long as I wasn't busting up your party."

"No. We just had a visit from the parents of a neighbor who died the other night."

"Geez, sorry."

"Yeah. It was an overdose. Bad stuff."

"Man. Those animals should be hunted down."

"Exactly. But I actually had a government guy tell me that law enforcement couldn't stop the other end of the pipeline, where it was coming from. I don't know."

"Why can't they?"

"Sovereign countries, international laws..."

"Yeah, right."

"I just feel bad for the parents. They don't understand why it happened. Now they just feel let down."

"By their daughter?"

"By the system."

"That's the trouble with systems, mate. They work for most of us, most of the time. But not always, and not for everyone."

"Who's the poet now?" Lenny shook his head. "I just saw the man's eyes, you know? He looked at me like it was his fault. Like he was responsible for bringing this little girl into the world and for protecting her, and now she was dead and there was nothing he could do about it. Not only is bringing her back impossible, but retribution is outside his skill set."

Lucas drank some beer. "But not yours."

"Huh?"

"Not yours. You feel bad for him? Don't bitch to me, do something about it."

"This isn't Kampuchea, Lucas."

"No, you've got better systems here. Better, but not perfect. And you're part of this one."

"What's your point?"

"No point, mate. Do something or do nothing, those are your

choices. But if it were me, I'd go with the one that helped me sleep at night."

"You sleep at night?"

Lucas smiled, the skin on his face pulled taut across his cheekbones. "Sometimes."

Lenny sipped his beer and looked across the bar. The room was buzzing with conversation and laughter, people not much younger than Lenny or Lucas but who would rely on the system to work for them for the rest of their lives.

"What would you do?" Lenny asked.

"Something."

"Be more specific."

"I'd find out who she got the drugs from and I'd encourage them to not give the stuff to anyone else."

Lenny started nodding and found himself moving in rhythm with a song that had started on the jukebox. Then the sound of Colin Hay from Men at Work rang across the room.

"*It's a mistake, it's a mistake.*"

"Is he talking to you or the bad guys?" asked Lucas with another tight grin.

"Maybe both," said Lenny. "I might have to cut out a little early. I just remembered, I've got something I need to do."

"You want a hand?"

Now Lenny was smiling. "I thought you'd never ask."

———

By the time the two men got back to Alice's apartment, the sun had fallen and the residential street was quiet. They had made a stop at a shop that was part liquor store and part office supply, and procured a six-pack of beer, a packet of gum, and a box of paper clips.

Lenny had a key to Alice's building, so they crept into the lobby without a sound. Then Lucas held the beer and the office supplies as Lenny used a paper clip to fashion a pick. It took a minute of trial and error before he got the door to Melodie Masters' apartment open.

It was as Lenny had left it. There was mail on the counter and an ashtray on the coffee table. Lenny parked himself on the sofa next to a side table, where he found a push-button telephone and beside it a Teledex directory. He held the directory up to Lucas, then placed it on his lap.

"You know the dealer's name?" asked Lucas.

"Nope. But if you want to hide a name in your Teledex, you either make up a code that you might forget or you put it on a page you don't use much."

Lenny slid the plastic selector down the face of the directory, through the alphabet, until he got to *WX*, then he pushed the button and the lid flipped open, revealing the page for the listings beginning with *W* or *X*.

"Anything?" asked Lucas.

"She's only written one name."

"For?"

Lenny smiled. "Damian."

"Now, I didn't do too flash at school, but I'm pretty sure that doesn't start with *X*."

Lenny picked up the phone handset, waited for a dial tone, and punched in the number from the directory. After a minute, someone picked up and said, "Hello?"

"Damian," Lenny responded.

"Who's this?"

"Ventura," he lied. "I'm a friend of Melodie Masters."

"Who?"

"One of your clients. Redhead from Georgetown."

"All my clients are from Georgetown, genius."

"Well, I need something and she said to call you."

"That right?"

"Yes. So can you hit me up, or was she telling a lie?"

There was a pause. "What do you want?"

"Couple eight balls."

"That's a lot."

"I'm having a party. Help me out."

"You have cash?"

"I didn't figure you'd take a check. I got cash, right now."

"Twelve Benjamins. It'll take me twenty minutes."

"Fine. Tell me where."

———

LENNY WANDERED ALONG THE ROAD NEAR YATES FIELD House at Georgetown University. It was the back end of the campus, butted up against the woods, cold and quiet. He was taking long, slow breaths, trying to calm himself. Having just met the parents of a dead girl, he wasn't feeling a lot of charity toward the lowlife who had supplied the drugs that had killed her, but Alice's voice rang in his head. He didn't want to do anything stupid, like kill the guy. Not yet, anyway.

Lucas was lurking in the shadows fifty yards behind, just in case the guy pulled a gun or did something equally asinine.

Lenny spotted the guy walking in from the center of campus, wearing a houndstooth jacket with the collar popped, his blond bangs swept sideways across his forehead.

He didn't look like any kind of drug dealer.

"Damian," said Lenny as the kid approached.

The guy gave a jink of his head. "You Ventura?"

"No, I'm Santa Claus."

"Smart guy, huh? Well, I think you'll find *I'm* Santa Claus." He smiled. "I've got the snow."

"Clever."

"You related to Melodie or something?"

"No, why?"

"Red hair."

"You remember her?"

"Sure. I've got a lot of professional clients."

"Well, now you've got one fewer."

Lenny didn't wait for the confusion to register on Damian's face. He stepped in and punched the kid hard in the stomach, and as he doubled over, Lenny grabbed Damian's belt front and back to check for a weapon.

Satisfied that he wasn't armed, Lenny took him by the popped collar and spun him around, slipping his hand into the jacket pocket and lifting the kid's wallet as he dumped him against a tree. Then he crouched down in front of him.

"Breathe," Lenny said.

As he waited for Damian to catch his breath, Lucas came up behind him. Lenny handed him the wallet, not taking his eyes off the young man. He was built like a man but now, hunched against the tree, he looked like a boy. His skin was smooth and unblemished by life, and Lenny got the sense that he had only been shaving for about five minutes.

Lenny reassessed his plan—even the best ones could go sideways as soon as boots hit the ground. And Lenny's had been simple: he'd give a drug dealer a beating for providing the narcotic that killed a woman. But now he wasn't so sure. This was not Lenny's idea of a drug dealer. He had imagined someone older and harder, maybe someone with a bodyguard and a nasty glint in his eye. But this kid was afraid. There was no snarl or attitude. Lenny leaned in close to him.

"What are you doing dealing drugs?"

"Just offering a service. I don't give anyone anything they don't want."

"Is that how you justify it to yourself?"

Damian's frown deepened, but he said nothing.

"Your drugs killed a woman."

"I'm sorry. But *I* didn't do that. I don't put the stuff up people's noses."

"But you supply something deadly to people not in a position to make good choices for themselves. Every man for himself is not an acceptable excuse."

"What do you want, man?"

"I want you to understand the error of your ways. Is this how you want your life to go? Dealing drugs on a college campus?"

"I have to make a living. I don't have a scholarship, you know."

"You're a student here?"

"Yeah."

"Well, there are plenty of ways to make a living that don't kill your customers. Get a job at Orange Julius. Malls are safer places to work, trust me. Because in this world you're involved with, there aren't a lot of nice people. There are bad often desperate people. Sooner or later someone like me comes along to beat you into the next life."

The kid recoiled as much as he could against a tree, and his eyes went wide.

"But I'm not going to do that today unless I have to. Here's what we're going to do instead. You're going to tell me where you get your drugs, and then I'm going to leave. And you're going to find a better method to pay your way through college. Because if you don't, I'll be back, and I won't be so chatty."

"You think they won't replace me?"

Lenny shrugged. "So, where? Who?"

"I can't tell you that."

"Why?"

"They'll hurt me."

"You can risk being hurt by them later or guarantee being hurt by me now. This is the bind you've gotten yourself into. But just so you know, I don't plan on advertising where I got my information from."

Damian pursed his lips.

Lenny punched him in the throat. It wasn't hard; he didn't want to crush anything. That would make getting information

from him trickier than it needed to be. Damian choked and spluttered and spat. Lenny waited. Then once the dealer had most of his
breath back, Lenny repeated his question.

"He cruises R Street. Lover's Lane, near the Oak Hill
Cemetery."

"When?"

"Every night."

"What's he drive?"

"A Ford. Blue."

"Name?"

Damian hesitated.

"Name?"

"JJ. But he's just the delivery guy. The boss's name is Crespi.
Roy Crespi."

"You know the boss?"

"No. Just heard JJ mention him, that's all."

"How does the drop work?"

"He cruises by at ten. If someone's standing there, he stops."

"All right. Here's what happens now: you go home. Where is
that?"

"Driver's license says Trenton, New Jersey," said Lucas.

"You're not in DC?"

"That's my parents' place," said Damian. "Here I'm at Henle
Village."

"Is that on campus?"

Damian nodded.

"Okay. Now, what you're *not* going to do? You're not to call
these people and tell them about our meeting. That would go
badly for you."

He nodded again.

Lenny stood and Lucas tossed the wallet into Damian's lap.

"Do better," said Lucas.

They made to leave when Lenny suddenly turned back to the
dealer and put out his hand.

"The merchandise."

The kid sighed. He pulled two small bags of white powder from his jacket and handed them to Lenny.

"I'm going to have to cover that," he said.

"Correct," said Lenny. "You're getting off easy."

As the two men walked away across campus, Lenny ripped each bag open and let the powder blow away on the breeze.

"We need some wheels," said Lucas.

CHAPTER EIGHT

They chose a Toyota Corolla in one of the college's parking lots. Lucas felt around the wheel wells until he found a magnetic box with a spare key. He tossed the key to Lenny, who unlocked it. Lucas got in on the passenger side and pulled a local street map from the glove compartment.

They drove out of the university district and across Wisconsin Avenue, then did a quick tour of the area. After finding their spot, Lenny parked on 31st Street so the car wouldn't be seen, while Lucas stood on the corner of R Street, within view of the cemetery and Lover's Lane.

It was five minutes after ten when the blue Ford Pinto cruised past the cemetery. It slowed as it reached Lover's Lane, almost to a stop, but then continued forward when no buyer appeared from the shadows.

Lucas jogged around the corner and got into the Corolla. "That's him."

Lenny eased out onto R Street and followed the Pinto onto Wisconsin. They drove a circuitous route for another half hour. The driver was clearly doing the rounds of his usual delivery spots. He slowed five times and stopped three, where someone appeared from the shadows and took care of business through the passenger-side window. The car was never stationary for more than thirty seconds.

Eventually the Pinto led them to the Adams Morgan neighborhood. The area was mostly row houses and condos, but the building where the Pinto stopped was a commercial space that stood apart, like it might have once been a storefront. The windows were blacked out. The side yard was now a gravel lot where four other cars were parked.

Lenny drove by and stopped around the corner, then he and Lucas returned to the building on foot. It was as quiet as the rest of the neighborhood. They stood in the darkness and watched.

"Five cars. Five people?" said Lenny.

"Maybe. But look at that tank."

"That's a Ford LTD Crown Vic."

"Nice-looking car. The others, not so much."

Lenny looked the vehicles over. Four of them were like the Pinto: small sedans or hatchbacks, the kinds college students or recent graduates might drive. The Crown Vic was something else. Not only did it look like the Queen Mary compared to the others, but it was newer. Two-tone brown with a half vinyl roof, and gleaming chrome bumpers and trim.

"The boss's car," Lenny said.

"I'd reckon."

"Plan?"

"This is a distribution hub, maybe a clubhouse, but not a residence. The grunts might sleep here, but the boss won't."

"So?"

"So that means he'll leave at some point. And then it won't be two on five."

"Roger that."

"I think we need some kit."

"Weapons? Our best bet is inside that building."

"I was thinking something else. Can I borrow your keys?"

Lenny dropped the keys into Lucas's hand.

"I'll be back in two ticks."

———

LUCAS DIDN'T GO FAR. HE DROVE OUT ONTO COLUMBIA
Road and then backtracked along 18th Street. Finding what he
wanted, he pulled in behind a strip mall and stopped by the rear
entrance to a sporting goods store. He took a minute to break in,
and then he went shopping. There were guns locked behind grates
that were way more secure than the back door, so he wasted no
time on them. Instead he collected what he thought he needed,
stuffed everything into a plastic shopping bag, and left twenty
dollars on the counter. As he walked out he found a maintenance
room and helped himself to a few tools.

When he got back to Lenny, the same cars were in the same
places.

"Nothing?" he asked.

"Nothing," said Lenny. "Looks like everyone's in for the
night."

"Then we wait." Lucas took a can of cola from his bag and
handed it to Lenny, then cracked open his own.

They were done with their drinks and had both relieved themselves beside a fence when there was movement from the building.
Warm light escaped from inside as the rear door opened and two
men appeared. They slapped each other a low-five, and one moved
toward the vehicles. He unlocked the Crown Victoria and got
inside. The guy at the building door waited like an anxious parent
until the engine started, then he closed the door, taking the light
with him.

"Let's go," said Lenny.

"You take this guy," said Lucas, handing him the keys. "I've got
a little plan for our friends here."

"Roger that. Let's rendezvous at that park back down Columbia."

Lenny jogged toward the Corolla. The taillights of the Crown Victoria spilled red across the lot. Its headlights flicked on and filled the space before it with a tunnel of white as it eased back onto the street.

Lucas watched the car drive away. He saw nothing for a moment afterward, then the Corolla pulled out and followed.

———

ONCE IN THE COROLLA, LENNY NOTICED LUCAS HAD left him a gift on the passenger seat: a rubber mallet. He followed the tank of a car south onto Connecticut Avenue then cut back northwest over the Taft Bridge.

The Crown Vic's driver didn't speed and always used indicators. Lenny held his distance until the driver pulled in near the zoo. The area was less residential—wooded and serene. Lenny's plan formed quickly.

He turned his headlights off and accelerated fast. The little Toyota was no match for the massive Ford in a race, but the Crown Vic was just cruising. As he approached the taillights, he eased off the gas just a touch.

The impact was harder on the Toyota. The rear of the Ford was heavy steel and had all the give of a granite mountain. Lenny doubted he had even damaged the paintwork as he hit the brakes and saw the rear of the Ford light up red.

Lenny pulled over but kept moving until the Ford came to a complete stop. He left the headlights off—he wasn't sure they would work now anyway—and grabbed the mallet, nestling the head in his left palm. He got out and held his hands out, signaling that he was no threat.

The door of the Crown Vic flew open. "What the hell!" The

guy spun toward Lenny as he stood in the light from the interior lamp. He was a big guy suited to the big car.

Lenny kept moving toward him, watching for a weapon. "I'm so sorry."

"You're gonna be sorry."

"I don't think your taillights are working."

"What the hell you talking about, man?" The big guy took half a step out of the light. Lenny closed the gap between them and saw him reach for something in his belt. *A gun.*

But the big guy came up empty-handed. He glanced toward the interior of the vehicle, which told Lenny the guy had taken the gun out from his pants in order to drive more comfortably. That wasn't his first mistake today.

"I've got my license and insurance," said Lenny, keeping the guy focused on his face as the mallet slid down his hand and he grabbed the wooden handle. He would have preferred to use his dominant hand, but coming from the left meant the arc of his swing wasn't disturbed by the Crown Vic, and most of it evaded the light spilling from the car.

The big guy did the rest as he took a step toward Lenny.

"I'm going to beat the living—"

He didn't finish the sentence. The mallet came out of the dark and clocked him in the side of the head. It was a measured impact —Lenny didn't want to kill him—but the lateral movement threw the guy's head sideways into the car's doorframe. The Detroit steel sent him into slumberland, and he dropped to the dirt like a dud mortar round.

———

Lucas waited to confirm no one else was leaving, then he casually walked across the street as if he were on his way home from the supermarket. Skirting the gravel and its collection of compact cars, he headed for the rear of the building. He moved quietly, keeping below the view of any windows, but in the dark he was confident he couldn't be seen from inside.

He found the meters for water and gas next to an access panel on the side of the building. He put his shopping bag down and gently removed the wire mesh panel, then took a flashlight from the bag and clicked it on. After collecting the bag, Lucas slid on his belly into the crawl space.

He followed the pipe he wanted all the way until an elbow joint sent it up through the floor, into what was either a back-office kitchen or a heater—he didn't care which. Lucas lay in the dirt and clamped an adjustable wrench and some vice grips around the joint in the pipe then, working quickly but carefully, he eased the pipe loose.

He heard the hiss of escaping gas just before he smelled it. Giving it a few extra turns, ensuring the gas was coming out nice and fast, he dropped the tools back in the bag and removed a coil of sporting fuse. The fuse was most commonly used on cannons in war reenactments or military ceremonies, but Lucas drove one end of it into the ground and began crawling backward, uncoiling the fuse and dragging his bag back toward the access hatch.

After checking that no one had stepped outside for a cigarette, he slid out from under the building and unwound the wire to the end. It was going to be an imprecise burn, so he readied himself to get away. Then he lit the end of the fuse with a Zippo lighter, grabbed his bag, and ran.

First he broke for the back of the property, flattening himself against the brick wall of an electronic parts store in the next building along. Then, checking the street was clear, he ran across to the other side of the road and stopped in the lee of a tall oak.

Lucas waited longer than he expected. He started checking the street for vehicles or pedestrians, resigned to dashing back across to relight the fuse.

Then it exploded.

The old place was sturdy, so the blast seemed to lift just the back half right off its foundation. Flames spewed from underneath as if the building were one of those new space shuttles launching from Florida. Lucas felt the percussion of the blast on his side of the street, but as quickly as it came, it disappeared. The launch flame receded back under the building.

Then the fun began.

The gas didn't stop flowing, so the floor ignited. Then something—Lucas had no idea what—exploded inside, shooting a second burst of flames out the window. The windshield of a two-door VW Rabbit cabriolet parked nearest the building shattered, and the car's convertible top began to burn.

At the side of the building, a window opened and a person dove out, landing hard on the gravel. Then a second person. A third ran out the front door, and all three gathered then backed away toward the street. Lucas waited for a fourth to emerge—there were four cars in the lot—but no one else did.

The three drug dealers attempted to get to their cars, but the flames grew higher and the heat more intense as gas filled the building and fueled the inferno. The fire had spread from one vehicle to the next. Lucas watched the men pace the sidewalk, trying to solve an impossible problem. The building was burning, and it wasn't going to stop until the gas was turned off, and that wasn't going to happen unless someone from the gas company went in with an asbestos suit.

The three men continued watching the blaze and looking at one another as if it were the other's fault, perhaps trying to think up how they were going to deflect the blame. They stayed on the sidewalk as the sound of sirens drew closer. But as the first flashing red lights came around the corner, they must have decided that discretion was the better part of valor and ran away in the darkness.

Lucas watched the first fire engine pull up. It didn't take the fire fighters long to figure out that the building wasn't going to be saved. The one in charge directed a team with a hose to protect an apartment block at the rear. When the second engine arrived shortly after, they took up position on the opposite side from where Lucas stood under his tree, trying to save the storefront along the main street.

He didn't wait to see a third truck arrive, instead slipping back into the side street and disappearing into the cool night.

CHAPTER NINE

THE DRUG DEALER WOKE SLOWLY, NOT WITH A START like in the movies. First his eyes opened as tiny slits, next he moved his head, and then his breathing picked up. He widened his eyes to make out his surroundings, but it was dark, so he blinked a few times. It was then that he seemed to realize he was tied up. He began to pull at his binds—wrists strapped to the arms of a chair, his ankles tied to its legs.

An unforgiving spotlight hit him, and he recoiled. Lucas had aimed the hunting light from the sporting goods store at the dealer's face, then followed him as he turned his head away. The massive warehouse was cold and damp, but the open space felt closed in by the darkness surrounding them.

Lenny stepped closer to the guy but remained mostly in shadow.

"How's your head?"

The dealer frowned and then instinctively tried to touch the lump that had formed. Realizing again that he was bound to a chair made him snarl.

"You're a dead man," he said.

"Today you're closer, Roy."

"How do you know my name?"

"I know plenty about you, Roy. I know where you live, I know where you work. I know that you used to have a nice ride."

"What? Used to?"

"Sadly, your Crown Vic is now a burned-out shell on the side of the road."

"I'm gonna kill you!"

"Not today. See today, it's your turn to be tied up in a warehouse. And the reason for that, Roy, is that I know a lot about you, but I don't know everything that I need to. So you're going to tell me everything."

"I'm telling you nothing."

Lenny slapped him hard with a wet rag. The dealer's head snapped back. Stunned, the guy's eyes began to water and he coughed.

"Yeah, I know," said Lenny. "My rag is doused with gasoline. It stings, don't it? Kind of permeates the eyes, burns the skin. The best thing is to avoid getting hit by it."

"Who the hell are you?"

"An interested party. Now, let's talk about your drug dealing business. I need to know where you're getting your product from, Roy."

The dealer spluttered. "I'm not telling you—"

The sound of the wet rag slapping against Roy's face echoed around the warehouse. He clenched his jaw and turned his face as if showing defiance. Lenny slapped him again on the other side, then he poured a little more gasoline on the rag.

"Where do you get your product, Roy?"

"They'll kill me."

"Only if they know you talked. But I won't tell them. Plus, you have a more immediate problem."

"What?"

"Getting out of this room alive. See, if you don't tell me where you get your product, I'm going to have to the take this rag covered in gasoline and shove it in your mouth. Then I'll have no choice but to punch you in the nose, repeatedly, until your nose bleeds and then clots, and you can no longer breath out of it. Then you'll be sucking every bit of air you can through the rag, which won't be much. What you will suck into your lungs is petroleum fumes."

Lenny stepped in and dangled the rag so it dripped onto Roy's nose.

"Now, you feel that sting on your cheeks, the burn in your eyes? That's going to happen to your lungs. The fumes are going to eat at them. And trust me when I tell you this is not something you come back from. If I leave the rag in you'll suffocate, and if I take it out, you'll never breath properly again. Walking up stairs will become a thing of the past. You'll probably have to wheel a bottle of oxygen around with you for the rest of your life."

Lenny retreated into darkness.

"So, Roy. Time to choose. A chance to see tomorrow fit and healthy, or not. All I need to know is who sells you your product."

The dealer didn't talk immediately. It took several more slaps of the rag—the last one across the mouth so he could taste the gasoline—for him to become a touch more cooperative.

"They'll kill you."

"Let me worry about that, Roy. Who are they?"

"The Esposito syndicate."

"Where?"

"Baltimore. They own the docks and half the city. A good chunk of DC too. You'll never get near them."

"I don't need to."

Lucas killed the light, and the warehouse succumbed to blackness. They took some time to acclimate their eyes, then Lenny stepped in behind the man in the chair.

"We're going to get some coffee," he said. "We'll be back shortly."

Lenny and Lucas walked toward the door behind the dealer. As Lenny pushed it open, he saw the needle of light across the horizon, the first glimpse of a new day. They returned to the Corolla, and Lucas dropped the spotlight into the trunk.

Lenny drove them back into Georgetown and parked the car in a slot one row away from where they had taken it. He then pulled a wallet out from inside his jacket and removed the cash.

"Two thousand bucks," he said. "I don't think Roy will be needing it. You need any cash?"

"The army gives me a bunk, a feed, and a few beers," said Lucas. "I don't have much need for anything else."

"Well, this poor old car took some damage, so let's make sure the student who owns it isn't out of pocket." He plucked a twenty from the stack and handed the rest to Lucas.

"Roy can buy us breakfast."

"Good call." Lucas flipped open the glove compartment and tossed the money inside, then they both got out and strode away.

They walked until the dawn had well and truly broken, then found a little diner on Wisconsin Avenue. They ate full breakfasts with sausages, hash browns, pancakes, and coffee. When the server came to refill Lucas's mug, he frowned.

"I'm only half done," he said.

"You don't want anymore?" she queried.

"Sure I want more, but how do you know how many I've had?"

"Why do I care how many you've had? I'm not your mother, darlin'."

"But how do you charge me?"

Lenny laughed. "The refills are free."

"They're what?"

"Free. You pay for a coffee, you get refilled until you're done."

Lucas looked at the server. "Is that true?"

"Yes, darlin'."

"Wow. What a country. In that case, fill me up."

After Lucas sipped his brand-new coffee, he asked Lenny what his plans were now.

"Follow the chain," said Lenny with a mouthful of sausage. "One link at a time."

"Who was this woman?"

"What woman?"

"Alice's neighbor. The one who OD'd."

"Melodie? I didn't know her."

"So why all this business?"

Lenny sipped his coffee. "I don't like the idea of good people dying for no reason."

"I get that, but you gotta admit, it happens every day. Why this one?"

"Let's just say that there are people in my government who are a little sick of all the drugs on our streets."

"Glad to hear it, but don't you have people for that? You lot have more law enforcement acronyms than I've had fried dinners, mate."

"We do, and they're doing what they can, but the rules favor the bad guys. I'm talking more about the other end. The administration wants action where this junk is coming from, you get me? It just so happens that I've now been exposed to this side of things. So I'm thinking, why not dig from this end of the tunnel and see where I pop up at the other end?"

"A Hogan's Heroes thing. I get ya."

"And if I dig from the other end as well, maybe the tunnels will meet."

"Or maybe not. I doubt these guys are using just one method to get their poison into the country."

"Agreed. All the more reason to dig from both ends."

Lucas shrugged and sipped. "Hey, if you're on the clock, it's as good a way to spend your time as any."

"What about you? Why are you really in the States?"

"Told ya, a yacht race."

"You sail?"

"I do, but okay, that's not why I'm here. Important people

think there's some funny business going on with this race in Rhode Island, and I've been ordered to go take a look, make sure everything's on the up and up."

"How long will you be there?"

"I'm told the whole thing finishes by the end of September, so I'll be free sometime after that."

"And then?"

"I guess I'll go where the wind blows me, until I'm told otherwise. So if you find yourself in a spot of bother at all, give me a holler."

Lucas took a napkin from the steel dispenser and asked the server if he could borrow her pen. He scribbled a number down and handed it to Lenny.

"Message service," he said. "Just give 'em my name."

Lenny tucked the napkin in his jacket pocket. "Roger that."

They lingered over breakfast and drank their fill of coffee. The twenty covered the bill and a large tip, so Lenny dropped the dealer's contribution on the table as they left.

"Where you off to?" asked Lenny.

"Train station. You?"

"I'll drop by Alice's, then it looks like I'll be getting a train too. Just the other way."

"Say hi to Alice for me. I'm sorry we didn't get a chance to catch up."

"Will do."

"And keep your wits about you, hey. You go further along that tunnel, the people aren't gonna get nicer."

"Roger that. Union Station's about three miles east," said Lenny. "I'm going this way."

The two men shook hands.

"Stay well," said Lucas.

"You too. Enjoy the sailing."

Lucas winked and walked away.

CHAPTER TEN

Lenny met Ventura at the zoo. He found all the cloak-and-dagger stuff hilarious. He understood the need for secrecy in intelligence just as much as in the military, but he couldn't see how meeting in front of the gorilla enclosure was any more secure than behind the doors at Langley.

Wearing a greatcoat, Ventura was nibbling on popcorn—eating one and tossing one to the gorillas despite the sign asking him not to.

Lenny shoved his hand deep in his jacket pockets against the growing afternoon chill and came up alongside the CIA man.

"Were you followed?" Ventura asked.

"There was a suspicious-looking group of elementary kids coming in behind me."

"This is serious."

"Are you going to give me the launch codes for the nukes?"

"I don't have access to that material."

"Then I don't think it's that serious. What did you find out?"

Ventura flicked a kernel across the moat toward a quizzical silverback. "The Bahamas are a problem."

"How so?"

"The place is a hotbed of merchandise."

"Merchandise? You mean drugs."

"We don't say that word in public, Cox. It spooks the natives."

"I'm sure it does. So, Bahamas."

"The stuff is everywhere."

"How?"

"Every way imaginable. But mostly they fly it in."

"From where?"

"Colombia. See, their problem is this: aircraft large enough to make it from Colombia to the US are too big to land at clandestine strips. They have to land at airports, and obviously the cartel wants to avoid that. But smaller aircraft that can land on a postage stamp can't make the trip without refueling."

"So they're refueling in the Bahamas?"

"Sometimes. But one of their top guys, Carlos Lehder, came up with the idea to fly a larger aircraft onto a proper strip in the Bahamas, unload, and then have smaller aircraft come in to bring everything into the US."

"They land at airports in the Bahamas?"

"Sometimes. But this Lehder guy, he bought into an island, a place called Norman's Cay. It's sparsely populated—even more so after he threatened all the homeowners and chased them off the island. It's got a nice long tarmac for a landing strip, and he basically controls the island with his private army."

"And the Bahamian government does nothing?"

"You saw the TV report. They're on the take. Our boys gave them a kick up the pants last year and they went through the motions of clamping down on it all, but it was for show. And there are other places. Any small airfield in the islands can be a refueling depot. My sources say Grand Bahamas is the latest. From there, boom, straight into Florida, Georgia, or the Carolinas."

"Where do they land in the US?"

"Tiny airfields, sometimes landing strips in the woods, other times they drop the stuff into the water just off the coast, and they have boats ready to collect it."

"What about the DEA?"

Ventura laughed. "What about them? If they find a spot to stake out, the cartel stops using it."

"How do they know?"

"How do you think? The DEA is a leaky ship, my friend."

"Probably because they don't meet at the zoo."

"You're hilarious, Cox."

"I'm here all week."

"No you're not. If you want to get the lowdown on where they're flying in and out, I have a contact in Savannah you need to talk to."

Ventura offered the bucket of popcorn to Lenny, who shook his head.

"No, thanks."

"Holy crap, Cox. In my hand."

Lenny glanced at the hand holding the bucket to see a piece of paper hanging out from underneath. Lenny took the paper.

"Don't look at it now."

"Okay. Who is it?"

"A pilot."

"An informant?"

"Let's just call him a pilot. Go to Savannah. Use my name. He'll show you what's what."

"Okay, sounds good. Does Greyhound go to Savannah?"

"Talk to your CO. I'm sure there's a military jumper you can get on."

"Yeah."

"Short of that, your friends at the NSC can cash you up for a plane ticket."

Lenny nodded and watched Ventura stuff a handful of popcorn in his mouth. "Stay in touch," he said with kernels falling out onto the concrete. He walked away and tossed the popcorn bucket into the trash as he went.

Lenny stayed and wandered around some of the exhibits. None of the animals looked ecstatic about being behind bars. He didn't blame them. It was a high price to pay for a couple of meals a day and free lodging.

As Lenny stopped by the lemurs, he noticed the cage looked empty. A few school kids were pointing, trying to find the lemurs hiding inside. Lenny watched for a minute without seeing the animals, and the kids lost interest and walked away.

But Lenny couldn't walk away. His brain was trying to formulate a question, but the words wouldn't come. Then something from left field popped into his head: *How did Ventura know he had friends at the NSC who would bankroll him? There hadn't been any CIA representative at that meeting.*

The thought passed as a sliding door opened and the lemurs charged into the enclosure, standing up like sentries to give Lenny the once-over. He wanted to call out to the kids, but they were long gone.

———

LENNY AND ALICE SIPPED ON BEERS AND SHARED nachos at a local college bar. She had discarded her workwear for an oversize woolen sweater and jeans.

"So you're going to the Hostess City of the South?" she said.

"Huh?"

"Savannah, Georgia."

"Ah. It would seem."

"When?"

"In a few days."

"You going back to Quantico first?"

"You trying to get rid of me?"

"The contrary, actually. I'm just starting to get used to having you around."

"Is that okay?"

"Yes, it is." She took a drink and looked at him over the top of her bottle. "You ever thought about doing a secondment in DC?"

"An office job? That's not really my bag."

"Maybe. But I think you're more versatile than you let on."

"Not sure that extends to living in a cubicle."

Alice shrugged and picked up a corn chip with guacamole.

"So, have you ever heard the name Carlos Lehder?" he asked.

She finished chewing. "The cartel boss?"

"I think so."

"What are you into?"

"Do you really want to know?"

"I don't think I do. But Carlos Lehder is bad news. He's basically Pablo Escobar's right-hand man in the Medellín cartel."

"Do you know anything about his operations in the Bahamas?"

"He bought an island, I think. Norman's Cay. He was flying drugs in and out of there. But if I remember correctly, the administration put pressure on the Bahamian government to stop it. I'm pretty sure he fled to Panama."

"Panama? Why not Colombia?"

"I'm not on that task force, but I think he's made himself unpopular in Colombia, and I mean beyond the normal cartel business. He and Escobar are meddling in politics, and that's raising some hackles down there. Escobar has gotten himself elected to their congress. But I do know the DOJ considers Lehder a person of interest."

"What does that mean to the Department of Justice, a person of interest?"

"It means that if somehow we were to get our hands on him, we would look to prosecute him in the United States."

"How would you get your hands on him?"

"We wouldn't. We don't do that. But someone might. We have agencies, and we and the State Department have worked with the Colombian government and others to write extradition treaties. Those would enable us to prosecute here, because it's here that they're doing the most damage."

On the walk home, Alice slipped her arm through Lenny's and nestled against him. It was cold out but he felt warm. It was the kind of walk he could get used to. Better than marching. An easy pace where the purpose was the walk, not the destination.

He tried to enjoy it while he could.

CHAPTER ELEVEN

THE ESPOSITO SYNDICATE WAS HEADED BY THE FAMILY patriarch, Francisco Esposito. It was known as a syndicate rather than a garden-variety crime family because Francisco had pulled together the networks of four families to create it. Lenny had no idea what the politics was like within the organization, but it was clear that, either through prudence or fear, the other families had ceded the head seat at the table to Francisco.

That was why Lenny found himself hiking through woods in the rolling hills outside Baltimore. The Caves Valley Golf Club was private, and exclusive enough to ensure that Lenny would not get past the front gate. But golf courses were expansive venues with plenty of access points for people as resourceful as Lenny.

He made his way through the trees to the side of a lush fairway and up past a practice putting green. His attire—chinos, polo under a knit sweater, and white walking shoes—had all been procured on a shopping spree under Alice's guidance. It was as good a camouflage as he could have under the circumstances.

Francisco Esposito was no golf fan, but he was reputed to be a member of the club, which prided itself on hosting meetings and functions for the rich and powerful, away from prying eyes. His youngest son's birthday didn't fall into such a category—Lenny had read about it in *The Washington Post*—but it was most definitely a guests-only affair.

Lenny saw the security detail from halfway along the fairway, so he bypassed the main clubhouse and came in through the service entrance, carrying a fold-up table. He left the table in a corridor, made his way through the kitchen, and entered the banquet hall behind a waiter carrying a shiny tray of hors d'oeuvres.

The room was filled with white cloth–covered tables. A band at one end was playing a Hall and Oates song. Suddenly Lenny wasn't as well camouflaged in his golf attire—everyone in this room wore evening dresses or tuxedoes.

Lenny spotted a security guard near the bar and walked over to him. The guy turned to him as he approached and offered a frown from his heavy brow. Lenny jinked his head in response.

"Hey," said Lenny, patting the guy's arm like an old friend. "You got a problem. The entire federal government is about to rain on your boss's parade, so you better find me a room where I can talk to him, or this party is going to go sideways real fast."

The guy moved his hand toward the holster under his ample wing. Lenny pinched the nerve in the security guard's elbow, causing his arm to spasm.

"No need for weapons or a scene. I'm not armed, and I'm here to help your guy, not hurt him. So how about you go find a suitable place to meet, and then you come back and get your boss."

The guard frowned deeper as if the whole thing was a trick.

"I know, that's right. I'm giving you a way to get me out of this room quietly. You'd best take it."

The guard nodded and moved toward the door, shepherding Lenny against the wall the whole way. They stepped out of the room into a foyer. The guy then jerked his head, and Lenny followed him into a smaller room being used as a repository for coats and birthday gifts.

"This place looks like Aladdin's cave," said Lenny.

The guard pulled the door closed, slipped out his gun, and pointed it at Lenny.

"I told you, you don't need that. And shooting me will only make your pain come faster and hurt more. So I'm going to sit, and you're going to get your boss. Mr. Esposito, right? Otherwise everything that happens from this point on is your fault."

The guy eyed him down the barrel then holstered the weapon, not taking his eyes off Lenny as he walked backward out of the room and closed the door. Within a few seconds another guy came in, similarly dressed like a Blues Brother, and pointed his gun at Lenny.

"This is a lot of presents," said Lenny. "How old is this kid?"

The guard didn't answer. A minute later the first guard returned and told the second one to search for a weapon. Lenny put his arms out and let the guy pat him down, then he stood at ease as the second guard shook his head.

"You came in here unarmed?" said the first guard, with an accent that sounded fake, like he'd watched too many Pacino movies. "You are one dumb SOB."

Lenny smiled. "Your boss on his way?"

"He'll be here if and when he decides."

"Okay. Just saying. Clock's ticking."

The clock ticked for twenty minutes before the door opened and a third Blues Brother stepped into the room followed by Francisco Esposito, wearing a tux with a bright white tie—the same snowy color of his hair, now thinning at the temples but otherwise lush.

"You better talk good, and you better talk fast," he said through flabby, purple lips.

A guard pulled a chair out for him, and he sat. Lenny got his own chair and sat opposite.

"You got a problem with your narcotics business," said Lenny.

"I don't know what you're talking about."

"But the federal government does. And there are people in it—people very high up—who are getting sick of the bad press coming from all these people overdosing on our streets."

"I told you, I don't know what you're talking about."

"I'm talking about the full force of the United States government aimed right at your organization."

"You don't say."

"I do say."

"Who do you work for?"

"You're not getting it, old man. I work for the people of the United States. And the people are fed up. So the folks who hold the power want action. They want wins. They want to prove that they're doing something about all these drugs. You familiar with the Manhattan Project?"

"I'm familiar."

"That's the approach these folks would like to take. Atomic bomb stuff. Blow you off the face of the planet at whatever cost."

"Is that so?"

"It is."

"And if they are going to do all that, why are you here disturbing my son's party?"

"To warn you."

"Warn me? Okay. Let me tell you something. The US didn't warn the Japs about the bomb—they just dropped it. So I think you're full of it. You're nobody and you got nothing. You want to take me to court? Go ahead. Then we'll see who's got the nukes."

Lenny smiled. "I'm sure you're used to playing cat and mouse with the local PD, the Capitol Police, the DEA, the FBI, whoever else. But my people don't operate like that. They're not interested in courtrooms or subpoenas or rules of evidence. They know who you are and what you do, and they are ready to wipe you and your organization off the face of this earth. You have become an enemy of the state."

The old man frowned, intensifying his already wrinkled forehead.

"So you think getting rid of me will somehow solve this problem? You think the flow of goods will stop because what, you kill me and my people? You're wrong. What you will create is a power vacuum, and power vacuums lead to instability and chaos. They lead to bloodshed. The merchandise will continue to flow, but the street will also be full of blood because less scrupulous people will see the opportunity. You don't know what these people are like."

With the hint of a grin on his face, Lenny stared at the man and said nothing.

Esposito took a handkerchief from his jacket and wiped the corners of his mouth. "But you're not here to kill me, because if you were, you would have tried already. So what is it you want?"

"The administration needs a win. A public victory in the war against drugs."

Esposito nodded slowly. "I see. And if I were to offer this win, I would want something in return."

"What's that?"

"Restraint. Your administration can't eliminate the product any more than I can—the demand is too great."

"We need to show that things are progressing. This fight is happening in the court of public opinion, and the people I work for do not want to lose there. We know the merchandise is coming in through Georgia. We want to capture a shipment—a significant haul—*and* the people bringing it in. You will tell me when and where."

"You think I'm going to give up my men?"

"I doubt very much that your men are the ones bringing it into the country, but either way, you can pay them for their sacrifice later. You can look after their families as your conscience sees fit. Provide them lawyers. They probably won't get more than a few years anyway, but we have to show something."

"And the merchandise? What becomes of it?" asked Esposito.

"It becomes a PR tool. You can write off a shipment on your balance sheet."

"But the government's process is to destroy it after trial. I want your assurance that when the PR event is done, it gets destroyed by one of *our* people. You understand?"

"I understand."

Esposito smacked his lips together. "I will arrange it, after I verify who you are."

"Sergeant Lenny Cox, United States Marine Corps."

"Marines?"

"I told you, this is war."

With a wave of a finger, the old man called forward one of his minions. They whispered for a moment, then the minion left the room. Esposito sat motionless. Lenny wasn't sure if he had stopped breathing until his guy came back in and handed Esposito a piece of paper. The old man looked at it, then handed it back to his man who passed it to Lenny.

"You will call this number tomorrow. Then you will learn whether or not I will help you. If I do, you will have the information you need. If not..." The old man shrugged.

"Okay," said Lenny.

"I must return to my son's party. You will be escorted from the grounds."

"That's not necessary. I know where the gates are."

"Oh, I insist."

Esposito used the back of the chair to stand, then one of his men got the door. Before he reached it he turned to Lenny.

"I don't expect we'll meet again, but if I should see you anywhere near me or my family without an invitation, I won't be as hospitable."

"If I'm anywhere near you or your family again, neither will I."

CHAPTER TWELVE

VENTURA TOOK THE ELEVATOR UP A COUPLE OF FLOORS from his cubicle. This time he was expected, so Erica held him for only a few minutes. When she gave him the word, he stepped into the office.

"What's happening?"

"Cox went to see Francisco Esposito in Baltimore," said Ventura.

"He did what?"

"I know this guy. You can expect the unexpected."

"What happened?"

"I don't know what he said, but this morning he requested a plane ticket to Savannah from the NSC."

The man in the suit nodded. "So he's buying it?"

"It would seem."

"But the Esposito visit is a concern."

"He's verifying his information."

"But how does he even know to go to a man like Esposito? And how does he get in to see him?"

"He's a sneaky piece of work, sir."

"Why isn't he working for us?"

"He has, but he's a Marine—he takes all that semper fi crap pretty seriously. A bit of a boy scout."

"I'll get a message to a contact in Baltimore PD. One of Esposito's guys. You get down to Georgia, keep eyes on our Marine. Make sure he follows the leads we want him to."

"Yes, sir."

"Is that it?"

"For now, sir."

"All right. Get out of here."

Ventura was already at the door. He strode past Erica with a nod and tried to keep the smile off his face. It was becoming a habit when leaving this office. But things were finally going his way. He could see his career getting back on track. He had been read in on some pretty high-level actions, and he was about to get back in the field, where he belonged.

———

WORKING FOR THE NATIONAL SECURITY COUNCIL wasn't like the Marines Corps. The Corps required requisition orders in triplicate and more signatures than the Declaration of Independence. And then the answer was usually *We don't have the budget for that*.

But one phone call to Ray Caan and he had a ticket for the following day to Savannah, Georgia, with a hand-delivered envelope containing two thousand dollars in cash for supplemental expenses. Lenny was starting to wonder if he was in the wrong business.

Before he left the capital, he had a couple of things to check off his list. He arranged the second thing first, ate a steak and baked potato at a Greek diner for supper, and then set out to take care of the first thing.

He hoped the first thing had taken care of itself, but in his short time on earth he had come to understand that people didn't always do what was in their own best interest. Decisions were rarely binary, this-or-that type scenarios. There were often multiple options at play, each muddled by its own series of considerations. And all of these considerations were often confounded by the greatest complication of all: money.

Lenny's drill instructor at MCRD San Diego had yelled a lot of advice at him and much of it had stuck, but nothing more than this: *Hard choice, easy life. Easy choice, hard life.* It was the reason Lenny started every day with a century each of pushups, sit-ups, and squats. He didn't enjoy the workout, but he survived because of what it gave him.

He knew not everyone thought like a Marine. Most people went the other way, making the easy choice in the short term and paying in the long term with a harder life. So Lenny wandered through the Georgetown University campus to see which option a young man had taken.

He waited opposite the Yates Field House, his jacket pulled tight and a beanie on his head, and nibbled on sunflower seeds, spitting the hulls onto the grass. The lights were on inside and a few people came and went from the fitness facility, but as the night settled in, the traffic dwindled close to nothing.

A guy came around the corner and headed for the rear of the field house, away from the well-lit entrance, and disappeared from view. Lenny waited.

A few minutes later, a second person appeared with a popped collar on his houndstooth jacket. Lenny sighed.

Easy choice, hard life.

Lenny stepped across the road, avoiding the building, and cut in behind Damian. The customer was waiting in the same place Lenny had waited, and he saw Lenny coming in behind his drug dealer.

"Who's this guy?" he asked.

Damian made to spin around but got only halfway there

before Lenny nailed him in the stomach with his fist. He doubled over then dropped. Lenny looked at the other guy.

"Time to go."

"But my stuff."

"You want a beating, or you want to leave?"

The guy didn't need long to consider the options. He shoved his hands into his jean pockets and hustled away.

Lenny turned back to the man on the ground. He was attempting to stand, so Lenny put a boot into his chin and sent him flying.

"You're an indictment on our education system, Damian. You have the opportunity to earn a degree from a fine institution and you're blowing it by making poor choices."

Damian rolled over and looked up at Lenny. "You."

"Yeah, me."

"I've got no new merchandise coming in right now 'cause of you."

"I'm glad to hear it. But apparently you don't hear so well. I told you to find a better job to pay your way through college. You remember that?"

"Do you know what Orange Julius pays?"

"I neither know nor care, Damian. That wasn't the point. For a guy smart enough to get into Georgetown, you sure are dumb. The point was to stop dealing drugs. To stop killing people. And I told you if you didn't do that, I'd be back."

"So what now? You're gonna beat me up some more?"

"Yes, I am. But first, I want you to understand why. This is the wrong path you're headed down. You can try to wash the stain from your hands, but you are killing people. I want you to lead a long and productive life, Damian. But this isn't the way."

"If I stop, they'll come after me."

"Who will?"

"Crespi."

"No, I don't think Roy will come after you anytime soon. So you can stop right now and get on with your studies. Construct a better building, design an artificial heart. Or just get a job in a bank and be a good person. I don't care. And I could care less if they come after you. Leave and find another college if you have to. Time to make the *hard* choices, Damian. Because the other option is very painful."

"All right," he said. "I get it. I'll stop."

"Good. But the thing is, I gave you that option before, and you lied. Now we have a trust problem. So I have to make sure."

"So you're just gonna beat me up?" he asked again.

"Correct."

Lenny pummeled the dealer with kicks to the shins and the gut and the ribs. When Damian curled into a ball, Lenny went at his back and his kidneys and the rear of his head. He stopped short of knocking him out and well short of killing him, but he figured the kid didn't know the difference.

When he was done, Lenny stood looking at him. He wasn't a kid, not really. He wasn't that much younger than Lenny. But he hadn't seen the world, hadn't explored its underbelly the way Lenny had.

"Just stay down for a while," Lenny said, crouching down close. "Then go home. Take a few days off class if you must, but don't ever forget this. I won't. I'll be watching. If you change schools, I'll know. When you graduate, I'll know. When you get a job and find a girl and get married and have a kid, I'll know. And if you deal again, I'll know. Next time the beating will stop only when you're dead."

Lenny stood. All Damian could do was groan, and Lenny hoped the message had gotten through. He was about to leave when he thought of something, so he squatted again and reached into Damian's coat, removing two bags of cocaine. Lenny stood then ripped the bags open and watched the powder blow away toward the woods.

"Do better," he said, then he turned and walked away.

ALICE WAS SITTING ON THE SOFA WITH A GLASS OF Chardonnay and a pile of briefing papers when Lenny arrived. She took one look, and her jaw dropped.

"What happened to you?"

"Me? Nothing. Why?"

"I don't know. You just looked different."

"Different how?"

"Maybe it's your eyes?"

"My eyes?"

Lenny flopped down onto the sofa. There was something going on with him. Something different. Not just in his eyes or his overall look. Something in... his scent—he smelled different. An aroma was pulsing off him, yet it wasn't something she could put her finger on. There, but not there. Strange. She knew this man. They had not spent large chunks of time together, but she enjoyed his company and they had shared things that suggested they had common ground on the big issues, and were prepared to stay quiet on the other things—things that a lawyer would worry about and a solider might have to work around.

But this was new. This was... feral. Something human but not, or maybe extremely human but not of polite society. It was like he was giving off vibrations into the universe, something basal.

"You want some wine?" she asked.

"No, I'm good. Listen, I'm going away."

"Back to base?"

"No. I'm sort of being deployed."

"Sort of being deployed?"

"Yeah."

"Is this like the Thailand thing?"

"Kind of, but different."

"But you can't tell me about it."

"Probably better if you don't know."

"But it's about the Medellín cartel."

Lenny frowned. "What makes you say that?"

"Because you don't generally begin conversations with 'So, what do you know about Carlos Lehder?'"

"I don't get much past you."

"You don't get anything past me. When are you leaving?"

"I'm on a flight at noon tomorrow."

Alice put her papers on the coffee table and placed her wine-glass on top. Then she stood.

"Then let's not waste any time."

"Doing what?"

"Doing nothing."

She put out her hand. He took it and rose from the sofa. Then she led him to her bedroom. She didn't know what this animal vibe thing was, but she wasn't planning on squandering it.

CHAPTER THIRTEEN

THE CALL HAD BEEN A QUICK ONE. THE NUMBER
Esposito had given Lenny did not go back to him. It was a Baltimore number, but a Boston accent told Lenny where he needed to be and when. Then he hung up without saying goodbye. But it made Lenny's next move as logical as it had been before.

As Lenny's plane landed at Savannah International Airport, he watched a C-130 taxi across the far side of the airfield. Maybe a Georgia Air National Guard aircraft.

With his pack, he wandered off the airliner through the Jetway and noticed a man sitting in the gate lounge. Ventura had said look for a pilot, so Lenny was on alert for a captain's hat and blue blazer with gold-striped cuffs. This guy was the other kind of pilot. He wore tortoise shell Ray-Bans and a battered brown leather jacket with an insignia patch of an eagle and the word *Airborne*. He had an unnecessary buzz cut, as most of his hair had gone the way of the dodo. But according to Ventura, his defining feature was the permanent cigarette attached to his lips.

Lenny stepped out of the traffic flow to the row of seats where the man's ash dropped from his cigarette onto the carpet. The pilot pushed the glasses down his nose and checked him out with a squint that gave Lenny the sense that the lenses might have been prescription.

"101st Airborne," said Lenny.

The guy nodded. "Once upon a time. You?"

"Marine Corps."

"Jarhead."

Lenny said nothing.

"Let's go," said the pilot.

He led Lenny outside into sunshine that was brighter than the stuff they got inside the beltway. There was a briny scent in the air, similar to Camp Lejeune but with an overlay of something vegetal. Walking over to an old Willys Jeep, Lenny got the sense that the pilot might have been living in the past.

The wind whistled through Lenny's tight haircut as they screamed into town. The pilot wound around a series of squares plotted throughout the city—each featuring a fountain or a statue with benches for folks to rest under the shade of massive, ancient oaks. Tendrils of Spanish moss hung from trees, and Lenny wondered if that was what he was smelling.

The pilot parked down by the river but made no attempt to get out of the Jeep. He lit another cigarette, and Lenny watched the breeze off the water blow the smoke away toward the old town.

"So is this the full-day tour or what?" asked Lenny.

"You don't like Savannah?"

"Never been. Looks nice. Quiet."

"I like quiet," said the pilot.

"Good for you. But I didn't come here to retire."

"No. You want to know how the merchandise moves."

"You saying it comes through here?"

"No. It usually flies into the low country."

"And where does it come from?" asked Lenny.

"You might be interested in Freeport."

"What's happening in Freeport?"

"Nose candy comes in, nose candy goes out. Ends up here, the Carolinas. As far as Maryland sometimes."

"How does it get to Freeport?"

"It's all fly in, fly out. What I know about, anyway."

"You've made these flights?"

"You trying to get me to incriminate myself, sunshine?"

"I'm not empowered to arrest you. I'm not a cop."

"What are you?"

Lenny smiled. "I'm a troublemaker."

The pilot nodded as if this were a legitimate job title.

"So Freeport, then?" asked the pilot.

"Actually, I'm hearing about a place called Deep Water Cay. An airstrip maybe?"

"I know it. It ain't Freeport."

"I'd like to take a look. Can you get me there?"

"Sure."

"What's it gonna cost me?"

"It's been taken care of. I'll let you know if we start running up the tab."

"Okay. Let's go."

"Later."

"My information is only good until tonight."

"We'll be there in time, don't worry. I'll pick you up here in two hours."

"And what do I do until then?"

"Take a walk along the riverfront. Eat some taffy. What do I care?"

Lenny got out and grabbed his pack from the back of the Jeep. The pilot zoomed away as if the vehicle had a third gear and nothing else. Lenny did as directed and wandered along the water. The touristy stores and restaurants held no interest for him, so he cut away from the coast and wound his way through the city streets. The Spanish moss gave the place an ethereal charm, and the brick buildings and humongous oaks offered a sense of permanence.

He wandered down Jones Street, filled with 19th century brick buildings, and happened upon a line of people outside a row home with nothing about it to explain the gathering. He asked what the deal was and was told it was the best southern food in town. Lenny didn't really know what that meant, but he was a believer in the idea that if he was in a place, he should really be in that place. He might be in Savannah for no more than a few hours and life might never bring him this way again, so the best southern food in a picturesque southern town sounded like something worth his while.

Mrs. Wilkes' Dining Room was all that and more. He waited in the shade of the live oaks with the other patrons before the door opened and they were ushered into what felt like someone's home. White-covered tables were served family style. Lenny sat with a couple from Indiana and a family from California as they were served on mismatched plates and hand-me-down flatware. Food was placed on the table on floral serving platters: fried chicken and beef stew, fried okra, collard greens, black-eyed peas, red rice, mac and cheese, and candied yams, with mounds of cornbread and gallons of sweet tea.

Lenny ate for a platoon and sat back with a warm glow when he was done. The service was all the southern hospitality he had heard about, with a dash of grandmotherly charm. When he stood to leave he thanked his lunchmates, then he strolled back toward the river.

The pilot was waiting in his Jeep, but he gave no indication that he was bothered by this. Instead he just put the vehicle into gear and sped away. He drove west out of town, into the wide, flat countryside. Lenny started to understand why they called it the low country.

The airfield wasn't much more than a cut strip and a few

sheds. There was a canvas sign for a flight club, and Lenny saw a phalanx of single-prop aircraft around the main hangar.

They parked and walked over to a Cessna 210. The pilot walked around the aircraft and did his inspections, then he told Lenny to get in. Lenny stepped up into the cockpit and looked around the cabin. The aircraft was designed to be a six-seater, but all the rear seats had been removed to leave a metal shell. He tossed his pack in the back and tried not to think about what was usually carried back there.

The pilot put on his headset and directed Lenny to do the same, then he started the engine and let it warm up as he checked his instruments. The fuselage vibrated and then dropped to a steady hum, and Lenny was reminded that most aircraft had the feel of a tin can.

There was no traffic control and no tower, so the pilot taxied straight out to the end of the strip and turned right. Before the turn was completed, he pushed the throttle and they hurtled across bumpy ground until the pilot was ready. He lifted the nose and the shuddering stopped as they soared into the air.

He radioed what Lenny assumed was the tower at the commercial airport, then they banked around over South Carolina and headed between Fort Pulaski and Hilton Head Island and out to sea.

The roar of the engine and the wind rushing around the fuselage kept the chitchat to a minimum. The pilot said nothing as the sun dipped, and he dropped altitude until Lenny could see the tops of the ocean swells throwing shadows across the troughs. Then the water changed from deep blue to turquoise, and to starboard he could see a distant island.

The pilot came in low and wide around Grand Bahama and banked back from the east. He was only feet from the water as it morphed into scrub, and suddenly they were over an airstrip in the middle of the island.

They landed with a casual thud, and the pilot eased off the

throttle, using the full length of the long strip to save his tires. He taxied back to the midpoint of the runway then pulled off onto the grass like he was parking his car at the county fair.

When he cut the engine he removed his headset. Lenny did the same as he surveyed the airfield. There were no buildings or any other aircraft.

"The main airport is back to the west, just north of Freeport," said the pilot. "There's a secondary airfield at the west end. I prefer to avoid both."

"So what's this?"

"I'm told it's an old military strip, but I'm not aware of the Bahamas having an air force, so I couldn't tell ya."

"Is this where the drug flights come in?"

"You'll go further in this business if you don't use that word."

"I don't want to go anywhere in this business. I'm here to take the business down."

"Ventura said you were a live wire."

"So is this the place?"

"No. Your place is a small private strip at the east end of the island. Deep Water Cay. Almost no one lives down there, just a fishing resort and a handful of houses. It's quiet, and there's beach access if they want to transfer to boats."

"So how the hell do we get there?"

"This is the Bahamas, bud. We take a boat."

Lenny grabbed his pack as the pilot closed up his craft, then he led Lenny along a parched road toward the water. It was a ten minute walk, and Lenny removed his jacket half way to the main road, carrying it over his shoulder like the war correspondents did on TV. They crossed the hyperbolically named Grand Bahama Highway without seeing a vehicle and then continued along the road for a few hundred yards until they came to a sparse township. A few buildings, one of which proclaimed the best conch fritters on the island, were dispersed between vacant plots and scrubland. The pilot cut down a side street that rapidly became a sandy track, and after a few minutes they hit the beach.

It was paradise. Lenny couldn't figure how a postcard could have made it any better. White sand swept into turquoise water that just begged to be swum in, the departing sun lighting it like a jewel.

The pilot stepped to a dinghy with a small outboard attached and made to drag it down to the water.

"We're stealing a boat?" asked Lenny.

"Belongs to a buddy of mine. I brought a bottle of rum to cover the fuel."

Lenny nodded and grabbed the other side of the boat, then dragged it into the water. The pilot started the outboard. Lenny pushed the bow out and jumped in.

They puttered along the shoreline toward the eastern end of the island, where a series of cays broke away like a smashed dinner plate. Darkness was consuming them as the pilot glided up to a dock on the back side of one of the cays. Lenny saw the warm lights of a colonial-style structure.

"Fishing resort," said the pilot. "They've got a bar."

"We staying here?"

"Not me, pal. Bit rich for my blood. I'll sleep in the plane."

Lenny shrugged at the guy's life choices. He couldn't see the value of risking jail smuggling drugs for the return of sleeping on the steel floor of a Cessna.

They walked up to the place, crossing its wide veranda. Inside, rattan stools surrounded a horseshoe bar. Lenny's boots made solid thuds on the hardwood floor. Everyone else was either barefoot or wearing flips flops and dressed in T-shirts and shorts, except the guy at the far end, who sat alone over a dark and stormy, in a polo shirt that made him look like a lost golfer. He didn't raise his head, but he watched the pilot walk in and sit at the other end of the bar, then he took a long look at Lenny before refocusing on his cocktail.

The pilot asked if it was Lenny's round. He said yes, although it was technically Caan's money or more specifically the US taxpayers', which Lenny figured was his money after all.

They each got a beer and nodded to the sunburned faces around the bar. After the two touched bottles and took a sip, the pilot leaned in.

"So the strip's a couple hundred yards down that way."

"Is it lit?"

"Nope, but the lights in this building will provide the heading, and there's another restaurant on a cay farther down. You line 'em up and in ya come."

"Doesn't anyone notice?"

"I'm sure they do, but folks keep to themselves."

They sat in silence until they finished their drinks, then the pilot ordered another beer and a plate of conch fritters. Lenny shifted to soda but declined food, still full from his meal in Savannah.

And he operated better when he was a little hungry.

CHAPTER FOURTEEN

The pilot went to the bathroom, and the bartender asked if Lenny wanted anything before they closed.

"I'm good," he said. "So, you get a few people flying direct to go fishing?"

"Sure. Not scheduled flights but GA, for sure."

"You know any good pilots?"

"I know a few, but aren't you drinking with one?"

"He's got to get back home, and I was thinking of doing some island hopping."

"Well, there's—" He glanced at the other end of the bar. "Ah, he's gone."

"The guy in the polo?"

"Yeah. Renquist. He's a pilot. Lives back near Freeport."

"Why does he come all the way out here?"

The bartender smiled. "'Cause we're good company."

Lenny nodded. "Fair enough." He pulled some cash from his pack and handed it over. "Sorry, do you take US dollars?"

"Of course. The Bahamian dollar is pegged to the greenback one-to-one, so no problem, man."

"Good to know. You know where I might find this Renquist guy tomorrow?"

"Here, I'd reckon. He's bringing a party in from Miami."

"Roger that."

The bartender drifted away and last drinks were called. The pilot returned. Lenny told him he had paid, so they waved to the bartender and walked out.

Back in the dinghy, the pilot puttered along the bay side of the cay, pointing out the runway that sliced right up the middle of the narrow strip of land.

They stopped at the far end of the cay and pulled the boat onto the beach but stayed put.

"They'll come in from the other end and taxi right down here," said the pilot. "We're as far from the resort as you can get and still be on the cay. What time did you say?"

"My information was eleven."

"So what will you do?"

"You got a gun?" asked Lenny.

"Nope. Don't want to enter the Bahamas with a gun."

"They won't have guns?"

"They will, knucklehead. They're smuggling narcotics. Guns don't make that worse. But when I've got nothing on board that I shouldn't have, I don't invite trouble."

"Okay."

"So what's the plan?"

"No plan. I'll call an audible once I see the defense."

"What do you want from me?"

"To stay in the boat and wait for me."

They waited for about forty-five minutes before the sound of a light aircraft grew louder from the darkness in the west. It swooped in low over the resort then flicked the landing lights on and eased down onto the tarmac. After coasting to the end of the landing strip, the pilot did a tight U-turn right above where Lenny and his pilot sat in the dinghy. The aircraft shut down, but no one got out.

"That's a Cessna," whispered the pilot. Lenny nodded.

Within a few minutes, another plane dropped in from the west and turned on its lights at the last moment before landing and doing the same tight U-turn. It then came to a gentle stop just short of the first aircraft.

"Piper Saratoga," said the pilot. "Looks new."

When the engine noise of the second aircraft died, Lenny heard the cabin doors open on both planes. He squatted in the dinghy and glanced at the pilot.

"Stay here," Lenny said, then he stepped up onto the grass that fringed the asphalt strip.

The two pilots had turned all their lights off, so Lenny was able to quickly step around the rear of the Cessna and watch the men. He was surprised there wasn't more security but figured fewer men meant less loose talk.

The pilot from the Piper walked over to the first man, who opened the cockpit door on the starboard side and removed a bag or duffel. As he handed it to his colleague, Lenny moved. He was behind the Cessna pilot in a flash, thrusting a boot into the back of his knee. The man collapsed backward, but he didn't let go of the duffel that both pilots had hold of, so he pulled the Piper pilot forward toward Lenny. As the Piper guy lurched toward him, Lenny punched the second pilot in the throat. He fell with a thud and wasn't popping back up, so Lenny turned to the Cessna man, who was trying to stand up. Lenny kicked his chest, sending him hard onto his back. Lenny rolled him over and forced his knee into the man's back. Then he patted him down and found an old revolver tucked into his jeans.

Lenny left the man lying on the ground and moved to check the Piper guy for weapons. On hands and knees, he was gasping and coughing, so Lenny ran his hand down the man's back but found nothing. He cocked the revolver, the unmistakable sound piercing the night air. Lenny pushed the barrel against the man's head.

"You have a gun?"

"No," he croaked.

"I don't believe you."

"It's in the cockpit."

That was sloppy. Lenny ordered the two men to lay on their stomachs on the asphalt with their hands behind their heads, then he moved to the Piper Saratoga, turned on his flashlight, and slipped the revolver he found there into the back waistband of his trousers.

Lenny climbed up into the cockpit and checked out the cabin. It was not dissimilar from the aircraft he and the pilot had taken from Savannah, except all six seats were in place.

He jumped down, strode past the men on the ground, and opened the door to the Cessna. It was essentially the same, with a few more nautical miles on the clock.

Lenny cast his light across the cabin, then got down and walked back over to the bag that had been dropped onto the tarmac. Lenny crouched down and unzipped it. Casting his light inside, he saw them: six bricks of white powder wrapped in plastic.

He stood and tapped the Cessna man's hip with his boot.

"You speak English?"

"No."

"No? You know enough English to understand 'do you speak English,' but that's it?" He touched the other guy's shoulder the same way.

"What about you, genius?"

"Yeah, I speak English."

"American? Okay. How much are you supposed to pick up tonight?"

"The duffel."

"That's it? There's only six keys in that bag."

"Yeah."

"You can fit a lot more than that in a small plane."

"We move what we're told. That's three hundred grand's worth."

The guy had a point. It didn't take a lot of the stuff to make a plane ride worthwhile. Lenny stood there and thought. He had two guns, a duffel of narcotics, and a mandate to cause mayhem. But on a private strip in the Bahamas, the options seemed limited. He could shoot the men and burn their aircraft, but his mandate didn't include killing unarmed men, and the folks with the three-letter acronyms had made it clear they weren't interested in prosecuting these people. Plus, two charred aircraft on their tarmac was going to put a dent in the business of the fishing resort, and the worst thing they had done was to ignore it.

That was all it took, Lenny thought. *For evil to prevail, all it took was that good men do nothing.*

"All right, boys, here's what's going to happen. I'm going to let you go. You fly back to wherever it is you came from and you take your licks. Tell your people that this strip is closed for business. At least for the business you do."

Lenny grabbed the duffel and set it in the grass next to the runway, then he directed the Piper pilot at gunpoint into his aircraft, which was now at the front of the line. Next he pointed the Cessna guy into his cockpit. Each of them started their machines. The first aircraft moved away, gaining speed as he went, before he eased into the air.

The Cessna was moving before the Piper was airborne. It took off right behind, banking hard to head south. Lenny stood on the asphalt until the sound of both aircraft had been consumed by the darkness. He collected the duffel, tossed the guns inside, and walked back to the dinghy.

The pilot was sitting in the boat where Lenny had left him. "So?"

Lenny held up the duffel.

"Nice," he said. "What will you do with it?"

"I don't know yet."

"I know people."

"I'm not going to sell it."

"I'm just saying, that's probably a lot of cash you've got there."

"It's a lot of ruined lives is what it is."

"You say potato. You want to hop in? We should get going."

"No, you go."

"You can't walk back to Freeport from here, you know."

"I know. Don't worry, I'll find my way back."

"Your call. I'll be at the bird when you're done."

"Don't wait for me. Just go back to Savannah."

"You're sure?"

"I'm sure. No problem. Thanks for the ride. And the tip." He held up the duffel.

The pilot shook his head. "You're the boss, but I'm telling you, the resort's all locked up tight by this hour."

"That's okay. I'll survive."

The pilot shrugged, moved to the back of the dinghy, and tossed Lenny his backpack, which Lenny dropped on the sand with the duffel. After pushing off from the beach, the pilot lowered the outboard into the water and then started it. He backed away a little farther from the cay, then he waved and disappeared into the night.

Holding the duffel, Lenny walked back up the sand to where the scrub started and dropped it. Then he wandered back up onto the landing strip. The black sky was barely discernible from the ocean. The gentle lapping of water on sand was the only sound. A small light glowed like a beacon at the other end of the cay—the resort, indeed closed up for the night.

It wasn't a bad place for a rendezvous. A long way from anywhere crowded with people but not too far for a light aircraft to reach foreign shores. Lenny wondered how many strips like this the cartel had access to. It might have been sparsely populated but it was populated; the resort guests were transitory, but the staff were not. Anybody would question regular landings after hours on a dark strip, so if the cartel used the runway, it had to be only occasionally.

Lenny stepped back off the tarmac onto the sand and over to the duffel. He dug out a small hole there and lay down in it. Lumbar support was always better sleeping in a hole than on flat ground. He didn't use the duffel as a pillow, as tempting as it was. Restful sleep didn't come on a bed of narcotics. Instead he rolled up his jacket and shoved it under his head.

He lay in his hole in the sand and looked up at the stars. There were more than he could count. More than he could even comprehend. An entire galaxy's worth on a canvas painted for one. One simple Marine who had taken down a drug shipment without a weapon or a shot being fired.

Lenny drifted off to the soft sound of the breathing ocean, with only one thought on his mind.

That was too damned easy.

CHAPTER FIFTEEN

LENNY WOKE JUST BEFORE FIRST LIGHT. FOR A WHILE HE didn't move, letting the breeze caress the scrub grass so it whistled its morning song. The ocean was dark but placid. As the sun broke behind him, Lenny stood, shook off the sand, and rolled his shoulders. It was paradise. Then he glanced down at the bag of drugs at his feet.

He slipped his pack over one shoulder, carried the duffel in the other hand, and set off along the landing strip. There were fishing boats already out on the water, rods sticking upward like antennae.

As Lenny stepped up onto the patio of the resort, he heard chattering from a group on the dock fussing around a flat-decked boat. It wasn't evident whether they were preparing to go out or if they had just gotten back with nothing to show for it.

Lenny pushed in through the door into the bar. The same bartender offered him a nod.

"You're back."

"The early bird and all that."

"Sure. You want breakfast?"

"Wouldn't say no."

"Table or bar?"

Lenny glanced around the empty room and slipped up onto a barstool.

"How do you take your coffee?"

"Straight up."

The bartender took a Bunn coffeepot and poured a mug of hot black then placed it in front of Lenny.

"Food?"

"I'll take whatever you're serving."

"You didn't eat last night. Full breakfast."

Lenny took a sip of the hot coffee. "Sounds like a plan."

The bartender replaced the pot. "I'm Reg, by the way."

"Lenny. This your place?"

"It is."

Reg disappeared for quite a while, making Lenny wonder if the guy did the early KP alone. When he returned, he delivered eggs, toast, and bacon, with a half plate of crunchy breakfast potatoes.

"Dig in," Reg said, so Lenny picked up a piece of bacon and ate it.

"What sort of fish you catch around here?" asked Lenny.

"People come for the bonefishing."

"Bonefish? Doesn't sound very appetizing."

"They taste okay, but you gotta be a whizz with a filet knife or you end up with a mouthful of those bones."

"And people fly all the way out here for that?"

"They fly out for this," he said, waving toward the window and the water beyond. "And the bonefish is good catching. Quite the fighter. Most guys just toss them back."

"Fair enough." Lenny scooped up some potatoes.

"You lost your pilot," said Reg.

"He had to go back."

"That's right. You were looking to do some island hopping."

"Something like that. You said you expected the pilot from last night to be back today."

"Renquist. Yeah, after lunch."

"You got any rooms?"

"Fully booked, I'm afraid."

"Dock shower?"

"We have a bathroom for the boat captains to clean up in."

"How much?"

"If you're sticking around for lunch, I'll throw in a towel and some soap."

"You got a deal."

Reg filled up Lenny's coffee. "Where'd you sleep last night? I didn't see you come in on a dinghy this morning."

"On the beach."

"Doing it rough, hey?"

"Catching *z*'s in paradise is hardly roughing it. Listen, did you hear an aircraft landing here last night?"

The guy pursed his lips. "I was probably asleep."

"It wasn't that late."

"I don't hear anything."

"I get it. So how often might someone who doesn't hear anything not hear an aircraft landing after dark?"

"What's your interest?"

"Honestly? Someone I know died from a drug overdose, and I'm doing something about that."

"You brave or stupid?"

"They're not mutually exclusive." Lenny shoved some egg and toast in his mouth and looked at the guy.

"These are not good people," said Reg.

"I know. So how often?"

"Not that often, not anymore. Maybe once a month for the last year."

"And before that?"

"Weekly."

"And you didn't wonder what it was you weren't hearing?"

"Not my business."

Lenny nodded. "You get a visit?"

"Once."

"What did they say?"

"That it wasn't any of my business."

"And what was the incentive to keep it that way?"

"There may have been an implication that this place might burn to the ground unexpectedly."

"That can happen."

Reg shrugged. "Can I get you anything else?"

"I'm good."

"I'll grab you a towel, then." He walked away and returned with a thin blue towel and a cake of soap wrapped in paper.

"Imperial Leather," said Lenny. "Classy."

"Welcome to the Commonwealth. Nothing but the best. Just don't ask me where I got it."

"None of my business."

Reg nodded again and removed Lenny's empty plate. "I don't want trouble."

"That's why I need a pilot. The trouble won't be here."

Reg watched him for a moment. "Shower's out that door, then second on the left."

"Thanks. Say, you haven't got any matches, have you?"

"You're not planning on burning the place down?"

"Where would I get lunch?"

Reg grabbed a matchbook from a basket and tossed one to Lenny. He slipped it into his jacket pocket and stood.

"What's the check?"

"I'll put it on your tab."

Lenny saluted with the wrong hand then carried his two bags, towel, and soap out the door. He found the shower room, which was more private than a barracks but not quite as clean. He took his time showering, lathering everything twice.

Afterward he returned the towel and then took up station on the patio overlooking the shallows. The chatty group on the dock was gone. Everything was quiet for a several hours. Lenny just watched the wisps of clouds moving across the sun, altering the color of the water every minute.

Lenny did a lot of waiting. It was the fate of a Marine sniper. Shooting well was a necessary skill, but waiting was the majority of the job. In holes, in trees, in vacant buildings in various states of disrepair. Sitting in the shade on a Caribbean island, watching the world go by, was not exactly a chore. Lenny figured he could get used to this.

The small flotilla of flatboats motored into the dock at lunchtime. Bonefish anglers disembarked and wandered up to their rooms to wash off, then they adjourned to the dining room. Lenny saw no fish come off the boats, but spirits seemed high.

Lenny didn't move. He was waiting for one specific person and figured he could have lunch after the anglers had cast off for their afternoon session.

Some of the clients had finished lunch and were settled on the deck for cigarettes when Lenny heard the aircraft coming in from the southwest. The pilot banked wide to land from the far end of the runway. Then the plane taxied to the closest point to the resort.

Reg took off toward the strip in a golf cart to where the runway ended, about two hundred yards down a sand track. Lenny saw two male passengers in panama hats and loud shirts climb out of the aircraft and into the cart. Reg drove them back to the resort and took them inside.

The pilot got out of the aircraft and unloaded two suitcases. Leaving them on the tarmac, he closed up and walked down the track. He passed a young barefoot Black guy in a T-shirt and shorts going the other way. The young man collected the luggage, and the pilot walked up the steps, past where Lenny sat, and went inside.

Lenny gave it a minute, then picked up his bags and followed. There were still a few men at lunch tables, but only one person at the bar. The pilot, Renquist, had resumed his position from the previous evening and sat with a drink that might have been a gin and tonic or just water.

Renquist watched without watching as Lenny walked over and dropped his bags by a stool kitty-corner from the pilot. Lenny parked himself on a stool and waited for Reg to appear from the kitchen.

"Burger or conch?" Reg asked.

"You got any fish?"

"Tuna. Frozen."

"I thought this was a fishing resort."

"Bonefish, remember?"

"Conch, then. And a beer."

Reg opened a Kalik and then retired to the kitchen to place the order. Lenny took a sip and looked at Renquist, who was focused on his drink.

"You just flew in," Lenny said.

The pilot glanced at him. "I did."

"From the States?"

"Miami."

"Do that often?"

"Often enough."

Lenny sipped his beer then put his hand out. "Lenny."

The man took Lenny's hand and shook without effort, though his grip was strong. "Renquist," he said.

"You live here?"

"Outside of Freeport."

"I might be needing a ride, if you're interested."

"I'm not interested."

"No? I thought you were a pilot."

"I thought you already had a pilot."

"He had to go home."

Renquist lifted his head. "Says who?"

"Says me."

"Well, his Cessna was still parked at the old airfield when I flew over just now."

"Is that right? Maybe he had a change of plans."

"Maybe. You should call him."

"I'm looking for a fresh perspective."

Renquist twirled his drink and frowned. "I'm not in that business. You should look elsewhere."

"What business is that?"

"You know well what business."

Renquist returned his attention to his glass, and Lenny said nothing more until Reg returned with two plates of conch fritters. He dropped them off, then walked out to serve customers at the tables.

"Where'd you learn to fly?" Lenny asked before he bit into a piece of fried conch.

"The Marine Corps."

"You were an officer?"

"An O2, by the end."

"First lieutenant?"

"You know your ranks."

"They were drummed into us at San Diego."

Renquist glanced up from his drink. "You were in the Corps?"

"Don't spread it around, but I still am. Just a grunt though."

"You on leave?"

"*Detachment* might be a more accurate term."

"What's a Marine doing in the Bahamas?"

"The opposite of what you think."

Renquist took a sip. "Is this sanctioned?"

"That's an interesting word. Do you know anything about aircraft landing on the strip here late at night?"

"There are no lights on this strip."

"I know. But it happened anyway."

"I've heard them coming in, now and again. Never seen it."

"I did. And I sent them packing."

"That's not a Marine Corps op."

"Let's just say I know someone who was a casualty and I don't like that."

"So this is a crusade."

"Call it what you will." Lenny ate some conch and took a sip of his beer.

"Sounds like the sort of thing that gets a young man into trouble."

"I've never minded a bit of trouble."

"Then you were with the right pilot already."

"Maybe. Let's just say I didn't get the sense he was showing me his whole hand."

"How so?" asked Renquist.

"I might have tried to persuade the boys from the aircraft last night to reconsider their life choices."

"Good luck with that."

"Yeah, I'm not convinced they were listening. But they gave up their stash pretty easily. Too easily."

"You think it was a setup?"

"It occurred to me."

"And you think your pilot showed you what you wanted to see so you'd go away."

"Something like that."

"But you want to cause more trouble than that."

"Indeed I do."

Renquist bit into his conch and chewed, then pointed his fork at Lenny. "You need to talk to Barry Seal."

"Who's Barry Seal?"

"Pilot. The kind of pilot you're looking for."

"Can you take me to him?"

"I told you. I don't do that kind of thing."

"What kind of thing? I'm talking about a charter flight."

"I don't do low altitude, under-the-radar stuff. I did enough of that in Vietnam."

"So fly right. I don't need to sneak into the country. I'm a citizen. I have a passport."

"You have to pass through customs."

"That's okay. I'd just rather avoid commercial."

"Why?"

"If I'm going to leave a paper trail, I'd rather it be after the fact, not before."

Renquist wiped his mouth with a napkin. "Can you pay?"

"Cash."

"And what about your proceeds from last night?"

"I need to figure out how to destroy it. Maybe burn it."

"Weed?"

"No."

"Snow?"

Lenny nodded.

"It won't burn. Combustion temp is too high. You'd best dump it in the ocean."

"I don't want to kill all the fish around here. Reg will have me strung up."

"Fair point. How much are we talking?"

"Not much. Six keys."

"No one goes to all that trouble to fly in six keys."

"I wouldn't have thought so."

"Alright. Finish your lunch, and we'll take care of it."

Renquist seemed in no hurry, so Lenny took his time and had a second beer. When they were done, Lenny covered his tab and Renquist's, then they wandered out along the track toward his aircraft. Renquist kept his eye on the duffel bag.

Lenny got into the Cessna, and Renquist eased the aircraft around and took off away from the resort. He radioed in, saying that he was doing a tour from Deep Water Cay and would be landing at West End. Then he banked to the south, and Lenny saw the water change from turquoise to a rich blue.

Once they were over deep water and away from the island,

Renquist gave Lenny the go-ahead and he opened the duffel. He took out a Swiss Army knife and punctured the plastic of the top brick of cocaine.

"Not too big," said Renquist. "We don't want to fill the cockpit with it."

"Aye, aye," said Lenny.

He opened the latch on the cockpit window then picked up the first brick, pushed the window open, and slipped it out. He repeated the process—stab a hole, open the window, eject the drugs—until he was done. With the guns still inside the duffel bag, he pushed the whole thing out the window and let it drop toward the water below. As he relatched the window, Renquist banked back toward the west end of Grand Bahama.

———

DESPITE THE WARM AFTERNOON, THE PILOT STILL WORE his jacket emblazoned with the badge for the 101st Airborne. He sat in his buddy's boat offshore from Deep Water Cay as the Cessna carrying Renquist and Cox took off. He watched it bank south, but then it kept banking as if south was not the final destination. He took up the radio from the seat in front of him.

"Basecamp, this is Flyboy," he said.

A crackle and then a reply. "Cut the crap, just tell me," said Ventura.

"Cox has flown out with the guy I told you about."

"Where to?"

"Looks like they're taking a roundabout route to his home field."

"You're sure?"

"Nope. I can't read the guy's mind, but I can make out his general heading."

"You better be right."

"You'll know soon enough."

CHAPTER SIXTEEN

AFTER DEPOSITING THEIR UNWANTED CARGO INTO THE sea, Renquist banked wide around the narrow western tip of Grand Bahama and brought the Cessna down on a small runway that wasn't the same one Lenny had arrived at with the other pilot.

"West End Airport," Renquist said after noticing Lenny's puzzled expression.

Lenny looked around as they turned and taxied toward the end of the landing strip. There was nothing to see there—just water and what resembled a parched golf course. Calling it an airport was one hell of an exaggeration. When Renquist taxied off the runway he turned right into a square of tarmac that resembled a mall parking lot on Christmas morning. Not a single aircraft anywhere. He pulled over to the side as if parking in a slot, then shut the engine down.

"So what now?" asked Lenny.

"I'll get it refueled and we can head stateside tomorrow."

"Not today?"

"Can't get all the way to Arkansas before we lose the light."

"Arkansas?"

"Trust me. That's where you want to go."

They got out, and Renquist led Lenny through a line of palm trees to a smaller lot with a single car and a shed with a sign that, in the hyperbolic spirit of the place, read *Customs House*. It looked closed up for the day.

Renquist walked to a beaten and sun-bleached Toyota pickup. The door was unlocked and opened with a loud, haunted creak. Lenny tossed his pack in the bed and got in. It reminded him of a military vehicle: light on comfort, big on dependability.

They pulled out, and Lenny realized Renquist was driving on the left side of the street despite the wheel being on the left—an American vehicle on the roads of a former British colony.

As Renquist drove along the main road, he pointed out some of the developments that were ramping up on the island.

"There was a boom in the sixties, but it all died when the economy tanked after that OPEC business in the seventies. It's coming back though. The streets are busier with tourists than I've ever seen."

"Good for a guy in your business."

"I don't need too much business. Might be time to bug out, find somewhere quieter."

It looked pretty quiet to Lenny. All the buildings were low and stout among tall, proud palm trees. They passed the port, busy with cargo ships and cruise liners, and then continued into town.

Renquist pulled over and pointed to a two-story building. "That's as good a hotel as there is, unless you want waterfront prices."

"I'm okay without the view."

"Right, then. I'll pick you up here at zero-eight-hundred tomorrow."

"Is there a supermarket around here?"

"Not like in the US. There's a small place about two streets back. Foodmart. But there are plenty of restaurants down near the mall, toward Xanadu Beach."

"Foodmart. That sounds fine. Pick me up there. Zero-eight-hundred."

Lenny got out and grabbed his pack, then Renquist drove away. Lenny regarded the colonial-style hotel with its wide verandah and iron latticework. He walked inside and felt the temperature drop, and noticed an ancient swamp cooler moving the air around. A petite, balding man sat behind an ornate wooden desk.

"Good afternoon," he said in an English accent. "How may I help you?"

"Looking for a room. One night."

"You've come to the right place. Front balcony has the view, rear has the quiet."

"I'll take the quiet."

Lenny scribbled Ventura's name in a ledger book and passed over the cash. The man handed him a key on a stick that wasn't going to fit in any pocket Lenny had.

"Top of the stairs. Room four. Cocktails in the garden at five."

Lenny thanked him and ascended the dark wood staircase. He easily found the large but sparsely furnished room. A double bed, one side table, one chest of drawers. A single floor lamp and a chair in the corner. French doors led onto a balcony. As promised, the view was unspectacular. Lenny knew he was facing the water, but he couldn't see it beyond the cinderblock wall of the adjacent building. Below, five small tables with folded umbrellas stood mute in a tiny, grassy yard attached to the hotel. No one was out there. Cocktails weren't until five. Lenny cast his eye to the lane behind the yard. Then he stepped inside. There was no bathroom. He figured there would be one at the end of the hall.

That would do. It would all do.

————

VENTURA SAT BAKING IN HIS COMPACT CAR WHOSE vents blew hot like an oven—no AC. It had been tolerable while he was waiting for the aircraft to arrive. There was only one road out from the runway, so he had found a patch of shade to wait under. Then, as he followed the pickup into town with the windows down, the breeze kept the air breathable. Now it burned. Everything was still—the air, the streets, the palm trees. Very few people were out. He thought of Langley, where people were wearing jackets and coats already. Why was CIA business always done in blazing hellholes?

He watched the hotel. Cox had gone inside and not come out. Evidently he was staying the night. Perhaps he was waiting on a commercial flight out of the main airport the next day.

Cox had done what he was asked to, as pointless as it all seemed. He'd stopped a shipment of drugs without incurring damage to the aircraft or harm to the pilots, which surprised Ventura.

Four empty Coke cans lay discarded on the floor, and the sweat poured off him. Cox wasn't going anywhere for a while, and Ventura couldn't wait in the car any longer. He parked the car on the street and walked away, looking for somewhere to stay. He'd come back and check on Cox when the sun dropped below the yardarm.

———

COCKTAILS IN THE GARDEN TURNED OUT TO BE WARM sherry, which didn't really hit the spot. Lenny finished one and then begged off, looking for a beer. He found a French restaurant that served a beer called Kronenbourg 1664, and steak frites, which the waiter called steak and chips. Both were massively overpriced, but Lenny peeled off some of Caan's bills and made a silent toast to the American taxpayer.

After dinner, he walked along the streets and noted how few

people were around. He suspected the hotels and casinos near the water were where the action was, but he was okay with the easier pace of the locals. He wandered back to his hotel and opened the French doors in his room. He wasn't convinced the front was any louder than the rear, but figured his location suited his purpose.

Lenny slept well and woke before dawn. After using the bathroom down the hallway, he packed his gear and slipped the pack on his back. Then he stepped out onto the balcony and over the lattice rail. He shimmied down the spouting pipe and into the garden, then he eased the gate open into the lane and walked away.

Lenny took the long route, zigzagging his way through empty streets, until he found the Foodmart, and he settled in to wait for Renquist. He didn't know if he was being watched, but he suspected he was being played. And one often went with the other.

———

VENTURA SAT HIS CAR. EVEN THOUGH THE SUN WASN'T up and his windows were down, the car's interior radiated heat. It was supposed to be winter. He had watched Cox eat dinner and then return to the hotel for the night, then he had called Langley to confirm which flight Cox was booked on and found no such record. But in places like these, records were not always accurate, if kept at all. So he rose earlier to surveil the hotel and wait for Cox to appear. He wanted to be around for whatever the Marine did next.

———

RENQUIST PICKED LENNY UP AT 0800 SHARP AND DROVE out to the airfield. They parked under the same tree and walked out to the Cessna. There were no other aircraft and no sign of a fuel truck, but Renquist did his preflight checks as if all that had been taken care of.

Within minutes they were airborne. They headed northwest

and hit the Florida coastline in about the same time it had taken to fly from Deep Water Cay to West End. Lenny hadn't realized just how close the islands were to the mainland.

As they neared land, Renquist pointed down to the south. "Palm Beach."

"Nice area?"

"Millionaire's playground. But West Palm Beach is where the real folks live. Lots of good bars and plenty of sunshine."

"So where are we going?"

"Not Palm Beach."

They flew over flat countryside that left civilization behind quickly, then Renquist banked the aircraft around to land into the offshore wind.

Renquist glided onto a runway larger than the three Lenny had seen in the Bahamas but still not quite what he would call an major airport. He used one of the two taxiways on either side to roll into a holding lot. Unlike the West End airfield, this one was filled with light aircraft all lined up in neat rows. He stopped near a hangar attached to a modest office building, with a sign that told arrivals they were at Fort Pierce Airport.

"Fort Pierce?"

"Yep. Gotta check in with customs. Let's check in. I already phoned our arrival in before we left this morning."

They walked across the tarmac to the FBO building and found a man in a loud Florida shirt and jeans sitting behind a desk, using a Twinkie as a microphone to sing along to a tape of Jackson Browne. Renquist handed over their passports. The guy took a look and made notations in a ledger, never putting the Twinkie down, then handed the passports back. Renquist offered a nod and walked away as the guy stuffed the Twinkie into his mouth.

Lenny hustled out and followed Renquist back to the aircraft.

"That's it?" asked Lenny.

"What more did you want to do?"

"To hear the end of the song?"

"The man ate the microphone. The song was done."

Lenny shrugged and got in the cockpit. Renquist kicked over the engine and spoke to someone on a radio before taxiing back onto the runway.

"Where to now?" asked Lenny.

"Mena, Arkansas."

"What's in Mena, Arkansas?"

"The guy you want, Barry Seal."

Renquist hit the throttle and eased the bird into the air, then they continued out across the state, passed by Orlando and north of Tampa, then over the coast and across the Gulf of Mexico. He pointed out the endless beaches of the Florida panhandle and Alabama, then banked and landed for fuel and coffee in Biloxi, Mississippi. Next, they flew over the corner of Louisiana before crossing Arkansas and coming in to land at Mena, a tiny municipal airport.

Renquist taxied to the end of the tarmac, where two enormous hangars sat side by side. Only one had a sign, which read *Rich Mountain Aviation*. He pulled the aircraft in front of it as if he were dropping kids off at the mall. He didn't shut the engine down, and the prop kept spinning.

"Barry Seal, that's who you want."

"You're not coming?"

"I told you, I don't do this kind of thing."

"But you don't want to take a break?"

"I'll take a break somewhere else. Walk to the back of the plane. You don't want to run into the prop."

"Roger that."

Lenny handed Renquist money for the ride and fuel then grabbed his pack and slipped out of the aircraft. He strolled toward the rear of the aircraft, but Renquist pulled away before he reached the tail. For a moment Lenny stood in the warm, still air and watched the Cessna taxi back toward the runway. He turned and walked into the hangar.

A guy in a white button-up shirt and jeans eyed him from behind a counter.

"Looking for Seal," Lenny said.

"You have a booking?"

"Looking to make one."

"Not sure he's taking any charters right now, but I can hook you up with another pilot."

"This is a special kind of charter. Barry's the man for it."

The guy's eyes narrowed, and he picked up a phone. Lenny looked out the window at the quiet airfield as the guy dialed a number, whispered a few words, and replaced the handset into the cradle. He turned around. "Go to the next hangar. Someone will meet you."

Lenny thanked him and walked out. As he ambled toward the next hangar, a big man—overweight with a thick neck and brown tinted shades—stepped out then stood in the sun and waited for Lenny to reach him.

"I'm looking for Barry Seal."

"And you are?" he said with a Louisiana drawl.

"Ventura."

"Well, Mr. Ventura. I'm not currently in a position to offer a charter. Doing some repair work."

Lenny noticed the hangar was big enough to house a fleet of Cessnas, and it was closed up tight.

"My friends in DC said you were the guy to talk to."

Seal's expression loosened. "DC, you say?"

"That's right. Maybe I can buy you a beer?"

He gave Lenny the once-over. "All right, Mr. Ventura. You can do that." He offered his hand, and Lenny shook it.

"Barry Seal," he said, and he slapped Lenny on the back as if they were old friends.

CHAPTER SEVENTEEN

THE CAR GOT TOO DAMN HOT. AGAIN. VENTURA WOUND down the windows but the air was stagnant, so it didn't help. Eventually, he gave up and walked across the street to the hotel. Cox hadn't come out, and even if he had drunk a gallon of liquor, it was hard to imagine a Marine sleeping until lunchtime.

Ventura strode into the lobby and found a petite man sitting behind a desk that looked like it belonged in the Oval Office. The guy glanced up at him with a confused expression—one that Ventura assumed he wore all the time.

"I'm meeting a friend, but he didn't show. He's staying with you."

"With me?"

"You are a hotel, right?"

"Of course."

"My friend's got red hair, short cut."

"Oh, Mr. Ventura."

Ventura frowned. "How do you know that?"

"I checked him in. We *are* a hotel."

Ventura bristled; Cox was toying with him. "Can you call his room?"

"No phones in the rooms."

"Perhaps we should knock on the door."

"I don't like to disturb."

"Try it. He's not usually late for things. You have to service the room, right?"

The little Englishman didn't look convinced, but he stood, wiped the sweat from his shiny dome, and took a key from a hook. As Ventura followed him up the stairs, the man turned and shot him that confused look again. Down the hallway, he unlocked the door, and Ventura pushed his way in.

The bed had been slept in, but there was no one in the room. No bag, no personal items. Ventura opened the French doors and scanned the rear yard and the lane beyond.

"Bathroom?" he asked as he stepped back in.

"End of the hall."

Ventura strode past the little man and dashed down to the bathroom.

Empty.

Ventura ran down the stairs and got into his car, then raced through the streets of Freeport and along Queens Highway to the far western end of the island. He skidded to a stop in the parking lot beside the airstrip and saw the same beat-up Toyota pickup. He flung the door open and ran through the line of palm trees to the aircraft lot—empty. The Cessna was nowhere to be seen.

Cox was gone.

———

SEAL DROVE HIS TRUCK, WITH THE WINDOWS DOWN, FOR about thirty minutes until they crossed the state line into Oklahoma. After about a mile, he stopped outside what appeared to be two double-wide trailers attached to create one long structure. There was no signage, but the pickups in the gravel in front suggested there were others inside.

When Lenny stepped into the dark interior of the bar, he entered a familiar world. The only light came from neon signs for beer, the glow of the jukebox, and a single fluorescent tube that hung over the pool table.

The bartender and a few patrons offered Seal nods, and the pilot ordered two beers with two bourbon chasers.

He directed Lenny to a table by the wall. Seal threw back his chaser first then downed half his beer. Lenny left his bourbon on the table. If it was a chaser, it would come after the beer, despite Seal's misinterpretation. But Lenny had no plan to drink bourbon before or after his beer. He let Seal shoot the breeze for a while, talking aircraft and football.

Eventually Seal eyed Lenny's shot glass. "You gonna drink that?"

Lenny pushed it across the table. "All yours."

Seal slammed it down and then went to collect another round. He returned with two more beers and two bourbons. He kept both shots on his side of the table.

"So, DC, huh?" Seal said.

"That's where my boss works, yeah."

"You're not with Baton Rouge?"

"No."

"Not with Florida?"

"Not directly."

Seal sank a bourbon. "Those guys are yanking my chain."

"Baton Rouge or Florida?"

"Both."

Lenny sipped his beer. "Maybe we can help each other."

Seal leaned back in his chair and blinked slowly like an owl. "I'm listening."

"I'm told you're the guy to talk to about Norman's Cay."

"Norman's? That's old news."

"Not what I hear."

Seal ran his finger around the rim of his empty shot glass. "Is that what Washington thinks? That Norman's is in play?"

"That's what I'm told. Lehder's home base."

"Your information is bad. Sure, Norman's Cay was one of Carlos's hubs, but the locals have been cracking down."

"The Bahamian police?"

"Them, and the local people. Things were good there for a while, but they got too hot. Carlos has moved on."

"I need to see that for myself."

"It's a free country."

"Can you take me?"

"I've got other problems."

"Baton Rouge and Florida."

"Exactly."

"What sort of problems?"

"You don't know?"

"No. You just came onto my radar yesterday," said Lenny. "But I can know by tomorrow, or you can tell me now."

"Indictments."

"For?"

"What do you think?"

"You haven't made a deal?"

"These guys don't know what they've got, but no one in Washington returns my calls. I know people. But I know the Ochoas. I know Carlos. And I've met Pablo."

"Escobar?"

Seal shrugged and finished his beer. Lenny stood with his beer in hand and sipped it. "I need the john. You get another round, then we'll see how we can help each other."

Lenny walked to the bathroom, poured his beer down the sink, then used the facilities. Seal liked a drink and he liked to talk. Lenny needed to stay one step ahead. When he returned to the table, Seal had refreshed their drinks and already finished one of his own chasers.

"There are people in DC who will be interested in your intel," said Lenny.

"I know it. But you tell the yokels down here."

"My people can take care of that. But I need to see Norman's first."

"You've got a bug in your butt about that."

"I like to cross my *T*s. So what do you say?"

"Takes a lot of fuel to get down to Norman's."

"I'm good for it."

"Are you gonna write me a company check?"

Lenny reached into his pack and pulled out a wad of cash.

Seal smiled and burped. "And my other thing?"

"I'll take it to DC. If you know who you say you know, they'll be open to a deal."

"All right, Mr. Ventura. I'll take you down tomorrow. This round's on you."

CHAPTER EIGHTEEN

LENNY SLEPT IN SEAL'S SPARE ROOM. HE EXPECTED THE pilot to be sore and sorry the next morning, but the big man appeared showered and fresh. They drove back to the airfield, and Seal flipped open the door to the hangar. Inside, the Cessna looked unremarkable, a bigger version than Renquist's but not large at all.

The pilot walked around the aircraft and completed his checks then gave Lenny the okay. As Lenny climbed in, he saw Seal pull off a strip of plastic with a serial number stuck to the tail, revealing a different tail number.

Seal hefted himself into the cockpit, filling up the limited space. Lenny slipped on his headset as they taxied the short way out to the airstrip, then Seal called in his details and was told the path was clear.

Once in the air, Seal started talking. He really seemed to enjoy holding court, which Lenny figured was a no-no for a drug smuggler.

"You won't believe it when you see it, but Norman's Cay was like nirvana a couple of years ago. Like total party central. Drugs, girls, drinks. Anything you could want. Real Sodom and Gomorrah stuff."

"I thought it was just a waypoint."

"That was the idea—a landing strip partway between Colombia and the States—but it was a whole lot more than that, boy. Carlos turned it into his private utopia. He'd fly stuff in from Colombia, offload it, and those aircraft would refuel and return to Colombia. Then American aircraft would fly in, get loaded up, and go back with the goods."

"That part was you?"

"Sometimes. There were a lot of pilots and a lot of aircraft."

"And you flew into Arkansas?"

"No. That's where I'm based, but I never took Carlos's goods there."

"So how did you get them in?"

Seal smiled, his cheeks lifting his sunglasses a bit. "Can't give all my secrets away."

"I'm pretty sure that's what DC will want, if you don't care to spend time behind bars."

The smile faded. "I don't want that. I did time down in Honduras. Not fun."

"No. So you fly into the States where?"

"All over. From Texas to Florida to South Carolina. Even done water drops off the coast of Louisiana. Can't be consistent in this game."

"Why use such small aircraft?"

"That was Carlos's issue. See, before Carlos this whole caper was dependent on old-school delivery. A mule on a commercial flight with a key sown into his jacket, or even the goods ingested in little bags. At most, a suitcase full. But Carlos came up with the idea for bigger shipments. He'd love to fly in a 747 full, but you can't land that without drawing attention. So the aircraft have to be smaller. But then they can't get all the way from Colombia and back. That's when he figured he'd use strips in the Bahamas."

"So Norman's wasn't the only one?"

"Not by a long shot. But it was the main one, for a time. Carlos even lived there, more or less."

"Anyone else live there?"

"Once, sure. But over time Carlos persuaded them to sell up and move on."

"Persuaded?"

Seal ran his finger across his throat and focused on the horizon. Within minutes he began descending toward a carpet of green. Lenny saw the canopy of trees rise toward them.

"We're there?"

Seal laughed. "Need gas. Once upon a time we could fuel up on Norman's. Not anymore."

They landed on a strip that was paved but worn, and Seal taxied over toward a shed, before which stood a gas pump. He rolled up beside it like they were in a Cadillac at a gas station. As Seal killed the engine, a guy ran out from the shed to fill the tanks.

"I thought Norman's was halfway to Colombia."

"It's actually much closer to the States, but that's Florida or Georgia, not Arkansas. Most of our flight time today is over US territory."

"Why did you set up shop that far away?"

Seal smiled like he had all the answers. "Fewer eyes."

"But unnecessary stops," said Lenny.

"This bird goes farther than any 210 ever built."

"How so?"

Seal winked. "Trade secret."

Lenny suspected auxiliary tanks but didn't ask.

After refueling they took to the skies again, and cut a line back where Lenny had already flown with Renquist, across the Gulf, and then over Florida and out toward the Bahamas. Seal pointed out New Providence, the small island that was home to the Bahamian capital of Nassau. It was a speck of land surrounded by a turquoise ring in a dark blue sea.

Not long after that, he indicated Norman's Cay. It was a long, thin spit of land with a full runway slicing across it at the southern end, then the island curled around like a fish hook to the north, forming a sheltered lagoon. Other than the airstrip and a small marina, Lenny couldn't see much of a manmade presence at all. Seal banked around and swooped over the lagoon.

"Sharks?" asked Lenny, noticing movement in the water below.

"Hammerheads. They love it here."

Seal said nothing more as he landed the Cessna with a tiny bump. As they slowed, Lenny saw some storage sheds, a hangar, and behind some trees, a larger structure that had a different architecture from an airfield building. They eased past some townhouses, and Lenny noted all the buildings were different in design. Clearly they had been constructed over many decades but shared one common feature.

They were all abandoned.

Seal came to a halt then pulled out a revolver hidden under the console and slipped it into his waistband.

"I thought you said no one was here," said Lenny.

"Carlos isn't here. I can't speak for anyone else."

They got out, and Lenny was struck by the brightness of the sun. He had been in the Bahamas just a day before, but at Norman's Cay, the colors seemed saturated—the greens deeper, the turquoise water more vivid. It was an incongruous sensation, given the state of the buildings.

It looked like someone had conducted a nuclear weapons test on the island. Every building was a hollowed-out shell, windows smashed, walls charred, roofs caved in. It was clearly not the result of a hurricane. But it was familiar to Lenny.

"It looks like a war zone," he said.

"That's about right."

Lenny drifted toward a tall building visible through the trees. "What's this?"

"It was the hotel."

"Tourist came here?"

"Before Carlos, sure."

Lenny stood in the hot sun in the middle of the runway and did a 360. It was hard to imagine how the CIA or the NSC could believe this place was drug-smuggling central anymore. They had to know the history. They also had the capacity to do a flyover and take shots of the abandoned buildings, or even get images from one of Reagan's new secret satellites.

It wasn't that he hadn't believed Seal, but one man's abandoned was another man's run-down fixer-upper, and he wanted to see what the CIA was calling a hub for drugs. This place looked like a dystopian paradise, an apple rotting from the core out. Which begged a lot of questions, and at the top of that list was *why am I here?*

Lenny's thoughts were interrupted by movement in the trees. A shirtless man stepped out of the bushes brandishing a shotgun. His body was a glistening bronze. As he stepped closer, gun tucked into his hip but pointed at the men on the landing strip, Lenny noted he had long hair on the sides but was balding on top, and his scraggly beard gave him a wild look at odds with the calm and calculating look in his eyes.

"Afternoon," said Lenny.

The man stepped forward until he reached the edge of the asphalt. "Get off this island."

"We don't mean any harm."

"You need to leave."

"We will. Doesn't look to be much in the way of nightlife. But not until we're ready."

"This is a private island."

"So what are *you* doing here?"

"I have permission."

"So you work for Carlos."

The man raised the shotgun to his shoulder. "No, but you do."

"No I don't."

"He does." The man shifted his shotgun toward Barry Seal, who put his hands up and away from the revolver tucked into his pants.

"Not anymore," said Seal.

"Don't care. Time to leave."

"What's your name?" asked Lenny.

"None of your damn business."

"It's Novak," said Seal. "I remember you."

"Leave," said Novak. "I won't ask again." He looked down the barrel of the shotgun as if aiming.

"Seal, why don't you go back to the plane," said Lenny. "I'll be there shortly."

"It's your dime."

Seal backed away then walked toward the Cessna at the end of the runway. Novak aimed his weapon at Lenny.

"You too."

"What are you doing here?" asked Lenny.

"I could ask you the same."

"Easy. I'm here to shut down drug-smuggling operations. Are you a smuggler?"

"No."

"So what are you doing here? I mean, it's nice and all, but it's looking a bit past its prime."

"Reclaiming what's mine."

"And what is that?"

"My stuff. What's left of it. You with the DEA?"

"I'm kind of unaffiliated at this time."

"What the hell does that mean?"

"It means I fall between the cracks, down to where the trouble-makers are. Now, why don't you lower your weapon and tell me what the hell happened here."

Novak didn't move for a long moment, then he dropped the weapon to his hip. "Why are you here?"

"I was told this is where the drugs came through. But it seems like that intel might be older than the Grand Canyon."

"You missed the party, that's for sure."

"Were you here for it?"

"On and off."

"Tell me about it."

"Why?"

"So I know what I'm dealing with."

Novak eyed him but lowered his weapon farther. "Let's get out of the sun."

He led Lenny back toward the bushes, where Lenny noticed the last vestiges of a pathway that the island was reclaiming. Behind the trees was a line of villas all in disrepair. They walked into one and found a ransacked living room, with furniture broken or ripped open, and bullet holes sprayed across the walls.

Up close Novak looked almost malnourished. He offered Lenny a seat on a chair from which the back had been broken off, and he sat on a cushion that was split open like a ripe melon.

"You weren't part of Carlos Lehder's army?" asked Lenny.

"Hell no."

"But he took over the island?"

"He did. Turned it into a private fortress."

"So how did you get to stay?"

"Like I said. On and off." The thin man grimaced at the thought. "I came for the hammerheads."

"Sharks?"

"It's an interest of mine. I'm a diver, and the hammerheads migrate here to mate. There are a number here year-round, but mating season is something else. I planned to open a dive shop, and create a research station to study them."

"But Carlos arrived?"

"He was here already but just another resident at that point. He even offered to fund my business. He's a smarter guy than you'd think. He was interested in the research. So he let me stay.

But then the planes started coming every night, and I knew what they were doing. I couldn't stand by and do nothing."

"What did you do?"

"I reported it to the police in Nassau. At first they did nothing, then eventually they raided the island, but Carlos has people everywhere and he got wind of it. By the time the cops got here Carlos was off the island, and the only drugs found was a bit of weed that belonged to another resident. It was a farce. But he knew that someone had set him up, and he started encouraging people to leave."

"Encouraging?"

"Some he bought out. Some found their dogs floating in their drinking-water cisterns. Some just had their houses mysteriously burn down."

"So you left?"

"For a while, and then I came back. Don't ask me why. My son keeps asking me that and I can't even answer it for myself. There's something about this place. It's the hammerheads, but it's more than that. It's paradise. Or at least it was."

"So what happened to Carlos?"

"Eventually he got back to business and I came back to run the shop, but the truth is by that time I was working for you."

"Me?"

"The DEA."

"I'm not DEA, but go on."

Novak narrowed his eyes. "Who are you?"

"You can call me Ventura. Beyond that, it's better you don't know. All I can say is, I have some resources behind me and an agenda to disturb the flow of narcotics into the United States."

"You've started well by coming here a year too late."

"Tell me what happened."

"The local police put a team on Norman's to keep an eye on things, but Carlos paid them off, all except one constable. He and I spent our evenings sabotaging equipment, making a small dent in the process. But there were paid guards everywhere. Mainly I kept a diary of tail numbers and so on, stuff the DEA could use. Eventually there was enough, and the DEA raided the island with the locals again. This time it caught Carlos unawares. He knew it was me—he found me sneaking around one night—so he and his goons tried to kill me."

Novak pointed at the walls pockmarked with bullet holes. "But just in the nick of time, a Bahamian gunship turned up and Carlos fled. He knew the good days of Norman's Cay were over for him, so as he retreated, he took the island down with him, like a petulant child. Burned the hotel, the storage sheds. Most of these villas were already shells from machine gun fire. He destroyed his own house. He even scuttled my dive boat. I searched, but I never found it."

"Where did he go?"

"I don't know. I heard maybe back to Colombia, maybe Panama or Nicaragua. I left too, and I only came back to reclaim what was mine, and to get one last look at the hammerheads."

"You're leaving for good?"

Novak nodded and the grimace returned. "Carlos spoiled this paradise for me. It's tainted now. He might not be here anymore, but things still happen."

"What do you mean?"

"I've only been here a week, but I've seen boats, I've seen aircraft arrive and leave. Not like they did before, with a dozen a night. But one or two over the week. I think someone's still using the strip to bring drugs in and then offload them onto boats."

"You've seen that?"

"Not the loading. That's after dark, and I don't feel the need to get that close. They don't know I'm here, and I'd prefer to keep it that way. But I can hear boats and see some that come in close to the island—sometimes they stop. And the aircraft are obvious." He paused for a moment. "But it's none of my business now. I did what I could."

"So you don't know anything about them?"

Novak shrugged. "I write down what I see. Boat serial numbers or names, aircraft tail numbers. Force of habit. It's the scientist in me."

"Could I see the list?"

Novak levered himself up and walked into the kitchen, then returned with a tattered notebook. He opened it and handed it to Lenny. It was as the man had said: a methodical log of passing vessels, water and air. Serial numbers, names, dates, basic descriptions. Lenny noted that some boat names appeared more than once, as did several aircraft tags. When he was done, he closed the book and handed it back to Novak.

"How long will you stay?"

"A few more weeks."

"You have supplies?"

"Some. There's propane running to the hotel kitchen from an old tank that didn't blow up, so I use that. And I sleep in here, under a mosquito net. If I run out of anything, Highbourne Cay is only a few miles north of Norman's, and they have a small marina store. I don't need much."

Lenny stood. "You have a radio?"

"I do. I have a contact on Highbourne."

"I'd like to keep in touch, if that's okay with you. If there's something going on here, I'd like to know."

"You plan on doing something about it?"

"Maybe."

"I don't know," said Novak.

"I get that. I'm sure it's hard to know who your friends are around this kind of business. How about I give you a frequency and you check in daily on the eights. If I'm within earshot, I'll ping this frequency."

"I could do that, I guess. But we're pretty isolated. You'll need to be close."

"Understood." Lenny took the notebook back and wrote in it.

"I'm leaving a message service number too. If you leave the island and go back to civilization, I'd appreciate it if you could just let me know."

"Why?"

"So I don't worry. If I can't get hold of you on the radio, I'm going to assume the worst, aren't I?"

Novak nodded. "You should."

"And you should probably go see your sharks and then get the hell out of here."

"I don't like being told what to do."

"Me either. But sometimes listening to the coach is the best play." Lenny extended his hand and the two men shook, then Lenny made his way out of the villa. Novak followed to the edge of the strip, and Lenny walked back to the end where Seal was waiting in the shade.

"We should go," said Seal. "Be good to get back to the States before dark."

"Fire it up," said Lenny.

They got in the cockpit, and Seal did his checks.

"That guy's a kook," said Seal.

"He's his own man, that's for sure."

"I'm telling you. Carlos doesn't mess around. I don't know how he didn't kill that guy and feed him to his damned sharks. And Novak kept coming back, pushing his luck."

"He doesn't like to be told what to do."

"Like I said, a kook."

They accelerated along the runway. Lenny spotted Novak standing by the strip, and they sped past. He didn't wave or acknowledge them. He just watched them through wary eyes as they rose into the sky and flew out over the sparkling water.

CHAPTER NINETEEN

As they headed out over the glorious blue of the Bahama bank, Lenny put on his headset.

"So Carlos Lehder isn't there," said Lenny.

"If you had listened to me, you'd have saved yourself a bunch of cash and a day in this tin can."

"But I wouldn't have learned anything."

"You didn't learn anything."

Lenny didn't reply, but he knew he had learned plenty. Most of it was about the people he was reporting to. His mind wandered and something Alice had said triggered a thought..

"So where is he?"

"Who?" said Seal, handing Lenny a sandwich he pulled from a cooler on the back seat.

Lenny tugged at the cling wrap. "Carlos Lehder."

Seal took large bites as if there was a time limit to eating the sandwich. "Word is he's back in Colombia, but I've heard about shipments being set up out of Panama and Nicaragua. He's usually Escobar's point man on that."

Lenny recalled Alice mentioning Panama. "Can we go to Panama?"

Seal turned to Lenny, and his eyebrows raised above the pilot's dark glasses. "Are you kidding?"

"No. If that's where things are going down, that's where I want to be."

"Then when we get stateside, I suggest you catch a commercial flight down there."

"I'd rather avoid a commercial flight."

"I'm under indictment, fella. You know what they'll do if they know I'm out of the country?"

"You're out of the country right now."

"Bahamas is different. Panama is serious. I don't need that kind of heat."

"How would they know? Let's go right now."

"What? You want to turn this bird around and head for Panama?"

"Sure."

Seal laughed. "Do you know where Panama is?"

"Central America."

"Just. It joins South America, which means it's far away. This little bird might have some extra time in her, but not that much. From here we'd have to fly over Cuba, and they generally don't take kindly to unidentified planes in their airspace."

"What would they do, shoot us down?"

"Yes, that's exactly what they'd do. You wanna die and start a war in the process?"

"Not today."

"No. And we don't have the fuel to go around. So forget that."

"Then tomorrow."

"Pal, so far you've done jack for me."

"I paid you."

"A flight to Panama is a whole other budget item."

"I'll get the money."

"Cash is not my problem."

"All right, I'll call DC. I'll get things moving. You want a deal, I'll get a deal."

"You talk a lot, but I ain't seen the walk yet."

"You will."

"I told ya, Baton Rouge and Florida aren't interested. So unless you know the president..."

"You don't want the president."

"Why's that?"

"Because the vice president is in charge of the war on drugs."

"How do you know that?"

"He used to run the CIA."

"So you know Vice President Bush, I suppose." He laughed.

"No. But I know a guy who does."

———

THEY FLEW BACK VIA FLORIDA, WHERE SEAL REFUELED at Gilbert Field in Winter Haven without bothering to show anyone a passport, then set out for the mountains of Arkansas. The sun was dropping below the canopy of trees as they landed and coasted to a stop outside his hangar. Once out of the cockpit, both men stretched their backs in the twilight as the night critters began to raise their voices.

"You can have my spare room again," said Seal.

"Thanks, but no. Just drop me off in town."

Seal removed his sunglasses and frowned. "There's not much to the town."

"That's okay. I've got things to do. I'll call you as soon as I have something."

"Panama."

"Unless I learn something different. But can you do it?"

"I can do it."

"Not in this little thing." Lenny slapped the side of the Cessna's fuselage.

"I have other horses, don't you worry."

They got in Seal's truck and drove into town. Seal slowed as they approached the intersection at Highway 71. Lenny knew Seal's house was to the right and the town center was to the left.

"You want me to drop you at the hotel?" asked Seal.

"No, here's fine. I'll walk."

"Suit yourself."

Lenny got out and double-slapped the load bed of the truck. Seal turned right and drove away. Lenny walked to the first hotel he came upon, an outdated place that appeared to have two rows of rooms, one behind the other.

He had been trained at Quantico to never choose the first hotel on the road into a town. Psychological studies had shown that people on the run—fugitives, AWOLs, criminals—naturally chose the second hotel along the main road. It was something about not being too close to the center of things but still having a safety buffer between them and whatever they were running from.

Spooks loved to overthink that kind of thing. Lenny just wanted a shower and a phone. When he stepped into the reception area, a little bell rung. The weathered wallpaper looked nicotine yellow against the white floor tiles. A man who looked to be suffering from jaundice emerged from an office behind the front desk. Lenny perused a rack of brochures for local attractions that included a state park and a train depot and dropped his backpack.

"Evening," said Lenny.

The guy blinked.

"Need a room."

"How many."

"How many nights?"

The guy shook his head slowly. "How many people."

"Just me."

"How many?"

"I said, just me."

The guy shook his head again. "How many nights?"

"Let's start with one."

"Vehicle registration."

"I don't have a car."

The guy frowned. "How did you get here?"

"Friend dropped me off."

"Why ain't you staying with him?"

Now it was Lenny's turn to frown. "He needed some private time."

The guy shrugged and wrote in a book. "Twenty," he said.

"Does the room have a phone?"

"Sure. *E-lectricity* too."

"Long distance?"

"You'll need to leave a deposit. Another twenty."

Lenny fumbled in his pack for the roll of cash. It was almost depleted. He had to do something about that. He handed the guy a couple of twenties, put the rest in his pocket, and was given a key with a plastic weight on the ring, just in case he was thinking of running away with it.

"I put you in the back, away from the highway noise."

Lenny hadn't heard a single vehicle pass.

"Appreciate that. You got anywhere to eat in town?"

"Of course," the guy said as if it was the dumbest question he had ever heard.

"That you recommend," Lenny clarified.

"Try the cafe. On Mena Street."

Lenny held up the key. "Thank you." He walked out and headed around the first block toward the second. There were two vehicles parked in front, spaced three rooms apart. He read the number on the first door and walked past the pickup then headed for the end of the row. As he reached the second vehicle—a large sedan with a vinyl-lined roof—a woman rushed out of the room behind it.

"Just leave me alone," she said.

She looked close to tears. Lenny stopped short. A man charged out of the room, in pursuit. Lenny noted the snarl first and the clenched fists second.

"Kirsty!" the man screamed.

She kept walking, but the man moved faster and caught up to her as she reached the car. He grabbed her arm and flung her hard against the side of the vehicle. Lenny saw the shock in her eyes.

"I said leave me alone!" she said, wincing.

The man kept her arm pinned against the car's window. "I'll leave you alone when I'm good and ready. Now come inside."

"No, Reece. Get the hell away from me."

Kirsty tried to pull away, but he slammed her into the sedan again. She recoiled but slapped him across the face.

Reece took a half step back, wound up his arm, and drove a fist toward her cheek.

It didn't get there. His fist stopped midmotion, and the force drove his shoulder forward, almost dislocating it. He glowered at the man gripping his arm.

"She's not really in your weight class, friend," said Lenny.

Reece dropped the hand that was holding Kirsty and tried turning to Lenny head-on, but Lenny twisted his arm and pushed him into the side of the car in the space the woman vacated.

"You want to take on someone who is?"

The guy winced as Lenny twisted his arm more. Then he pushed away and let go. Reece took a moment to scowl at Lenny.

"Didn't think so," said Lenny.

"This ain't none of your business, pal."

"I represent the Marquess of Queensbury. When you choose to fight someone in a lower division, it becomes my business."

Reece stiffened, and Lenny sensed something stupid coming on. "Don't do it, Reece. Just go back to your room."

The guy pushed off the car with his hip and cocked his fists. "You don't tell me what to—"

Lenny didn't wait to get hit; he wasn't in the mood. He punched Reece in the nose. The guy's head snapped back into the

B pillar of the sedan, and he slumped to the ground, blood oozing down onto his shirt.

Lenny glanced at Kirsty. "You okay?"

"You killed him."

"No, ma'am. He's just out for the count. You have a room key? I'll put him on the bed. He'll wake up soon enough, just with a bit of headache."

Kirsty glanced at the man on the ground and then at Lenny. She reached into her pocket and tossed the key on the ground beside Reece. Then she made to walk away.

"You're leaving?" he asked.

"You think I wanna stay with that?"

"No. Leaving looks like a smart move. But don't you have any possessions in the room?"

"Nothing I can't live without, and I don't want to be here when he wakes up."

"Where will you go?"

"You think I'm going to tell you?"

"Not if you don't want to. I'm just concerned that you get where you need to be."

"You gonna offer me a ride now?"

"No. I don't have a car. But as long as you know where you're going, and you can get there, I'll leave you to it."

Lenny crouched, snatched up the key, and hefted Reece onto his shoulder in a fireman's carry. He opened the door and went inside. The bed was unmade, but the room wasn't messy. There were very few personal items. When he dumped the man onto the bed, he groaned, which Lenny took as all the proof of life he needed. He dropped the key on the bedside table and stepped outside, closing the door behind him.

Kirsty was still standing by the car. Her face was etched in uncertainty, but Lenny couldn't tell about what. Perhaps she was having second thoughts. He'd seen that before. Growing up in a military family, he saw it all, and some of it wasn't featured in the navy's promotional material. Some sailors brought their troubles home, and some wives took the brunt of those troubles. Some left because of it. Most didn't. Staying and dealing with a little abuse was often preferable to leaping into the unknown. Lenny didn't understand that, but he was never afraid of the unknown. Adventure lay on the path to the unknown. Abuse was just abuse.

"You okay?" he asked. He didn't move toward her.

"I'm going to get a bus to Hot Springs."

"Okay." Lenny had no idea where that was, but it wasn't here.

"Then I can get to Little Rock."

That he had heard of. "Sounds like a plan."

She didn't move, just stared at the asphalt.

"Where were you going together?" he asked. "Little Rock?"

Kirsty shook her head. "Atlanta. He's got family there."

"What about you?"

"No."

"Family anywhere?"

"I have a cousin in Denver."

"I hear it's nice there."

"She said I could stay a while."

"Sounds like a better plan."

Kirsty looked up at Lenny. "I only have enough to get to Little Rock."

"Does Sleeping Beauty have any cash?"

She laughed flatly. "Never."

Lenny stepped toward her and noted that she didn't flinch or move away. She was tougher than he had given her credit for. He pulled out the remaining money in his pocket. Two twenties and a ten.

"Here's fifty. Should be enough to get a Greyhound to Denver."

She looked at the money and then at Lenny again. "I can't take your money."

"Sure you can. You got somewhere you need to be. When's the bus to Hot Springs?"

"Any minute now. That's why I was leaving."

"Then no time for discussion."

"I can't."

Lenny grabbed her hand and stuffed the cash into it. "Go. Go now."

She started to turn away, then she stopped. "Why are you helping me?"

"Because I can. And someday you'll be able to do the same for someone, and you will."

She just nodded then turned and walked out to the road.

The bus arrived a few minutes later, and he watched her get on. It was old and dirty but looked capable of getting to a nearby town. She sat by the window and looked out at him. As the bus pulled away, Kirsty put the palm of her hand to the window. Lenny nodded, and then she was gone.

―――――

LENNY FOUND THAT HIS ROOM LOOKED EXACTLY LIKE the one Reece was snoozing in. It was basic and worn, but as good as a barracks and much more private. He picked up the phone and sat on the bed. He needed to make two calls. One now, one later. Both DC numbers. He knew the long distance calls would be expensive, but he had put a deposit down. He inserted a finger into the number-two slot on the rotary dial and turned it the short distance, then dialed the long zero and another two, and continued with the rest of the digits.

"Purchase," said the DEA man at the other end.

"This is Lenny Cox."

"Cox?" he sounded like he was trying to recall the name. "You still in the Bahamas?"

"No. Listen, how many missions have you done with Ray Caan?"

"We don't really call them missions."

"How many?"

"I've never worked with him directly. I've heard of him, but that's it."

"You deal with the NSC much?"

"Nope."

"So why now?"

"Drugs. That's kind of what we do."

Lenny said nothing.

"What's on your mind, Cox?"

"Do you know Carlos Lehder?"

"Not personally."

"But you know of him."

"Everyone in drug enforcement knows of Carlos Lehder."

"Do you know the Ochoas?"

"Major cartel family."

"I met a guy who claims to know them."

"Interesting."

"He's a US citizen, a pilot. He might have done some smuggling for them."

"Okay."

"He took me to Norman's Cay."

"What happened to Freeport?"

"I went to Freeport, Purchase. I interrupted a drug handoff."

"Good news."

"It was staged."

"How do you know?"

"I know BS when I see it, Purchase. The question I have is, was it put on by you or by Caan."

"I get evaluated by how many busts I can prosecute. I don't put them on."

"That's kind of where I landed."

"So how did you end up at Norman's Cay?"

"Long story. But before my quarters dry up, I need this pilot to get me in somewhere. Somewhere deep. And I need for Caan to know about it after the fact."

"How does that affect me?"

"The guy's under indictment from task forces in Louisiana and Florida."

"Ah. He wants a deal," said Purchase.

"He does. And my gut tells me he knows some very heavy hitters. He might be of use to you."

"Has he taken this to the local task forces?"

"He says they weren't interested."

"So maybe he's full of it."

"Then why indict him? I'm telling you, he's equipped to do what he says he does, and if he can get me where I need to go, you might have a way in to the cartel."

"Okay, Cox. Let me run it up the flagpole."

"Run it quick. I need this guy to get me where I need to go asap."

"You causing trouble?"

"Those were my orders."

Purchase laughed. "But you're not going to tell me where."

"I think it might be better if you don't know. Just in case."

"I can take care of myself."

"I don't doubt that, but if Caan asks questions you want to be able to be honest."

"Because he is with me, I'm sure."

"Yeah."

"If you find out something I should know…"

"You'll be my first call, if there's a public win in it."

"And if it's not so public?"

"I have my orders. Let me give you the number at my hotel. If I'm not here, leave a message and I'll get back to you."

Lenny gave Purchase the number. "Where the hell is that?" asked the DEA man.

"Arkansas."

"I'd ask but..."

"Exactly."

Lenny hung up and looked at the phone. He had his second call to make, but timing was an issue. He wanted to stay under the radar as long as he could. And how soon he left was in Purchase's hands. But he would need to make the call sooner rather than later. Logistics demanded it.

After spending the better part of the day coiled up in a small aircraft, he felt the need to get the blood flowing in his legs. Lenny took his key but left his pack and walked into town. Mena was a small place—not much more than a mile of commercial buildings scattered along a stretch of Highway 71, most of which was focused on the T-junction with Mena Street.

Lenny walked up Mena Street in the general direction that the hotel manager had given him for the cafe but without any sense of purpose. He wouldn't be eating today. He had no money in his pocket, and his checkbook was in a locker at Quantico. It didn't bother him. He was used to not eating for days at a time, and he had gotten two of Seal's sandwiches on the flight back from Norman's Cay.

So he wandered. Past a hair salon and a full-service gas station, both of which were closed up for the evening. He saw lights in the cafe and assumed it was the one recommended, perhaps more for its opening hours than the food. There were a few people inside, but the place wasn't doing any kind of roaring trade.

Lenny kept walking but quickly found himself standing beside a church with nothing more than trees and darkness ahead. He crossed the street and walked back, then right at the T and down the highway. Another gas station that had a light on inside but no sign of people, and a closed general store, and another hotel.

He marched until he ran out of town, thinking through his

options. His mission parameters were simultaneously clear and opaque. *Cause trouble* was specific to a point but left a lot of room for interpretation. Those giving the orders had made it obvious they wanted to be a step or two removed from the action, the old CYA strategy of which Colonel Yardley was not a fan. But that worked in Lenny's favor somewhat.

He stood in the quiet outside a feed store, listening to the sound of the wind in the trees and the night critters. His breathing fell into rhythm with the bugs, and eventually he felt fatigue ebb into his bones. He turned on his heels as if on the parade deck at Pendleton, and marched back toward the other end of town.

CHAPTER TWENTY

THE NEXT DAY BROKE SUNNY AND COOL IN THE mountains of Arkansas. Lenny showered, slid his clothes off their hangers, and tied up his boots. He was contemplating the day's activities when he heard the voices outside. He made out three distinct people, all men, but the one doing most of the talking was a voice he recognized.

Reece had woken up. Lenny knew that from the previous night because the big sedan was gone when he returned from his walk. He had wondered if he had chased after Kirsty, and hoped she had enough of a lead to avoid him.

Lenny peeked through the curtain and saw the three men standing around the car. No sign of Kirsty. Not in the car, not in their little group. What he did see was intent. They were waiting for someone, and it didn't take a five-star general to figure out who. All three cast eyes toward Lenny's door. The two newcomers were broad across the shoulders and capable of something, depending on intelligence and training. Reece was a known quantity. He had neither. Lenny didn't like the odds, but he wasn't afraid. He was trained—well trained—and one of the first things the Corps taught him was not to pussyfoot around in a wrestling match. He believed in the Marquess of Queensbury rules when the competition was fair and confined to the ring. Three on one in a parking lot was not that.

He stepped back from the window, thought through his game plan, and closed up his pack before dropping it beside the exit. Then he opened the door and stepped into the doorway.

Reece was looking at his car when Lenny said, "You still here?"

His head snapped around, and Lenny saw him wince.

"You messed with the wrong guy, pal."

"If you're talking about you, I'm gonna start laughing."

Reece moved around the front of his car and took the lead that Lenny wanted. The other two guys spread out behind in a lazy attempt to box him in.

Lenny smiled. "Go home, loser."

Then he stepped back and slammed the door. Lenny stood still in the dark, leaving his hand on the doorknob, and counted. He estimated five steps from the front of the car to the door. He figured Reece would hesitate a second, but then be driven to action by his staring buddies. He would stride out but not run. After five Mississippis, Lenny pulled the door open.

Reece was standing right in front of him, fist held high about to knock on the door. But a fist held high was useless. There was no momentum behind it. He was going to have to draw it back to give it any power. There was no time for that.

Lenny grabbed Reece's shirt collar and yanked him forward into the door jamb. His head hit with a crack that dazed him, so Lenny pushed him back and repeated the move. The second crack dropped him to the pavement.

Without stepping out of the doorway, Lenny eyed the other two. They looked confused.

"You guys know him well?"

"Met him last night," said the left guy.

"Did he tell you he was beating on a woman when I ran into him yesterday?"

They looked at each other, and the left guy spoke again.

"No, he didn't. He just said you had a bag full of cash."

"Boys, I don't have a bag full of cash. In fact, I don't have a red cent to my name. I gave my last dollar to the woman he was beating up so she could get away."

The left guy considered this for a moment. "I don't believe you."

"Fair enough. Let me put it this way, then. There are two of you and one of me, so the odds are in your favor. But I'm military trained, and when I say trained, I mean *well* trained. So you might win, but there's a hundred percent chance that at least one of you never walks again after this. Not without a cane, anyway. So you gotta ask yourself, which one of you wants to get crippled today. All for zero cash, and on the word of a guy who abuses women?"

The two guys looked at each other again. There was no verbal communication and no nods or shrugs, but these guys knew each other well, because they both made the same move. They took several steps backward then turned and walked across the lot to a pickup truck. Once inside, they each gave Lenny a scowl, and they drove off.

Lenny patted Reece down and found two keys—one for the room and another for his car. For a second time he got into a squat and lifted Reece into a fireman's carry, and took him back to his room. He dumped him on the bed and turned him sideways. He moaned but didn't wake up. Lenny tossed the room key on the table and closed the door behind him.

It was time to make a call or two.

He returned to his room and dialed the number again.

"Purchase."

"You're in the office early."

"Cox, I've got something for you."

"You didn't call."

"Like you said, it's early. But you struck a nerve. This one went all the way to Bud."

"Who's Bud?"

"Mullin, my boss. Administrator of the DEA."

"Does he make the calls?"

"He runs the place. He reports to the attorney general."

"Okay, important guy. What'd he say?"

"He wants to talk with this Seal guy."

"You want his number?"

"Yes."

"When will Mullin call him?"

"When you give me the number."

Lenny gave him the number.

"I've gotta go," said Purchase. "But I should tell you, this won't happen super fast. Even if he could get in a room with Escobar, we'll need to vet him and his story."

"Just keep him on the hook. I'll do the rest."

"You got it. Stay in touch."

"Roger that."

Lenny tapped the switch hook to kill the call, then he dialed the next number.

"National Security Council."

"It's Cox. I need to speak with Caan."

"One moment."

There was a good half minute of static, and Lenny could almost hear the dollars ticking over on the long distance call.

"Cox?"

"Caan."

"Where the hell are you?"

"Do you really want to know?"

"You left the Bahamas."

"How do you know that?"

"You used your passport to enter the United States in Fort Pierce. Are you in Florida?"

"Not exactly. Listen, Caan, I don't have a lot of time."

"What's wrong?"

"I'm out of cash."

I gave you two thousand dollars."

"You and I both know how far that went because I gave half of it to your pilot."

"He's the CIA's pilot, and you ditched him."

"He wasn't up for the kind of troublemaking required."

Caan coughed. "What do you need?"

"Five thousand."

"Are you kidding?"

"Nope."

"You think I can just click my fingers and make five grand appear out of thin air?"

"Yes, Caan, I do."

"This isn't your retirement fund, Cox."

"And I'm happy to get receipts for everything, if you want that kind of paper trail. Look, you don't need to yank my chain. The Bahamas are islands. Getting around takes fuel, and fuel costs money. You get me?"

"All right, but this isn't an endless spigot, you got me?"

"Roger that."

"Where are you?"

"Mena, Arkansas."

"What the hell are you doing in Arkansas?"

"Preparing to cause trouble."

Caan expelled a long breath. "I've never heard of Mena, Arkansas."

"It's not a big place."

"So they might not have five grand on hand."

"There are banks, Caan. And e-lectricity."

"Still, we'll split it up. Call back in thirty."

"Roger that."

"And stay in touch, Cox."

"You want me to send you my itinerary? I could copy in the vice president."

"That's not funny. This isn't a secure channel."

"I'll talk to you in an hour."

Lenny hung up, grabbed his pack, and walked out of the room. He used Reece's key to start the sedan, which turned out to be a Chrysler Newport. The rear floor was covered in trash and the vehicle smelled like a Marine Corps personnel transport after a long deployment. Lenny put it into gear and pulled out, then he drove the short distance into town.

The town had woken up but only just. Stores were open, but there were few people around. The busiest establishment was the cafe. Lenny pulled into the lot and parked at the rear, then he ratcheted the seat back and closed his eyes. He had slept well but it was always good policy to get a nap in when there was time to kill.

He dozed for an hour then headed into the cafe. When the server offered him a smile, he asked about a pay phone.

"In the back. How do you take your coffee?"

"Straight up, but I'm waiting on a money transfer to come in, so I'll need to leave before I can pay."

"A coffee won't break us."

Lenny thanked her and found the phone on a wall by the bathrooms. He dialed 0 for the operator, who helped him make a collect call.

"National Security Council."

"Will you accept a collect call from a Mr. Lenny Cox?"

"I will," said the voice without hesitation. Clearly NSA agents got caught without change on a regular basis.

"You're on the call, Mr. Cox," said the operator.

"Thank you, ma'am."

The NSC voice said, "We'll call you back. What's the number?"

Lenny recited the number off the pay phone and the other party hung up. The phone rang about ten seconds later, and he picked up.

"One moment," said a voice on the other line.

There was an electronic thunk and then another voice Lenny didn't know: "Sergeant Cox, do you have a pen?"

He snagged a felt-tip pen from a passing server and scribbled on a napkin. He was given four account numbers and four locations: two banks, one gas station, one general store. The banks were cash advances, the other two Western Union outlets.

"That was fast," he said.

"Yes, sir."

"Well, thanks."

There was no reply, only a click and dead air. Lenny hung up and returned to the dining room, and was directed to a table where a coffee sat waiting for him. He drank some and instantly felt his stomach rumbling. The server arrived and asked if he got his money.

"Yep. And I borrowed a pen. Do you know which of these places is closest?"

She leaned over. "The gas station. About a hundred yards down the street."

"I'll be back."

"Give me your order and we'll have it ready."

Lenny ordered eggs, bacon, and potatoes, with a side of pancakes. Then he walked to the gas station, showed the clerk his passport, and was handed five hundred dollars. He returned to the cafe, ate breakfast and several cups of coffee, left a tip the value of the entire meal, and thanked the server.

He drove Reece's car to the general store just off the highway, where he got another five hundred. He noticed a poster for an international calling card, so he bought one and put some cash on it. Then he hit up each bank for two thousand. Only one teller gave him a sideways look and made a comment on carrying that much cash.

"Buying a car," he said.

"Would you prefer a cashier's check?"

"The guy I'm buying from is funny about banks. He thinks the federal government is watching."

"Oh, they are. Have a nice day."

With his cash in hand, he drove out of town. It took only a few minutes to reach the airfield. He parked and then banged on Seal's hangar door.

The pilot's bleary eyes suggested he had gotten into a few drinks at home.

"Ventura," he said.

Lenny smiled. "That's me. What's new?"

"I got a call from some guy called Jacobsen, from the DEA."

"Good."

"He had a lot of questions."

"He needs to make sure you're worth the effort, Barry."

"I'm worth the effort."

"I hope you proved that."

"He seemed convinced. Wants to meet in person."

"Good."

"He said he doesn't report to the task forces down here."

"Nope. He reports to Bud."

"Who?"

"Bud Mullin. Head of the DEA. He's in the vice president's war on drugs group. So you're in with the big boys, Barry."

"I ain't seen nothing in writing."

"It takes time. But I said I'd get you at the table with the movers and shakers, and I did."

"Yeah, you did."

"So how about Panama?"

"I'd told you. I don't have anything signed yet."

"I'm not asking you to do it for free."

"We're talking thousands just for the fuel alone."

Lenny pulled out his wad of cash.

"And then there's my time."

"The fuel I'll cover. Your time is yours. But if you prefer me to call my buddies in DC and tell them it turns out you're a flake and they should toss you to the locals, we can go that way."

Seal growled and rubbed his head. "How much you got there?"

"Three grand. And I don't want any messing around with immigration."

"Me either. But fuel's gonna be four."

"Deal." Lenny counted off nine hundred and put it in his pocket, then he handed the rest to Seal.

"You said you only had three."

"And you work with drug smugglers, Barry, so you shouldn't trust every word you hear."

"Whatever. We go tomorrow."

"Why not now?"

"Because it's eight hours of flight time, for starters, and for seconds, I've got a headache."

"All right. Tomorrow. I'll bring the sandwiches."

Lenny got back in the car and drove into town. He returned to the cafe and asked for directions to the post office. Once there, he slipped his passport into a fresh manila envelope, wrote Alice's address on it, and closed it up.

From here on in, he didn't want anything identifiable with him. It was time to become a ghost.

He drove back to the motel he had previously stayed at and parked the Chrysler in front of Reece's room. The guy was only passing through himself so he might have already moved on, or without his car he might be stuck in town. Lenny didn't care either way. He left the car with the key on the driver's seat and walked away.

———

VENTURA WAS SIPPING ON A TAB WHEN HE GOT THE call in Miami.

"He's in Arkansas."

Ventura spat cola through his nose. "What?"

"We don't know why."

"Are there goods running through Little Rock?"

"Nothing different from anywhere else."

"Eyes?"

"None. We don't want to spread this one too far and wide."

"So?"

"So get your backside on a plane, Ventura."

"Yes, sir."

Ventura placed the phone in its cradle and slammed down the remains of his drink. Then he picked up the phone again, hoping the pilot wasn't too far into his bottle of rum.

CHAPTER TWENTY-ONE

LENNY WOKE UP FROM A RESTLESS NIGHT'S SLEEP ON THE sofa in Seal's airfield office. He stepped out into the predawn and stretched muscles that were tired just from sitting in aircraft.

He made coffee using the office machine and was sitting in a camp chair sipping his second cup when Seal arrived. The pilot nodded good morning and set about opening the big hangar.

Lenny did a double take. This was no six-seater Cessna but a huge silver bird with patches of gray and blue, the kind the Marines might use for troop or equipment transport. At least seventy feet long with a massive prop engine on each wing.

"What the hell?"

Seal smiled like a proud daddy. "Fairchild C-123 Provider. This baby was at Khe Sanh."

Lenny walked into the hangar and examined it in wonder. "How did you get it?"

"I bought it. The US Air Force offloaded them after 'Nam to the Department of Agriculture. I know a guy who knows a guy."

Lenny thought about the quantity of drugs such an aircraft could hold. "And this will get to Panama?"

"Nonstop."

"Seriously?"

"She's got two Benson auxiliary tanks. Can get to Panama and halfway back on one load."

"Well, let's do this thing."

Seal did his checks while Lenny drove Seal's truck into town to collect the sandwiches and drinks he had ordered from the café the previous evening, and left another fat tip. He was becoming very popular.

When he returned Seal had lowered the ramp, and Lenny grabbed his pack from the office and stepped up into the dark, cavernous belly of the beast. It was not designed for moving civilians, but something else far more hideous.

When Seal was ready, he fired up the C-123. The noise was palpable, hitting Lenny in the chest. Seal pulled out of the hangar toward the runway, then stopped. He unbuckled, ran back down the open ramp, rolled the hangar doors closed to lock up, and jogged back. He was puffing heavily when he slid into the pilot's seat. He raised the ramp and taxied out, then punched it, and they rattled down the runway and into the sky.

It was a long flight, out over the Gulf of Mexico, in between Cuba and the Yucatan Peninsula, and then across the Caribbean toward South America. The loud aircraft vibrated and bounced through the air. Lenny was used to it. He'd been in worse but rarely for so long.

"How do they package the stuff?" Lenny asked.

"Kilogram bundles. They call them 'keys.'"

"I know keys. How many in a shipment?"

"How long is a piece of string? If it's a drug mule on a commercial flight, they might only have one key separated and spread across them. A small aircraft could carry up to a hundred keys, and an aircraft like this? Hell, maybe a ton."

"Is one key worth the risk?"

"They've been flooding the market with bigger shipments, so

the price has fallen. But in New York I hear they're still getting as much as forty thousand dollars a key."

"A hundred keys is four million."

"You see what you're up against?"

Lenny let out a low whistle. He saw it, alright.

It was late afternoon when land appeared on the horizon. Seal checked his instruments and eased along the coastline until he banked around a port town.

"Colón," he said. "It's where the Panama Canal ends. Or begins, depending on your point of view."

They flew on along the coastline, and Seal pointed out a series of bays. "Puerto Escocés. Nice little bay for moving things you don't want anyone seeing."

"They don't fly it?"

"Sure they fly it, but they also have a hundred other ways to transport it." Seal banked inland and pointed out across Lenny. "See that?"

Lenny saw mountainous jungle that seemed to go on forever. It reminded him of Southeast Asia.

"We're over Panama, but that's Colombia, right there. Problem is, there are no roads of any use between the two. It's a national park or something, and it's just mountains and jungle. Can't move anything by land."

"So they use boats?"

"Right. They drive the stuff down from Cartagena and then use boats to Panama, or across the water direct to wherever."

"Why Panama? Why bother with the extra step?"

"Well, they don't include me in their planning, pal, but I figure it's the canal. A lot of container traffic goes through there, to all parts of the world. Farther than any aircraft can go."

Seal banked around and headed away from Colombia. After a short while, he switched frequencies on his radio and made a call, which received a garbled response Lenny couldn't decipher.

Then, slowly, they glided downward toward the green carpet

below. At the last minute, an airstrip opened up before them. Seal landed the big aircraft with a thud that might have raised eyebrows from airliner passengers but not anyone in the military.

A fuel truck waited at the end of the strip. Seal killed the engine. A man drove the truck toward the C-123.

"Welcome to Panama," said Seal.

"I take it this is not Panama City International."

"No, that would be Omar Torrijos International Airport. This is actually an aero club strip. Not many craft this size can land here, but this baby was designed to land on short, bumpy strips in Vietnam."

"It seems to do that all right."

"Not as well as the air force hoped. Maybe the 'Nam strips were too short or too bumpy, but either way, it gets the job done here."

"So what now?"

"Now you get out, and I refuel and fly away before anyone asks questions."

"We're in the middle of the jungle."

"The guy in the fuel truck will drive you into the city. Give him ten bucks and he'll be happy. Just don't ask his name."

"Roger that."

Lenny unbuckled and slipped out of the seat.

"I won't be coming back," said Seal. "You're on your own now."

"That's how I want it. Thanks for the ride. I'll put in a good word with the higher-ups when I get back."

"I'd appreciate it."

Lenny was about to move into the cargo hold when he stopped. "What's the currency here?"

"The locals use the Panamanian balboa. Like Rocky."

"Or Vasco Núñez de Balboa," said Lenny.

"Who?"

"Spanish conquistador."

"Whatever. But it doesn't matter—the US dollar is also official currency."

"Really?"

"Yep. The greenback, baby. Don't leave home without it."

Lenny nodded then walked down the cargo ramp and out onto the dirt strip. The ground was moist and sticky like clay, and despite the clear skies, the trees dripped as if it had just rained. He wiped the humidity from his brow and moved to the side of the runway, where he watched the guy fueling the C-123.

Seal went down the ramp but stopped at the end, as if he refused to put a foot on Panamanian soil. He stretched out his back. When he heard the fuel lines being uncoupled, he wandered back up into the cargo hold.

The fuel truck backed away. The big propellors started turning, and the cargo ramp closed. The truck stopped near Lenny, and the driver gave him a nod. He was all mustache and trucker's cap, and he said nothing but Lenny got the message. He jogged around the vehicle to get the blood flowing, then he climbed up into the cabin, and they pulled away. Lenny wasn't sure if he heard the roar of the aircraft engines as Seal charged down the primitive runway, but he didn't see it. All he saw was a tunnel of foliage ahead as they bounced along the dirt road.

They drove from jungle to the outskirts of the city in under an hour. Lenny noticed poorly constructed buildings, with sheets of corrugated iron fixed to rickety board walls or cracked cinderblock. People loitered, some talking in groups, others just watching the truck pass by.

Soon tall buildings and logos of US and Japanese corporations appeared. The city felt modern but a little tired, the way hot places often did. The driver directed the truck from the wide boulevards of downtown into the tight lanes of the old town. Then, without notice, he braked to a stop and pointed.

"Hotel Turistico."

They were the first words spoken on the ride, but Lenny

didn't reply. Instead, he handed the driver a twenty and got out. The driver rumbled away, and Lenny surveyed the scene. The area had an old European feel. Cobbled streets and wrought iron balconies like he had seen in pictures of New Orleans. The people here didn't stand around. They were moving, doing, going. A restaurant glowed warmly out onto the dimming light of the street, and people sat at tables drinking and talking and laughing.

Lenny glanced at the tourist hotel and gave it a hard pass—too nice, too upmarket. The kind of place where English would be widely spoken and passports would be checked and questions would be asked. He set off walking, through lanes and sprawling streets that felt like they had been designed by someone with vertigo.

He guessed he was about three blocks off the main drag when he came upon a suitable candidate. It was marked with a hand-painted sign by the door that read *pensión*. Lenny went through a small dark foyer, with a fan blowing from a wooden desk. A tiny woman with hair in a bun smiled at him.

"Hello," said Lenny.

"*Buenas noches,*" she whispered as if in a library.

"*¿Tienes un cuarto?*"

"*Sí. ¿Solo tu?*"

"*Sí.*"

Lenny took out some cash so she could see he had US dollars.

"*Ocho,*" she said.

Lenny handed her two tens. "*Dos noches.*"

"*Bueno.*" She took a key from a hook and opened a drawer to make change.

Lenny waved her off. "*Está bien.*"

"*Gracias. El primer piso.*"

"*Gracias,*" said Lenny. The first floor would do fine. "*¿Tienes un mapa de la ciudad?*"

The woman spun in her chair and pulled a folded map of the

old quarter from a rack. Still smiling, she handed it to Lenny. "*Desayuno a las siete.*"

Lenny thanked her again. He wasn't sure he would be awake for breakfast at seven, because the flight had been long and tiring, and he expected to be up late. As he took his pack and headed for the stairs, he wondered for a moment how Seal could do two eight-hour flights back-to-back. There had to be a regulation against that, but he concluded that drug smugglers didn't care much about that kind of red tape.

Lenny found his room to be basic but comfortable. A bed, a dresser, a chair, a sink. No balcony but a view of the terracotta roofs. He didn't linger at the window. Instead he stripped off his clothes, hung his shirt off a knob on the dresser, and folded his pants. Then he slipped into bed and was asleep in minutes.

———

VENTURA WAS TIRED AND IRRITABLE, BUT HE WAS happier to be in the field than behind a desk. No time for sleep though. He needed to rent a car and find this Podunk place called Mena, Arkansas. First he'd check in with Langley. He found a pay phone on the airport concourse and called.

"Where are you?"

"Little Rock. I'm about to drive out to where he is."

"He's not there."

Ventura clenched his jaw.

"He's in Panama City."

"Florida?"

"No, Panama."

"He's in Panama?

"That's our intel. One of our people just saw him get dropped off in Casco Viejo—it's the historic quarter. He didn't check into our hotel, so we're working on an exact location."

"I'm still at the airport."

"Good. There's a flight out of Atlanta. Get on it."

"Yes, sir."

"When you get there, don't go straight to Cox."

"Sir?"

"There's someone down there who wants to see you first."

When Ventura hung up, he stared at the pay phone. What on earth was Cox doing in Panama? The guy was really sticking in Ventura's craw. He walked over to the Continental Airlines ticket desk and asked for the next flight to Atlanta. It was in forty-five minutes. Time to splash some water over his face. Then he asked about a flight to Panama and was told there was nothing direct with them, but Delta might have something out of Atlanta. Ventura thanked the agent, took his boarding pass, and returned to the bank of pay phones to call someone at Delta.

"Damn Cox," he muttered, as he picked up the handset and tucked it under his chin.

———

JUST AFTER MIDNIGHT, LENNY WOKE WITH LIGHT FROM a streetlamp slicing in through a crack in the curtain. He checked his watch and padded to the sink, where he used a washcloth to wipe himself down. Then he got dressed, turned on the light, and spread the map out across the bed. He found his location in the historic quarter and ran his finger across the folds, looking for the name of the area that Seal had given him. He double tapped the spot then traced a route back to his hotel. He traced it again, from his hotel to the destination, just to get a feel for the lefts and the rights. Then he folded the map, slipped it in his pocket, and headed out.

The lobby was dark and quiet, so he eased the door open and shut it gently behind. Outside it was muggy but cooler. A neon *farmicia* sign buzzed across the street. Lenny marched away, noticing that even the tourist section was calm. He covered a lot of ground walking for thirty minutes. When he reached a district known as Curundú, he rechecked his map then went down the kind of alley his father had always said to avoid.

The dive bar had no sign, but the Spanish music was a give-away. Lenny pushed open the heavy wooden door and stepped in. It could have been in Washington or Albuquerque, with glowing beer signs and a quiet clientele who mostly kept to themselves.

Lenny took a stool at the bar, and the bartender ambled over to him.

"*Cerveza*," said Lenny.

The bartender took a bottle from a fridge and popped the top. "One dollar."

Lenny put a ten on the bar top but anchored it with his fingers. There were better ways to do these things, but he didn't have time to get cute.

"The rest is yours for some information," he said.

"What information?" The guy's accent indicated he wasn't a native English speaker, but Lenny had heard worse on the streets of San Diego.

"I need a firearm."

The guy furrowed his brow like this word evaded him.

"A gun."

He shrugged. "I don't know nothing about that."

"Who does?"

The bartender's eyes flicked toward a couple of brooding char-acters sitting at a corner booth.

"Them?"

He shrugged again. Lenny lifted his fingers off, and the bartender took the note. Lenny slipped off his stool and strolled over to the two men. He stood before them, sipping his beer.

"*¿Qué?*" said the guy in a leather vest, attempting to dress like a biker.

"I need a gun," Lenny said.

The guy chortled. "*¿Qué?*"

"A gun. *Un arma*."

"Go away, gringo."

Lenny smiled and drank again. "I have money. *Dinero*."

Leather vest looked at his buddy then back at Lenny. He smiled with alarmingly perfect teeth. Then he jinked his head toward the back door.

"Outside."

Lenny put his beer on their table, and the guy slid out from the booth. When the second man started to move, Lenny put his palm out.

"Just him," said Lenny.

The man made a face like he didn't care either way, and he moved back into the booth. That told Lenny plenty—like they were underestimating the gringo with no weapon, and that his buddy either had a gun to sell or had one to pull on him once they were outside.

It was the latter.

Lenny followed him into the alley behind the bar. The door closed behind them. Lenny had barely stepped onto the pavement when the guy pulled the gun out from under his leather vest and pointed it at Lenny's chest.

Lenny craned his neck as if inspecting the weapon from all angles. What he noticed most of all was that it wasn't cocked. "A revolver. What is that, a thirty-eight? You don't have a Glock, do you?"

"Give me your money," said leather vest, jutting the gun at Lenny.

"I'll take that as a no. Do you have rounds for this thing? I'll need a box if you have it."

"I said, give me your money."

"Patience, friend. You'll get your dough." Lenny pulled a hundred from his pocket. "Let's say fifty for the gun and fifty for a box of ammo."

"I'll take it all."

Lenny laughed. "That's funny, because if I didn't know better—"

The next part happened like magic, as if the hands were faster than the eye.

Lenny grabbed the barrel of the revolver and forced it downward with one hand while holding the guy's wrist with the other. His trigger finger snapped, just before the pollicis tendons in his wrist reached tearing point, and he let go of the gun. Lenny pulled it away with his right hand and used the opportunity to put a left jab into the guy's throat.

He dropped to the moist asphalt, trying to decide whether to reach for his wrist, his finger, or his throat. Lenny dragged him against the side wall of the bar and crouched before him.

"Now, how about that ammo?"

Leather vest shook his head.

"No ammo? That's disappointing. So let's just say, then— since I only got half of what I needed and you tried to rob me and all—that I just take this demo model for a test drive and we call it even. All right?"

The guy gasped but didn't seem capable of words.

"I'll take that as a yes."

Lenny stood and took one last look at the guy. The throat would recover first—he'd have a raspy voice for a week. The finger would be out of action for a month. But the wrist was a bear. Lenny had seen fellow Marines that took six months to recover from wrist injuries. The pain rendered them unable to make a fist. Or eat soup.

He pulled the door open and walked back down the dark corridor into the bar. He stopped by the booth and picked up his beer. The second guy's jaw nearly hit the table top. Lenny slugged his beer back and placed the empty back on the table.

"Gracias," he said, sauntering past the heavy wooden door, and set off marching toward his bed.

CHAPTER TWENTY-TWO

Lenny slept late, missing breakfast. He walked to a nearby restaurant and ate a lunch of steak and eggs and drank heart-starter black coffee, all for a few bucks. He bought a map of Panama, then he retired to his room to look it over. Of particular interest were the bays at the eastern end of the country, near the Colombian border. But getting there was going to be a problem.

He went back down to the lobby and asked the woman if there was somewhere he could get a motorcycle.

"¿*Alquilar?*"

"*Alquilar o comprar.*" He could rent or buy, he didn't care.

She showed him a place on the map. He thanked her then set off with the revolver stuck into the back of his pants. As he wandered past a street vendor selling clothing, he made a point to circle back later; a change of clothes was in order.

The place with the motorcycles was a parking lot outside a boarded-up factory. He had expected some kind of low-rent dealership. This was individuals selling their own stuff, or at least items they were claiming to be theirs. Provenance was sketchy. He walked around the lot like he was at a flea market. There were cars and trucks and an ATV. He saw a Jeep that looked like it might have carried MacArthur. And lots of motorcycles: road bikes, dirt bikes, scooters.

He settled on a dirt bike that was being offered by a young guy with a bandana. He was also selling bananas by the box, and loud Florida-style shirts, except they were emblazoned with palm trees, container ships, and the word *Panama* written in cursive. It was an *ask no questions* kind of deal. Lenny haggled with the guy for good form and agreed on two hundred US dollars.

"*¿Gasolina?*" Lenny asked.

"*Lleno*," said bandana.

"Gracias."

Lenny left with a bike with a full tank, no paperwork, a new shirt, and a free banana, which he peeled and ate on the ride out of town. He stopped several times to check his map and a couple more times to ask for directions when the map lacked detail.

It was only a touch over a hundred miles to Puerto Escocés, but the ride took three hours and proved to be a bust. The highway became a road, which turned off to a dirt track, which then became nothing more than a hiking trail. There was no way into the large bay that Seal had shown him from the air. Not in a vehicle, anyway. And they weren't carrying large quantities of narcotics out on the backs of burros.

Before calling it quits, he decided to follow the dirt track to the end of the line. The track led south of Puerto Escocés but was enough to drive a small truck or van through. He veered around potholes for another mile until he broke from solid jungle to an opening.

It was a village. Thatched-roof huts clung close together like cows in a field. The cluster of homes opened up to a wide beach punctuated with lazy palm trees. Beyond the sand was the most gorgeous turquoise water Lenny had ever seen. He pushed the bike off the track and into the scrub, then wandered down onto the beach with his daypack across his shoulder.

This was no tourist hotspot. The beach was littered with palm fronds and seaweed, and a line of fishing boats reclined on the dry sand, the epitome of the word *beached*.

Lenny loved it. He felt his blood pressure decrease as he inhaled the Caribbean air. It was the kind of laidback place he could see himself after the adventures were done and the pace of youth lost its luster.

He glanced along the shoreline. Three men worked together to untangle a fishing net, paying no attention to the red-haired white man standing on their beach. He spotted two women with bronzed skin looking at him. They didn't approach, as if assessing a mountain lion from a safe distance. Lenny offered a gentle wave but got nothing in return.

Then he heard the vehicle. It was the rattle of body and parts bouncing around the unkempt road rather than engine noise, but it definitely didn't belong. Lenny wandered back up through the palm trees and into the foliage beyond. There he crouched and watched the van stop at the end of the track, only ten feet from where he had left his motorbike in the scrub.

There were two men in the cab. The driver switched off the engine, and the scene fell silent but for the lapping waves. They just sat with the windows down, smoking and waiting. Perhaps they were looking to buy that day's catch from the fisherman, but none of the villagers approached the van. Lenny could hear the men speaking Spanish but wasn't able to decipher the nature of the conversation.

Lenny sat down in the scrub to wait. A half hour went by. Then an hour. Then women emerged from thatched homes and moved toward a central point in the village that was out of Lenny's line of vision. Shortly after, a plume of smoke lifted into the evening sky, and Lenny caught the scent of fish cooking over wood fire.

After their meal, Lenny saw children playing soccer on the beach. They went at it hard, sliding in for tackles, sand spraying into the air. Then, in an instant, it was over. Mothers called, and all the kids scattered as if late to watch their favorite television program. But there were no TV antennas and probably no televisions. The approaching night wrapped itself around the village.

It wasn't more than twenty minutes before the sound of the outboard engine tore through the noise of the bugs. In the moonlight, Lenny saw the white hull of a speedboat appear like an apparition. The men crushed out cigarettes, and the cab light came on momentarily as they stepped out of the van, and they ambled down the beach to the boat.

Lenny fumbled in his backpack and found his binoculars. The speedboat landed no more than twenty yards from him, but he wanted to see the whites of their eyes. Or the white of whatever else they had on board.

Two men on the boat passed small parcels to those on the beach, who carried the parcels up past the water, placed them on dry sand, and returned for the next round. They weren't in any hurry, but they didn't stop for chitchat either.

The whole thing took ten minutes. When the last package was dumped on the beach, the two men from the van pushed the bow of the boat out until the sandy bottom released the hull and the engine started. The boat chugged out a little in reverse, then the driver turned on a dime and hit the throttle hard.

The men on the beach didn't watch them go. They had work to do. They each scooped up a stack of parcels and carried them to the van. One guy slid the side door open. The interior light illuminated the men stacking the parcels into the cargo space.

As the men moved between the beach and the van, Lenny eased through the jungle. This time, when both men were heading back toward the beach, he took the chance to prove his hunch. He stepped out onto the track and over to the van, and peeked in through the open door. Plastic-wrapped parcels of a white powder. Lenny thought about taking a key for evidence, but that wasn't his job. Besides, someone was going to count these things at some point, and he didn't want to raise suspicion, at least not yet. He wasn't about to taste it, like on TV. It might be pure, which could kill him, or it might be baking soda, which would render it pointless as evidence.

He crept back into his hiding place. He knew it wasn't baking soda. That got delivered on grocery chain trucks in the middle of the day. It wasn't coming in on boats near the Colombian border under the cover of darkness. He knew just as well as the villagers, who had made sure they weren't around to see any of it. And he didn't need to present the evidence in a courtroom. He was just there to cause trouble.

So he waited. When they were done and the door to the van was slammed home, Lenny got ready to move. The men got in. The van started, and the headlights pierced the night. As the van turned around and the light swept across his position, Lenny ducked. Then he moved fast.

The van rattled away slowly. Lenny ran behind it to the spot where he had left his bike.

He pulled the motorcycle out of the scrub, threw his leg over the seat, and rolled it forward as he started it. He left the headlight switch alone, and he set off after the van. It was risky. The road was visible but the potholes were not, so Lenny bounced along, barely in control of the bike.

Every muscle in his body ached from the effort by the time he reached the paved road. Lenny had lost the van's taillights in the distance, but now it was either left or right. Not a complex choice. Left was back toward Colombia, which seemed to defeat the purpose of the exercise, so Lenny cut right, flicked the headlight on, and gunned the throttle.

The chewed-up asphalt was only marginally less risky than the dirt track. But Lenny was moving much faster than before, and speed brought results. Within five minutes he saw the glow of taillights ahead, so he eased off the throttle and kept his distance.

As they reached the outskirts of Panama City and hit traffic,

Lenny closed in. The van moved invisibly through the city, one of a thousand dirty white vans, even at night.

The van meandered through downtown and into an industrial area of low-slung warehouses. Here the traffic was light, so Lenny dropped back a touch, but the guys in the van showed no sign of looking for, let alone noticing, a tail.

Lenny pulled over alongside a chain-link fence when the van stopped at the gate to a warehouse facility. In the distance, maybe a mile away, he could see the lights on the cranes at the port of Panama.

The van didn't go into the warehouse. Instead it drove over to a semitrailer that sat waiting in a loading bay. The van backed in toward the cargo container on the trailer. Lenny saw the rear doors open and one of the men get out. From his vantage point he didn't see any of the parcels get loaded, but it didn't take Sherlock Holmes to figure out where the drugs were now.

The operation was faster than on the beach—less than five minutes—and the van doors closed. The van drove away, back through the gate and out toward where Lenny was squatting with his binocs. He dropped to the grass against the fence as the van's headlights splashed across him and continued on.

Once the darkness returned, Lenny sat up but saw no more movement, until another van drove by. Again he dropped, and a blue van pulled in through the gate and backed up to the container. Five minutes later it too was gone. Lenny scribbled down its license plate under that of the first van, and jotted down the serial number on the side of the container.

Eight more vans arrived, unloaded, and left before Lenny saw a man emerge from the container and push the heavy doors closed.

A few more minutes passed, then the cabin lit up as the door on the passenger side opened and closed. Next, the driver got up into the cab, and the semitrailer pulled away from the loading dock and out toward the gate.

Lenny shoved his binocs and notepad into his pack and slipped it onto his back, then crouched low beside the motorcycle, hiding but ready. As it was, the truck turned away from him and headed toward the bright lights of the port, so Lenny pushed his bike up onto the road and took off after it.

The truck drove about a mile and a half before it hit a long line of prime movers hauling Conex containers into the port. The driver tucked in behind the last truck and killed the engine. It looked like part of the process, one everybody was familiar with. The driver and his pal got out of the truck and walked ahead to a van selling coffee and snacks. The group of drivers congregated there, waiting for the trucks ahead to get processed and offloaded, making room for them to move up. Nobody looked in any kind of hurry.

Lenny pushed the bike in behind a bush then wandered along the other side of the road, past the long line of trucks, to the port gate, where an enormous sign proclaimed the facility to be the Balboa Port. He watched how the security procedure worked, which included handing the gate guard some paperwork. The guard would look at it then count the number of containers on the truck—just one most of the time—and once a space in one of the lines ahead became available he would direct the truck into that line. Some of the containers were then unloaded and placed on the dock to await loading onto a future ship, while others were moved directly to a ship that was already at port.

No one was checking the trucks or the drivers. Lenny figured it would be an hour until his truck got to the gate, so he stood in the shadows and continued watching. The trucks nearer the gate moved in but the other drivers stayed standing around the food van. After about thirty minutes, all the drivers took to their semi-trailers and moved forward as a group. Those closest to the gate remained in their cabs, waiting to get processed, while those farther back got out again and returned to mingle around the food van.

The driver from Lenny's truck exited. Lenny figured he would be in the next batch to get through, so after everyone had resumed their places at the van, he ambled across the road as if he was just another guy, and walked along the trailer attached to the truck he was surveilling.

Behind the first set of tires he found a huge steel box attached underneath the load bed. It was a storage box, about six feet long and two feet deep, designed to hold ropes and chains when they weren't being used to secure a load. Lenny checked both directions then undid the latch. It wasn't locked, so he quickly lifted the front of the box open like a garage door, slipped inside, and pulled it closed.

It wasn't comfortable. There were a few chains and tools that dug into Lenny's ribs, and the air was thick and oily. He waited another twenty minutes before he felt the engine start and the box vibrate. As the truck eased forward, he had to work hard to hold the door closed. It slowed as the line regathered, but the driver didn't kill the engine this time. He sat for a few minutes, then advanced a truck length and stopped again.

Lenny waited for a longer acceleration, a movement that suggested they were through the gate, heading for whichever line they would join inside the port facility. A few more short moves forward, then he felt the engine rev a little harder, and the truck progressed slowly and steadily. Once in the new line, the engine cut out.

Lenny pushed the box open just a crack and strained to hear the slam of the cab door, but it never came. It suggested that at this point the drivers would remain in their vehicles, either because they would be inching forward more often or checked by port security, or maybe both.

Lenny didn't wait in his metal coffin anymore. He pushed the lid open just enough to roll out of the box and drop to the ground in a pushup position. He quickly bear-crawled under the truck and lay on the asphalt to survey his surroundings. To his left was an open expanse until another line of trucks—the ones whose containers were being stored at the port, awaiting their ships. On his right, a shorter distance of open tarmac before a line of stacked containers.

He chose option B.

Lenny crawled to the edge of the truck and was checking if the coast was clear, when the engine fired up and the humungous tires started moving toward him. Not waiting to get turned into a pizza crust, Lenny rolled out and dashed across to the nearest container stack.

After watching the truck drive forward and stop again, Lenny caught his breath. Then, keeping close to the container stacks, he made his way near the dock. Men in hardhats on a gantry supervised the loading of a ship so large Lenny couldn't see the containers once the ship-to-shore crane lifted them over the side of the deck. In turn, the trucks in the line would be ordered into place and have their container removed and loaded. Lenny figured each container had its prearranged placement, depending on weight and destination.

He stood in the shadows and watched the choreographed process. The scale of it all was hard to fathom. The ships, the cranes, the sheer number of containers was so massive he found it hard to believe the things would float.

Lenny had to duck back into the maze of containers a few times as dock workers passed by, but after about an hour he saw his truck move forward underneath the giant crane system. The spreader dropped down and was connected to the container. Then it lifted the box off the truck hoisted it high up into the air before moving along the boom and over the ship, at which point Lenny lost sight of it.

There was one more thing to know. Lenny jogged along the container stack toward the stern of the ship. Once at the rear of the huge vessel, he jotted down the name: *Murrieta Nord*, registration Panama. Then it was time to get out. He wasn't going to be able to use the rope-box trick again. Any semitrailer leaving the facility would have the boxes filled with the chains they had removed prior to unloading. So he took the old-fashioned route. He wound his way through the stacks to the darkest corner, where he climbed a double-high stack. He then stepped from one stack to the next until he was right against the fence. Beyond the fence lay dense foliage that looked like a black hole. Lenny took a deep breath, put a boot on top of the fence, and stepped over.

The drop was like falling out a second-floor window, but Lenny used his parachute training to hit the grass in a roll. It sent a shudder through his body and left him winded. He lay on the moist grass and let his breathing calm. When he was ready, he pushed his way through the foliage toward the road where he had hidden his motorcycle.

The line of trucks wasn't any shorter. It seemed like the flow of containers was constant. Lenny pulled the bike out of the bushes, started it up, and headed back to his hotel, where he hoped he would find a beer and a bed but would be satisfied with one or the other.

CHAPTER TWENTY-THREE

LENNY DIDN'T GET A BEER OR A BED. HE PARKED THE bike beside the hotel and walked into the lobby to find Ventura sitting in a rattan chair, reading *The Washington Post*.

"Fancy meeting you here," said Lenny.

"You're a regular Eddie Murphy, Cox."

"Eddie Murphy? That's a new one for me."

"You're also a major league pain in the—"

"Now, don't say anything you might regret, Ventura."

Ventura stood. "What the hell have you been doing?"

"My job. And you?"

He bristled. "That's above your pay grade, Marine."

"Probably. Well, it's been a blast catching up, but I really need a beer and a shower."

"Not right now, you don't. You need to come with me."

"It's been a day, Ventura. And a night, come to think of it. How about we chat tomorrow?"

"I got a lieutenant colonel waiting to speak with you."

Lenny cocked an eyebrow. "Marine?"

"Very."

Lenny sighed. He had no problem blowing off a spook from the company but not a senior officer.

"Let me just wash my face."

"No time, Cox."

"But I just got a new shirt."

"Put it on in the car."

Ventura led Lenny to a European car so small it looked like it was built on a motorcycle frame. Lenny changed his shirt as they drove, but in the tiny vehicle the effort looked like Houdini escaping from a straightjacket inside a locked box.

It was a mercifully short ride to Ancon Hill. Ventura stopped at the gate, where a sign read *Quarry Heights Military Reservation* and, in smaller script, *Department of Defense*. Ventura spoke to the guard, who made a call and then returned to tell Ventura where to go.

He seemed to know the way. They puttered up to a two-story colonial-style building with a wide verandah. Ventura led Lenny up the stairs, knocked on the door, and a lance corporal opened the door like he was a butler. He ushered Ventura and Lenny inside and directed them to a room that looked like a railroad baron's den. Shelves of uninviting books surrounded a large desk, and a set of four plush leather chairs encircled a cherrywood coffee table near the window.

The lance corporal disappeared. Ventura sat in one of the leather chairs. Lenny stood at ease. Fifteen minutes later, Ray Caan stepped into the room with another guy, who looked like either an accountant or an astronaut.

"Cox," said Caan.

"Caan. I wasn't expecting you."

"Funny. Cox, this is my boss. Lieutenant Colonel Oliver North."

Lenny snapped to attention.

North offered his hand. "No need for the salutes, Sergeant. Neither of us is in uniform."

"Yes, sir."

They shook hands. North was as buttoned-up as a guy not in uniform could be, with a collared shirt, pressed trousers, and a neat, conservative haircut that wasn't quite to Marine spec.

"I like your shirt," said the lieutenant colonel.

"Yes, sir." Lenny wasn't sure if the comment was a subtle dig at his unkempt appearance or just a good-natured jibe at the shirt's volume.

"Let's take a seat."

Lenny sat beside Ventura across the coffee table from North and Caan.

"You're with the NSC, sir?" asked Lenny.

"That's correct. On detachment in DC. Sort of like you, but the people I deal with are a tad less trustworthy." He smiled at his own comment.

"Yes, sir."

"So, what brings you to Panama, Sergeant."

"The mission took a turn, sir."

"I'd like to hear it, but first, have you eaten today?"

"I'll be okay, sir."

"A drink?"

"I'm fine."

North stood and walked to the desk, then picked up a phone. He spoke for a moment, then returned to the leather chairs. "Tell me about the mission."

Lenny explained that Freeport had been of limited value, and in line with his orders to "cause trouble," he followed the leads to Norman's Cay, which had been a stronghold of cartel boss Carlos Lehder.

"He was long gone," said Lenny. "The island is barely operational. But I learned that Lehder might be in Panama, so I'm just following the chain down into the sewer."

North nodded.

The door opened and the lance corporal entered, holding a

tray with four glasses of beer and a plate of sandwiches. When he left the room, North held his beer up. "Cheers."

The other three men took sips. It was the nectar of life to Lenny's parched throat. When each of them had grabbed a sandwich, North asked Lenny to continue.

"It seems the Colombians are moving narcotics via a number of channels."

"Multiple flanks, as it were," said North.

"Yes, sir. I have reason to believe they are still using locations in the Bahamas, just to a lesser extent, and that more stuff is moving through Panama and maybe other Central American countries like Nicaragua."

"You have any evidence of that, Sergeant?"

"Nothing concrete, Colonel."

North nodded, and Lenny took another slug of his beer.

"What do you know about the political situation down here, Sergeant?" asked North.

"Not much, sir."

"Well, let me sum it up in one word: *delicate*. As I am sure you know, the Soviets have their little foothold in Cuba, which destabilizes the whole region. Now the Nicaraguans are in bed with the Soviets. A few years back, the government was overthrown by a group calling themselves the Sandinistas. They are communists, Sergeant, pure and simple. But not everyone in Nicaragua is on their side. There is an internal group called the *Contrarrevolución*, who is fighting the red menace. We call them the Contras. Now, obviously the administration cannot directly act on a sovereign country, but we can certainly assist with aid."

"Military aid, sir?"

"Whatever aid is required, Sergeant."

"Troops?"

"No, no US boots on the ground. Our objective is to assist the Contras to destabilize the Sandinista regime and, in so doing, prevent the spread of communism in the region."

"Okay. What does this have to do with what I'm doing?"

"You've wandered into the hornet's nest, Sergeant Cox. See, the Panamanian administration is more friendly to the US. Their leader, General Manuel Noriega, has allowed us to use his country as a staging area for aid missions."

North picked up his beer and rested the glass on his thigh but didn't drink. "We have reason to believe that the Sandinistas are now working with the Colombian cartels, allowing the cartels to ship their dirty product by air and sea into Nicaragua, and then onto the United States. It's a double win for them. They hurt us by allowing narcotics to flood our streets, and they earn a decent cut of the profits to fund their communist agenda."

"And Panama?" asked Lenny.

"What about it?"

"What about drugs coming through Panama?"

"No, that's not happening."

"Are you sure, sir?"

"What do you know?"

"Just what I've been told. But it's the Panama Canal. Half the world's shipping comes through here."

"Well, if it were happening here, we'd know. And General Noriega won't stand for it. He doesn't want drugs in his country. Our focus is on the Sandinistas. If we don't stop the red tide there, we'll end up with Soviets on our borders. And that would be the end of life as we know it, Sergeant."

"Yes, sir. So where does that leave me? I should be looking at Nicaragua?"

"It's tempting, Sergeant, but I don't think the administration wants a United States Marine there right now. As I said, the politics of it are delicate. Better that we work back channels, help the local good guys fight the bad guys."

"Yes, sir. So what are my orders at this point?"

"The Bahamas are still in play. You said so yourself."

"With all due respect, sir, the Bahamas are a leaky faucet when we have a busted pipe under the house. Stuff is leaving Colombia from Cartagena and Barranquilla, and some of it is transiting through the Bahamas, but not like it was. It might be going through Nicaragua, but that can't be all of it. Besides, you have that in hand, I'm sure. But it's getting home somehow, and there's only so many ways it can get there."

North looked at Caan. Caan put his beer down as if he had been handed the microphone.

"You mentioned Carlos Lehder before. Lehder is the Medellín cartel's logistics guy. He was the point man behind using Norman's Cay. But you're saying that's not operational now."

"It's a waypoint, but it's not a hub. Not anymore."

"Okay, so that ties into some new intelligence. Our sources suggest that Lehder is working on alternative routes."

"Nicaragua? Panama?"

"Panama, no. As the lieutenant colonel has said, General Noriega is on our side. But Nicaragua, yes. He has met with Daniel Ortega, the leader of the Sandinistas. We're working on that. But our sources also say he has met with Raúl Castro."

"Raúl?"

"Fidel's brother."

"He's moving drugs through Cuba?"

"We have no hard evidence, but we believe so."

"But they're communists."

"They're all communists until someone waves some cash in front of them. With these guys everyone is equal, but some are more equal than others. Andropov and his Kremlin buddies aren't standing in mile-long bread lines during a Moscow winter, that's for sure."

"But how are they running the stuff through Cuba?"

"We don't know. Maybe boat from Colombia to Cuba, or aircraft, or both. Then maybe boat to the US? Aircraft would be harder. We watch the skies between the US and Cuba pretty diligently."

Lenny sat back in his chair and waited for Caan to continue. But he seemed to be done. There was a long silence that Lenny felt no compulsion to fill. Finally North spoke.

"Take a day off, Sergeant. Relax, get some sleep. We'll assess your information and provide your orders *a-sap*."

"Aye, aye, sir."

North stood, so Lenny did the same. The lieutenant colonel shook Lenny's hand. "Thank you for your service. The people of the United States appreciate it."

"Thank you, sir."

"Lance Corporal Bretton will drive you back to your billet. We'll be in touch."

Lenny left the three men in the study and found Bretton waiting for him. They got in a Ford Granada and drove the short distance back to the pensión. The lance corporal didn't engage in conversation, but Lenny was fine with that, as he was lost in thought. About Communists and Contras, Colombians and Panamanians and Nicaraguans and Cubans, about good guys and bad guys. How drugs could enter the US if not through the Bahamas, and how he could track down and watch a boatload of drugs come into Panama and get onto a ship bound for who knew where—and do that within a day of arriving, when General Noriega wouldn't stand for it, and the NSA and CIA had eyes all over town.

But mostly he kept asking himself why a Marine officer would thank him for his service. Marines didn't do that to other Marines. It was their job, their calling. It was who they were. They didn't thank each other for it, any more than ants thanked each other for help carrying a leaf. Thanking him for his service was something a politician would do.

That thought was going to fester.

————

Lieutenant Colonel North took a bite of sandwich and looked at Ventura. "So, you've worked with him? What do you think?"

"He's good at what he does," said Ventura. "But I think you've given him too long a leash. He's not with the program. I promise you, he won't see things the way you and I do."

"So he doesn't need to know. But my question is, is he keeping anything to himself?"

"You're a senior officer in the Corps. He takes that pretty seriously."

"So you don't think he knows."

"About the shipments we're turning a blind eye to? No, I don't think he knows. He only just arrived. I can't see how he would even know about them."

"He arrived yesterday. He's been doing something since then."

"You want me to grill him?" said Ventura.

"No. I don't want to put all the dots out there for him, even if we think he can't connect them. But we can't have him stumbling into it, all the same. The Contras are depending on that money."

"He did mention shipments through the canal," said Caan.

"Why wouldn't he?" said Ventura. "Name me one other thing your average Joe knows about Panama?"

"Still," said Caan. "I think we should point him in another direction." He glanced at his boss.

North nodded. "I agree. Let's put him to use elsewhere."

CHAPTER TWENTY-FOUR

LENNY WAS DROPPED OFF WITHOUT A WORD. HE STOOD in the quiet street and contemplated breaking camp and finding another place to bunk down. But it was late and he was tired, and anyone who might be watching—the CIA or the NSC or some other three-letter acronym—knew he was in town and without orders. Lieutenant Colonel North had told him to relax, but his brain was abuzz and needed to wind down.

He surveyed the scene once more and found no evidence of a watcher, so he set off through Casco Viejo, a tangle of streets lined with beautiful architecture that had lost its luster, as if the place had seen its peak with the building of the canal.

He found the Central Hotel Panamá, looking like a chateaux pulled out of the French countryside. It was after midnight and nothing much was open, but a five-star hotel was a 24/7, kind place. He walked in as if he belonged, which was a hell of a trick given he had spent the day lying in moist jungle and riding along dirt tracks. But his loud shirt emblazoned with Panama made him look like a tourist, and those were the kinds of people who wandered through hotel lobbies in the wee hours. Lenny made for the concierge's desk.

"I need to make a call to the United States," he said, putting a twenty-dollar note on the desk.

"We have direct dialing in your room, sir."

"Yes, I know. But my wife is asleep, and I'd rather this not appear on my bill." He smiled mischievously and got a look from the concierge that suggested he had seen it all before. The cash disappeared like a magic trick, and he passed the phone across to Lenny, who dialed the first number to get a line.

"I'll leave you to it," said the concierge. "Will five minutes be enough for you, sir?"

"Thirty seconds will be enough."

The concierge walked away as Lenny dialed the number. It was a message service, so the call took *less* than thirty seconds. He left a callback number and time, then he hung up and walked out of the hotel. The thoughts in his head would not stop immediately, but he knew the phone call he would get back would provide some clarity, if not answers.

Lenny walked straight back to the hotel, stripped off his clothes, splashed some water on his face and in his hair, and fell into bed.

When he woke, the sun was up and streaming into the room. He took a long shower and put on another loud shirt he had picked up in Thailand, this one with palm trees and wood-sided station wagons. Then he wandered out into the street. He walked back to the Central Hotel and ordered brunch in the lobby bar. There were businessmen doing deals around him, and he wondered how many of those were legal and how many were making money at the expense of others. He decided not to follow that train of thought.

After a meal of eggs and sausages with a glass of orange juice, he was reading the newspaper over coffee when a bellhop approached him.

"Mr. Cox?"

"Yes."

"I have a phone call for you. Would you like to take it here?"

"Sure."

The bellhop held an old black bakelite phone in his hand, which he placed on the table. He then took the cord and unwound it to the wall, where he plugged it into a socket. He returned to the table, picked up the handset, and told an operator that Mr. Cox was on the line. After handing the phone to Lenny, he took the dollar tip and walked away.

"*Buenos dias*," said Lenny.

"What on earth are you doing in Panama?" asked Alice Brooks.

"Canal spotting."

"And I'm supposed to ask for the gentleman in the Florida shirt?"

"I'm wearing that one I got in Bangkok."

"I would have thought that was a Hawaiian shirt, but it was the *gentleman* bit that I had more trouble with. What are you into? Or do I not want to know?"

"Are you in the office?"

"No. I'm at the Watergate."

"You're hilarious. So what do you know about Nicaragua?"

"I studied law, Len, not geography."

"I don't want you to name the capital, Ally. I'm talking politics."

"Well, Nicaragua lived under the Somoza dictatorship for about forty years until it was overthrown in 1979 after bitter fighting."

"By the Sandinistas?"

"Correct."

"Who are communists."

"Technically they would argue they are socialists."

"And the difference is?"

"The short version I recall from Georgetown was that in communism the state owns all property and distributes it to the people, whereas in socialism everyone owns property equally and it's distributed by a democratically elected government."

"The Sandinistas don't sound democratically elected."

"No. They took power by force from the Somoza family. But they were no angels themselves. The Carter administration withdrew aid for a time over their human rights abuses."

"And now the Sandinistas are supported by the Soviets."

"That's pretty much it."

"And our administration is supporting the other guys, the Contras."

"Not anymore."

"What do you mean?"

"I mean, have you heard of the Boland Amendment?"

"Not this week."

"The CIA was involved in direct acts of sabotage against the Nicaraguan regime without the knowledge of congressional oversight committees. Congress didn't like that, and public approval for direct support of the Contras is low. So the Boland Amendment disallows any funds appropriated by Congress to be used by intelligence agencies to support the activities of the Contras."

"So the CIA can't help them?"

"No. Congress closed the bank."

"What about the NSC?"

"Well, that's a gray area."

"What does that mean?"

"The Boland Amendment covers intelligence agencies. CIA funds are appropriated for intelligence and security purposes, for example. But the National Security Council is technically part of the White House, so while some of its activities might be considered intelligence, some can be positioned simply as policy determinations."

"That sounds like a load of fudge."

"That's one word for it. In short, Congress said no funding the Contras. So that's it. Except it isn't, is it?"

"I don't know."

"The attorney general is suspicious. He knows the Sandinistas are funded by the Soviets and Cuba, but the Contras seem to be able to match them for weapons and tactics, which should be beyond their means, if they're not getting aid from enemies of the USSR."

"Which would be us," said Lenny.

"Right."

"So are they getting money from us?"

"I don't know."

"But shouldn't they? I mean, they're fighting communists."

"And the previous dictatorship killed their detractors, stole aid money and property, while the new regime improves education and lowers poverty."

"So you're saying we should support the communists."

"I'm not saying that. It's not my cup of tea, Len. I'm just saying the people we were helping weren't saints. They committed genocide and who knows what else. I don't know what the answer is. I just know Congress has said this isn't our war to fund."

"And Panama?"

"General Noriega has been on the CIA's payroll for years. He supplies intel, and I believe lets the CIA and others base themselves in Nicaragua for operations."

"Which Congress doesn't allow anymore."

"Not into Nicaragua," she said.

"Is he in the drug business?"

"I don't know. All I can tell you is that he's suspected of money laundering on behalf of the cartels."

"So he's helping us but laundering money from the drugs that hurt our people."

"That pretty much sums it up."

"So why don't we arrest him?"

"The enemy of my enemy is my friend. Plus, suspicion is not proof, and he's essentially a head of state."

"So who are the good guys here?" asked Lenny.

"You recall Kampuchea?"

"There were no good guys. Not even us."

"Remember that. And keep your eyes open."

"Will do."

"Are you okay?"

"I'm doing just peachy."

"You coming back to DC anytime soon?"

"I really don't know."

"It's more fun when you're here," said Alice.

"Right back at ya."

"Well, I've gotta go. Stay safe, will you?"

"That's the plan. I'll catch you soon."

"I hope so. If you need help, call, okay?"

"Roger that."

Alice hung up, and Lenny listened to the dial tone for a moment, then he placed the handset in the cradle and tossed some cash on the table for the brunch. He was done eating. His mind was whirring again. He needed to walk.

Lenny wandered the streets like a tourist, but rather than taking in the architecture, he was focused on the middle distance, thinking logical trains of thought that fell into randomness, and random thoughts that solidified into logic.

There were communists and whatever the rest of us were. Capitalists? Lenny didn't feel like one of those. Those guys worked on Wall Street. He thought about Norman's Cay and the Panama Canal. Aircraft and speedboats. Nicaragua, Cuba, Panama, and the Bahamas.

It was politics and business, but it all revolved around the same thing: cocaine. The same source and destination. Many routes, numerous beneficiaries.

And losers like Melodie Masters, a woman he didn't know. And her parents, whom he met and whose lives would never be the same because of a powder that corrupted not only those who took it but those whose hands it passed through.

When Lenny arrived back at his hotel, Ventura was waiting again.

"Having a good time?" asked Ventura.

"I'm under orders to relax."

"That's over. You've got new orders. You're back in action. And I have orders to support."

"Support what?"

"They want to know if drugs are going through Cuba."

"Why?"

"To stop them."

"Really?"

"And it would be a win for the president. And a black eye for the commies."

"I thought a Marine wandering around Cuba was likely to start World War Three."

"It would. No one at Guantanamo Bay leaves the base. But you're not going as a Marine. You know that TV show *Mission Impossible*?"

"Sure."

"Your mission, Mr. Phelps, is to not get caught, because if you do, the secretary, the president, the governor of whatever damn state you come from, your best buddy, and the girl you took to the prom will all disavow you."

"That last one already happened."

Ventura stood. "You want to think through your support requirements?"

"I need a beer. So let's go get one and I'll tell you what I need."

"That's the smartest thing you've said so far."

"No, this is: you're buying."

CHAPTER TWENTY-FIVE

Lenny had to admit, the CIA was well resourced. He had no idea where Ventura got his toys, but he only took two days to gather the tools Lenny would need. Lenny spent the time discussing tactics with Ventura, updating Lieutenant Colonel Yardley, and thinking through the what's and wherefores. But mostly he was thinking about the why. Yardley articulated it.

"They're setting you up."

"How so?"

"They're worried about a Marine in Nicaragua but not about one getting captured in Cuba? Who are they kidding? Nicaragua is sensitive, but it's small potatoes compared to Cuba. The Soviets will go ballistic if you get caught in Cuba, and things are tense as it is. Andropov was the head of the KGB before he became the Soviet leader, and sources say he's extremely suspicious of US intentions. Basically he believes we're likely to strike them first in a sneak nuke attack."

"There isn't a winner in a nuclear war, sir."

"I know that, Cox. I can't speak for the Russian leadership. They're suspicious sons of guns. And finding a United States Marine in Cuba won't improve their mood."

"Then I best make sure I don't get caught."

"Got that right, but you're missing the point, Sergeant. These NSC and CIA guys are saying they don't need you in Nicaragua where they're fighting the red menace, but Cuba is okay? That makes no sense. Either they want to poke the Soviet bear, which could trigger a war, or they want you literally anywhere other than Nicaragua. Which begs the question, what the hell are they doing in Nicaragua?"

"Nothing. The Boland Amendment doesn't allow us to fund anything in Nicaragua anymore."

"Oh, you're a policy wonk now."

"I know a thing or two, sir."

"How is Alice?"

"I have no recollection of such a person, sir."

"Get used to saying that, Sergeant. You do get this, right? If you go into hostile territory, Ventura is on the money, they will play dumb and say you're there because you're a communist or something. They'll disown you."

"I got my orders from a senior officer. Are your orders different?"

"No. I don't like it is all."

"I'll be all right, sir."

"I know. But I've been wrong before. Just keep your head down, will you? And forget what Ventura says—if by chance you get out alive, give us a call and we'll come pick you up somewhere nearby."

"I could probably swim to Haiti."

"I hope so. Be safe."

"Aye, aye."

————

LENNY MADE HIS NEXT CALL IN A DIFFERENT LOBBY AT another hotel. He tipped the bellhop and used his calling card to reach DEA headquarters.

"You're really getting into this CIA clandestine stuff, Cox," said Purchase.

"It's a fat hassle, if you want to know. But I need to know something: do you have a way to track container ships coming into the United States?"

"Of course."

"Can you track them before they arrive?"

"I can call someone. Why?"

Lenny paused. Once he took this path, he was on it all the way. "I need to know the route of a container ship."

"In Arkansas?"

"In Panama."

"Florida?"

"No, the country Panama."

"What are you doing in... Wait, I don't want to know."

"Exactly. But can you track it? See if it's headed to the States?"

"Give me the details."

Lenny told the DEA agent the details of the ship he had seen at the dock.

"I'll call you back," said Purchase.

Lenny hung up, and the bellhop returned. He gave him another tip and asked for the next call to be routed to him. One cup of coffee later, the phone rang.

"Cox?"

Lenny heard noise in the background. "Where are you?"

"In a bar. This is a call I don't want going through the switchboard."

"What's up?"

"That ship is due to dock in the Port of San Francisco in three weeks or so."

"Is that right?"

"It is. So what gives? Why aren't you asking your buddies at the NSC these questions?"

"To be frank, Purchase, I'm not sure which side of the ball those guys are playing."

"And you're sure about me?"

"Not completely, but I think your interests are more in line with mine."

"Yours were to cause trouble, if I recall. Who are you causing trouble for?"

"Everyone, it seems. Look, the bottom line is, I saw a drug shipment get loaded onto that container vessel. At least seven or eight vans' full."

"And you didn't feel happy about blowing up a ship?"

"There's a lot of stuff on that ship that isn't narcotics. And the sailors are just doing their job."

"So what do you want me to do? Search every single container coming off it in San Francisco?"

"No. Just one. I've got a container number."

"You are thorough, Cox. You sure you don't want a career in law enforcement?"

"It seems a little too black and white for me, Purchase. Do you want the number or what?"

"Shoot."

Lenny gave him the details. "I'd keep this among people you trust, Purchase."

"What are you saying?"

"I don't know for sure. But certain parties might know about the shipment and be turning a blind eye. They might not want it to be exposed."

"Thanks for the heads-up. I know a guy in San Fran. We'll get into it. Damn those other guys."

"And I can't be the source."

"Hell, no. I've got an informant in Los Angeles I can use."

"What if someone asks him about it?"

"He's not talking anymore. Got hit in a drive-by last week."

"Dead men tell no tales."

"In my experience. Anything else?"

"Can you be at this number at eleven p.m. every night for the next week?"

"I've got a wife and kids."

"I wouldn't ask if it wasn't important."

"You're asking me to hang out at an Irish pub and watch football. I'll do this favor for you."

"You're a swell guy."

"My wife may not agree."

"I'll be in touch."

———

LENNY AND VENTURA HEADED OUT OF COLÓN AND across the Caribbean Sea on a fishing trawler. It took two days to make the crossing to Kingston, Jamaica. That gave Ventura plenty of time to run through the equipment. He had procured a radio, field glasses, a camera, and MRE packs. Lenny traded in his Florida look for a khaki shirt and pants that smelled like army surplus. Most important were the weapons.

"Didn't think American arms were the best idea, so this rifle is a Zastava M76," said Ventura. "It's Yugoslavian. Semiautomatic marksman rifle with detachable bayonet."

"As long as it doesn't blow up in my face."

"And this is the pistol."

"Makarov?"

"Yeah, Russian semiautomatic."

"You really don't want to leave a trail, huh?"

"That's the plan."

Lenny used the time on the crossing to toss buoys into the water and test the rifle. The optics were sufficient, and the thing seemed to shoot straight enough. The Makarov worked, but he stripped it and rebuilt it anyway.

When they reached Kingston, Ventura had a van waiting that

drove them to Port Antonio on the north coast of Jamaica. After a few hours' sleep, they took another boat, this one much faster, for the crossing to Cuba.

"We're gonna give Gitmo a wide berth," said Ventura. "Best our people don't know about you either."

"So going to Guantanamo for help is out."

"There's a gate, but no US personnel go through it. A few locals work on the base, but they're all old. Castro banned locals from getting hired in 1959, but the ones that were already working were allowed to stay until retirement or death. But you? Most likely the sentries will shoot you, which will result in questions we don't want to answer."

"Plus, I'd be dead."

"If your fellow Marines can shoot."

"That's always the best assumption."

They headed out toward Haiti then cut in to the western end of Cuba. The sun was long gone when they spotted a flashing light on the shoreline and began to cruise toward it.

"Where are we?" Lenny asked.

"Near a village called Cajobabo. You'll be met on the beach. Give the guy ten bucks and this." Ventura handed Lenny a carton of cigarettes. "He'll drive you to where we believe the drug drops are happening."

"Which is where?"

"North side of the island somewhere."

"And you trust this person?"

Ventura raised an eyebrow. "Rule number one in the company: don't trust anyone."

Lenny nodded. He was getting that message loud and clear.

The boat coasted in to the wide beach, and Lenny jumped off into the shallow water. Ventura handed him his pack and rifle.

"See you at Langley sometime."

"Beers are on you," said Lenny, as he turned to wade toward the man on the beach holding the flashlight.

"Turn that off, will ya?" he said.

"*¿Qué?*"

"*Apágalo.*"

The guy killed the flashlight and led Lenny up the sand to a turnaround, where a truck sat waiting. It looked about a thousand years old, and was a make and model Lenny had never seen before and probably never would again. Possibly Soviet. He climbed into the tight cabin. The springs in the seat had ceased working years before, and he sank into it like it was a marshmallow.

Lenny handed over twenty dollars, and the guy peered at him from under a dirty straw hat but said nothing in return, just started the truck turned around. They drove through a tiny village and, within minutes, were ascending into the mountains that ran through the middle of the island like a spine.

The road was pitch-black but for the weak headlights, and Lenny had no idea where they were going.

"*¿A dónde vamos?*" Lenny asked.

"Mata."

"*¿Cuánto tiempo?*"

"*Par de horas.*"

A couple of hours indeed. Lenny tried to settle in for the ride but found he had to hold on as he slid around the slick bench seat. His arms ached by the time they began to coast down from the mountains.

They entered another small township as the land flattened out near the coast. The truck rattled past an open cut section where a rudimentary landing strip had been carved out of the wilderness. The engine groaned as they rose back up a hillside with a series of ramshackle buildings then coasted down again, along what looked like the main street of the town. There were some mud brick buildings that appeared commercial in nature, and then a few more houses. As the buildings ended and the jungle resumed, the driver pulled over beside a rickety barn.

"*Vamos,*" said the driver.

Lenny grabbed his pack and rifle and followed the man into the barn. He was hit by the stench of feces and damp animal hide, despite there being no livestock inside. The man didn't turn on any lights.

"*Espera aquí.*"

"Wait here? For what?" He held up his palms and shrugged his shoulders.

"*Mañana.*"

"Tomorrow?"

"*Un hombre vendrá mañana.*"

"What man? *¿qué hombre?*"

"*Un hombre,*" the man repeated. "*Espera aquí.*"

The man backed out of the barn, pulsing his palms toward the dirt floor, telling Lenny to wait. Then he closed the door, got in his truck, and drove away.

Lenny didn't sit—it was too dark to see any furniture or equipment so the dirt was his only option. He waited five minutes until his eyes acclimated and his ears lost the hum of the truck and fell in tune with the silent town and its surroundings.

There was no way he was staying in the barn. If the smell wasn't bad enough, Ventura's words rattled around in his head.

Don't trust anyone.

Lenny eased out of the barn. In the moonlight, he removed the Makarov from his pack and clipped the holster to his belt. Then he slipped the pack onto his back and slung the rifle strap over his shoulder.

The tiny town was dead. A beach spread out down a grassy bank from the main street. Like the one he had seen in Panama, this was no tourist destination. He noticed only two vehicles—a motorcycle by a house and a silver van beside a mud-brick building that appeared to be a general store. It was here where Lenny looked up to see a telephone line from a pole down to the building. And an antenna had been erected on the roof.

In the east, the first indication of dawn was visible across the water, so Lenny headed up the hill, past a few more houses then a line of buildings. At a cinderblock building, broken farm equipment was scattered around the property. Maybe a repair shop. Lenny went around back and used an old oil drum to climb up on the roof. Its corrugated iron sloped slightly on one side, with a flat section covered in tar paper, where he removed his pack and lay down.

He pulled out his binocs and observed the town. In the predawn, people began appearing from homes, making their way down to boats on the beach and paddling out. As daylight slowly spread across a small bay, the water turned from black to gray. The telephone line fully revealed itself, and Lenny confirmed there was only the one building with a connection, likely the only place with electricity.

At the end of the village was the barn, and beyond it a field with some mules behind a post-and-rail fence, which seemed to be keeping the jungle beyond at bay more than any animals in.

Then he heard the familiar sound of boots on the ground. Six men marched in relatively tight formation. They weren't in uniform, just shirts and dirty trousers, but they each had a rifle slung over a shoulder. Bringing up the rear was the straw-hatted man who had driven Lenny across the island. They headed to the farm, where Lenny's driver pointed at the barn.

Don't trust anyone.

The men put their rifles to their shoulders. Two stood outside the door, while two jogged around the back. The last two advanced to the door, opened it, and went inside. After a long minute— likely checking all the dark corners for the hiding American—they reappeared. The obvious leader of their little militia, who had remained outside, turned on the driver, yelling at him. The driver shrugged like it made no sense. *He was in there*, Lenny imagined him saying in Spanish. The leader shouted some commands, and they spread out to search the farm.

When they came up empty, they took to the streets. The leader remained in the yard by the barn, looking up into the hills beyond the farm, his slack posture betraying his thoughts.

They had lost the American.

After the men searched the town, including a walk around the building Lenny lay on top of, they reconvened back in the yard. The morning was now in full sun, so Lenny reached into his pack and put on a khaki cap, then took out a pack of laminated papers secured on a keyring, copies of photographs. Pictures of men. All the major players: Pablo Escobar, Jorge Luis Ochoa Vásquez, Fabio Ochoa Vásquez, Carlos Lehder, and more. Lenny wasn't sure what Ventura was thinking. None of them were going to turn up in a rural village in Cuba. But some of the photographs were of more junior men, the ones who did the work, took the risks. They might be here, so Lenny looked one more time and compared them to the faces he saw through the field glasses. There were no matches.

Then a Jeep—an ex-army, American workhorse—roared into town. Two men were inside, their hair blowing in the breeze, sunglasses on. The Jeep skidded to a stop in the yard at the barn. The passenger jumped out and strode over to the leader of the militia group, who began to speak. The man took two quick steps toward Lenny's driver, waving his arms as he replied. The driver recoiled some, then pleaded his case.

The new man pulled out a revolver that was tucked in his jeans and shot the driver through the head. He almost flipped backward from the impact. The man didn't linger over the body. He spun around and shouted at the men around him to get out and look.

Lenny saw the flowing black hair and recalled something familiar. He flipped through his photo pack to check one specific picture. He checked again through the binoculars: same guy. He looked thinner than the photo, but it was him.

He was looking at Carlos Lehder.

CHAPTER TWENTY-SIX

LEHDER WAS WHISKED AWAY IN THE JEEP WHILE THE men swept the village one more time. Lenny held the Makarov in his hand in case someone got the idea to search the roofs. He rechecked his rear to confirm that no one could spot him from a higher position. He was safe, unless they came in on a chopper.

The driver's body lay in the yard as the sun rose higher. Lenny sucked water from a canteen and watched the militiamen wander the streets, looking for someone who wasn't there.

As the afternoon became evening, the men disappeared. Fisherman returned and the town came alive. People cooked food, children played on the beach, and the old truck Lenny had arrived in reappeared to carry the driver's body away.

Lenny used the cover of cooking food to eat one of his MRE packs. As the last light sprayed across the water the children were called in and the villagers settled in their homes. It was the rhythm of those who lived primarily without electricity, dawn to dusk, but it was also the familiar pattern of a community that had been overrun by the cartels, trying to mind their business and not get involved. Lenny wondered if the dead driver was a local or a cartel import.

It was dark when the glow of kerosene lamps appeared along the landing strip. Within twenty minutes came the thrum of an aircraft engine, and then a small aircraft landed hard on the rough surface. The silver van burst to life and drove up the dirt road to the runway. The urgency Lenny saw on the beach in Panama wasn't here. Men stood around chatting in the lamplight before opening the hold of the aircraft and forming a human chain to the van, along which was passed the keys of narcotics.

Lenny lost count at fifty, but they kept going and filled the van. A hundred kilograms was the weight of a tall man. Not a massive weight or volume, but when it was sold by the gram, it would hit a lot of customers. Ruin a lot of lives.

After they had finished, the pilot closed up the hold then wandered into the jungle to relieve himself. He didn't seem in any rush to leave. There were no police here, and Lehder had bought everyone else. He owned the silence of the villagers through good old-fashioned fear. As at Norman's Cay, he was acting with impunity.

The pilot appeared from out of the foliage, zipping himself up, then he ambled around the plane, checking the tires and struts and inspecting the prop. Lenny glanced at his watch. The van drove back into the village while all the men but two went down to the beach.

The boat came in within minutes. Lenny assumed it was floating offshore, waiting for a signal. Perhaps a light, perhaps a radio call. It coasted in close to the beach but not all the way; the draft was too deep. It was a pleasure cruiser with three large outboard engines in back, more than enough room for a hundred or so keys of cocaine. Lenny took down the boat's details as the men formed another human chain, from the van down to the beach and into the shallows. The drugs were passed along and then up to two people on the boat. Once they were done, the cruiser was pushed out, the outboards fired up, and it pulled away, destination USA.

At the closest point, Cuba was only about ninety miles from the United States. But from where Lenny lay, watching through his binocs on the eastern end of the island, it was more like three hundred miles. Which got Lenny thinking. Why so far? Sure, this was an isolated area where the Medellín cartel could do whatever they pleased. But the other option wasn't downtown Havana. There had to be plenty of rural options at the other end of Cuba, closer to Florida. Perhaps they preferred to stick closer to Colombia. Maybe the DEA watched the Florida Straits more intensely than the east coast. But extra time on the water surely meant greater risk.

Lenny focused on the airstrip. The pilot had finished his checks, so he got into the cockpit, started it up and turned around, then bumped along, looking like he was never going to gain enough speed. Finally the plane lifted into the air, just over the canopy of trees, and banked away to the south. Back to Colombia.

The two men left at the strip doused the kerosene lamps, and the van returned to its position beside the old store. The men all met in the center of the village, then dispersed to act as sentries. Lenny knew the sentries were for him. There was no reason for guards otherwise. So for the next part, he was going to have to be careful.

He waited for a few hours. The sentries grew slack and bored. Not even a dog barked. He left his rifle on the roof but took his pistol and eased himself down, dropping to the grass with barely a sound.

Lenny moved like a cat through the village. The sentries had made the greatest mistake: they were stationary. Sentry duty was obviously not a regular task. There were no patrols and no rotations. It meant there were routes they couldn't see, but more than that, it kept their energy low. Two men outside the store, just near the silver van, were leaning against the wall, whispering in the moonlight, occasionally peering down the main street. But they expected no trouble.

They didn't get any. Lenny cut around the rear of the buildings and across the yard behind the store. He glanced once more at the phone line. It was a risk, but one worth the effort. Plan A was preferable to Plan B. And he wasn't sure Plan B wasn't really Plan H, where everything had gone to hell. Ventura had been clear. So had Lieutenant Colonel Yardley. No one was coming to help. If he tried to get back across the island to Guantanamo, he would probably get shot by his fellow Marines, if he wasn't captured by the Cubans watching the base. Getting off the island was going to take more than a fishing boat with two oars. And the way things were playing out, a fast escape was likely to be the only kind available to him.

Lenny pulled a kit from his pack and picked the old lock on the back door of the store, then he slipped inside. He waited for his eyes to adjust, preferring not to alert the sentries out front by using a flashlight. There was a line of shelving on which in the US he might have seen corn flakes, or bottles of Coke, or laundry detergent. But the shelves here were all but empty.

He moved to a long counter that acted as the checkout, although there was no register. Cans of some kind of meat and a few cans of beans lined shelves built in the wall behind it. There was a sack of cornmeal on the floor. Then he noticed a large metal box. A shortwave radio, which explained the antenna.

He stepped over to a sign that read *Correos de Cuba* and wondered how much mail actually got sent from such a place. Perhaps it was a lot, given the dearth of phone lines. Lenny found the phone tucked in under the counter. He picked up the handset to check it was connected and heard a garbled but definite tone.

Lenny removed his shirt then flipped up the collar and pressed where the material came to a point. There were two stitches missing in the trim seam, and he squeezed a small piece of paper out of the hole. Then he unfolded the paper on which he had written the important numbers that he hadn't commitment to memory. One was the number for his calling card. There was no local number in Cuba to call, so he had jotted down the number for the Bahamas.

He dialed, unsure if a call to the Bahamas would even go through. When it did, he let out a sigh. He asked to be put through to the second number on his list. When he was connected, the sound of the voice on the message service was garbled as if transmitted from a tin can down a string. After a beep, he whispered his message, hoping it was loud enough to be heard at the other end: *2300 tomorrow, call this number*. He read off the digits written in the middle of the phone's dial. Then he tapped the switch hook to end the call, and he made another.

He winced, trying to hear through crackling and background noise.

"O'Malley's."

"Can I speak to Brian Purchase?" he said, as loud as he dared.

"Hold on."

There was a cheer in the background, then, "Cox?"

"Do you guys ever impound drug boats in Miami?"

"It happens."

"I need a fast one. For at least a few days."

"You're in Miami?"

"Negative. But I got a guy who can pick it up. I hope. Can you do it?"

"I can try. What's this about?"

"You know the answer to that."

"I don't want to know. Okay. I'll see what I can do."

"I'd appreciate it. My life might depend on it."

"I'll try hard."

"Roger that. I'll call you tomorrow. Same bat time, same bat channel."

"What about bats? I can't hear you."

"Forget it. I'll call tomorrow."

Lenny ended the call and tucked the phone back under the counter. He stood, shirtless, for a long while, listening for sounds of movement from outside. When it was quiet, he slipped his shirt back on, retreated out the rear door, and headed back to his rooftop to get some sleep.

CHAPTER TWENTY-SEVEN

THE NEXT DAY WAS A LONG ONE. LENNY WAS TRAINED to stay still and silent for long periods, but he never learned to enjoy it. The sun beat down on his rooftop. The business below him opened up, and two men spent the day doing not much of anything other than talking, listening to anti-American propaganda on the radio, and smoking.

Lenny used the time to scope out targets around the village. There wasn't much to see. A few buildings, a few farms, the barn. There was the airstrip and, about a mile to the west, a wisp of smoke from a small camp where he assumed the guards were bunking down. He wondered if Lehder was there. It was hard to imagine the boss staying in such poor conditions, but he seemed like a hands-on kind of guy. Perhaps the downfall of Norman's Cay had spooked him.

The rhythms of villages were driven by the environment, not the people. Day was for working; night was for sleeping. When it was hot, people kept out of the sun, conducting their business in the cool of the morning and evening. Meals were eaten then, and kids played on the beach. There was a monotony to it but also a dependable constancy.

The drug smugglers kept to their schedule as well. The sentries largely abandoned the village during the day, retreating to their camp for siesta. Then, as the sun fell, they ambled back into town. The landing strip was lit at the same time as the previous night. Aircraft arrived like clockwork, the van fired up, and the drugs were moved down to the beach.

A boat came in that night. This one was a cigar boat, shaped like a bullet, full running lights on as if they didn't care who knew they were there. The human chain loaded the drugs, and the boat was pushed out. As it turned around, Lenny wrote down the name on the transom. It sparked half a memory, as if he had heard it somewhere before. The plane departed, the van returned to its post by the store, and the sentries retook their positions.

Lenny kept his schedule as well. He eased down off the roof and stretched his back out, then he crept through the village to the store. The guards weren't there. He saw their silhouette on the other side of the street, sitting on the grass bank that led down to the beach. They were smoking and talking in whispers.

He made his way inside and sat on the floor behind the counter with the phone in his lap. When it was time, he used his calling-card number and was put through to a bar in DC. He asked for Purchase.

"Cox?" asked the DEA man.

"Yep."

"Where are you?"

"You keep asking that."

"But this time I want to know. Where am I sending a boat impounded by the United States government?"

"Cuba."

"I'm sorry, I thought you said Cuba."

"You asked."

"Are you trying to cause an international incident?"

"Not today. You got something for me?"

"I do, but I'm not sure it's a career move."

"The container you intercept in San Francisco will be."

For a moment there was nothing but crackle down the undersea line. "Alright, Cox. There's a boat at South Beach Marina."

"It would be best if it wasn't US registered."

"They're drug boats, Cox. They're never US registered. That's why they're so hard to impound."

"Give me the details."

Lenny scribbled down information on the boat and told Purchase who to expect, if anyone.

"And if he doesn't show?" asked Purchase.

"Put it back in the impound. And forget we ever met."

"You want me to keep hanging out here?"

"At the pub? No, go home to your wife."

"You're sure?"

"I appreciate your help."

Lenny hung up and waited. The clock ticked over to eleven. He heard no sounds from outside and realized he was holding his breath. This was not a call he could make. It had to come to him. Which meant the phone had to ring.

He snatched it off the hook midring.

"Yankee Doodle, that you?"

"Lucas," said Lenny. "Thanks for calling back."

"No worries, mate. How's things?"

"Delicate. Did you finish your thing up in Newport?"

"Yeah, mate. We won the whole bloody thing."

"You won the America's Cup?"

"Australia II, yep."

"And your thing?"

"Like a joke, mate. A Frenchman walks into a bar. Clunk."

"I don't know what your plan is now…"

"I was headed home when I got your call."

"Where are you?"

"You said you needed me in Miami."

"I did. I do. So where are you?"

"Miami."

Lenny smiled. "I might need a little bit of help."

"Causing trouble."

"Something like that."

"My specialty, mate. What do you need?"

Lenny told Lucas where he was, what he planned, and what he needed from him.

"No worries," said Lucas. "I'll go see your guy."

"I appreciate it."

"Your shout when we get back."

"First round's on me. I better get off."

"Yep, I reckon you should. I'll catch ya on the flip side."

Lucas hung up. Lenny stashed the phone under the counter and was about to get up when he heard the rear door open. He froze, unsure if he had forgotten to close it properly. He pushed back into the shadows at the counter and watched two sentries step quietly through the store. There was no time to move and nowhere else to hide. Lenny put his hand on his sidearm and held his breath.

Both men moved toward him. One glanced out the window right above Lenny. Then the second one called the first, and they moved to a cupboard, which they opened.

Lenny watched the second guy take two cigars out, hand one to his buddy, and close the cupboard. Then they walked across the store and out the door.

After expelling a long breath, Lenny waited. He sat in place for another half an hour, in case the men were waiting in ambush. But there was no movement, so eventually Lenny got up to a crouch and looked through the window. The men were sitting back on the grass, gazing at the moonlight on the water, the orange glow of cigars between their fingers.

Lenny left via the rear door and snuck back to his position on the roof.

CHAPTER TWENTY-EIGHT

LENNY GOT THREE HOURS SHUT-EYE THEN SET OUT WITH his pack and the Makarov, leaving the sniper rifle behind. He kept to the edge of the jungle, where the foliage threatened to overtake the fields. He eased up the rise to the flat clearing behind the village.

The airfield was dark. Lenny could make out the open field and the outline of trees on the other side. There was no movement other than a breeze, and he had seen no evidence that anyone was guarding the space. There really wasn't anything to guard—no hangar, no fuel depot, no terminal. He hunkered down by the edge of the field for a while, then removed his pack and pulled out one of the toys Ventura had given him.

Lenny lit a flashlight but kept it inside his pack so it offered a subtle glow. He took some C4 explosive and inserted a detonator. Then he removed a timer and connected the detonator wire to it. After taking one more look around, Lenny dashed out onto the runway. He glanced back toward the village to get his bearings then moved to the spot he wanted and dropped to his knees. The rough ground was pockmarked already, so he turned over some soil to make a divot and pushed the explosive into the hole. After covering it with a piece of grass, he ran back to his position in the trees.

It wouldn't pass close inspection, but he hadn't seen anyone checking out the landing strip at all. He hoped it would stay that way. He dashed back to his pack then wended through the jungle vegetation and down to the barn. After he was done there, he crept into the village to where the silver van was parked. He left gifts behind everywhere he went.

Lenny returned to the repair shop and was lifting himself up onto the roof when he saw the light coming from the west. It was a dull glow about a mile away, as if someone had gotten up in the night and turned the kitchen light on. Except there were no houses west of the village, and no electricity even if there were. Something was happening at the camp.

Lenny dropped back to the ground and set off for a look. He kept to the periphery of the village then took the jungle route in favor of the track leading out to the camp.

It was predawn when he reached it. There were about ten tents scattered in a small meadow, and a wooden hut that might have passed for an old man's garden shed back home. A man tended a campfire, over which he was cooking something in a large pot.

The illumination was from a collection of kerosene lamps hanging near a Jeep—the same Jeep that had taken Carlos Lehder to the barn, before he had shot the driver dead. A canvas cab had been installed. Two men in dirty jeans and work shirts were moving from the hut to the Jeep, carrying something small and delicate in their hands as if baby birds were about to hatch. When each man reached the Jeep, he held his cupped hands up to a third person in the rear of the vehicle who took the objects from them and placed them gently into the Jeep.

Lenny tried to discern what they were but, in the dim light, couldn't tell. The men didn't move quickly, each one reaching the Jeep every five minutes then returning to the hut.

Lenny crept around the camp until he was behind the hut. He

slipped out of the thick trees to the back side of the only solid building around and placed some C4 against its base. As he did, he listened keenly for any noise inside, but heard only the sound of bugs in the night. He moved away, back into the jungle, and hung his pack in the fork of a tree, then slowly eased around toward the Jeep. Whatever they were packing sure didn't look like bricks of cocaine.

The sun was throwing its first light across the Caribbean, but the jungle kept the camp in darkness. Not for long. Lenny saw one of the men deposit his offering, then the man in the Jeep jumped out and together they walked across to a tent and disappeared inside.

Lenny watched. The guy tending the pot over the fire had his back to the Jeep so, before daylight broke and everyone appeared for breakfast, Lenny stepped from the shadows and hustled over to the vehicle. He lifted up the canvas top and looked inside.

The back of the Jeep was empty.

He frowned in confusion for a moment, but it was a moment too long.

The sound of weapons being cocked jerked his attention from the Jeep. He turned slowly and raised his hands away from the Makarov holstered on his belt. Three men each pointed a rifle at him. A fourth man wandered across the camp with a broad smile.

Lenny watched Carlos Lehder saunter over to him.

"Curiosity killed the cat," said Lehder. "Isn't that what they say?" His English was accented but perfect. Lenny noted that despite his swagger, Lehder's eyes were bloodshot, his face haggard. "My name is Carlos."

"Morning, Carlos. I'm Armand. Armand Hammer."

"Hammer?" Lehder cocked his head. "I like your name."

"Thanks."

"So you are here to what, arrest me?"

"No, Carlos. I'm not a cop."

"Oh, you're not a cop. You're a soldier?"

"I'm a tourist."

"A tourist? I don't think American tourists are welcome here."

"Of course they are. I've been to Jamaica many times."

"This is not Jamaica, señor."

"You're funny, Carlos. I like you."

"I am a very likable fellow. I have many friends, including President Castro."

"You've been to Cuba?"

"We are in Cuba now."

Lenny chuckled. "You keep saying that. I don't think Jamaicans like being confused with Cubans."

"I don't either, but the mistake is yours. So, Mr. Hammer, or whatever your name is, why don't you step into my office." He jutted his head toward the hut.

"I think I'm good here."

"Oh, I insist."

One of the men held his rifle at Lenny's chest, while a second stepped forward and took the pistol from Lenny's holster. Then they moved aside to allow him a path to the hut.

The sun was spreading across the camp, but the hut swallowed all the light it was offered. As he ducked inside, Lenny realized it really was more like a garden shed. There were no windows at all; the only light broke in through the door. He stood there, allowing his eyes to adjust a touch, until he was manhandled into a chair. His hands were pulled violently behind him and his wrists were tied to the chair, then Lehder stepped into the small space and lit a kerosene lamp. The others retreated outside and closed the door.

Lenny saw a military cot and a table with another chair. It wasn't exactly the Four Seasons. Lehder lit a cigarette and took a single drag before setting it in an ashtray on the table.

"I don't think living rough suits you, Carlos."

"I assure you, I can do it as rough as you, Señor Hammer."

"You look tired. I'm just saying that as a friend."

"Thank you, but I won't be here much longer. You, however, are going to die here."

"What makes you say that?"

"Because I learn well. I have been too lenient in the past, given chances to people who betrayed me. I give no such chances to you. So you will tell me what I want to know, and then I will end your life mercifully. Or, you will hold out or lie to me, so then I will pull all your fingernails out and then you will tell me. After that, I will hand you to my Cuban friends, and mercy will become but a dream for you."

"That doesn't sound like something a friend would do."

"I know you are a spy. But for who? The DEA?"

"I work for a property developer. He wants to build a resort here."

"There are no resorts in Cuba."

"Of course not. But this is Ochos Rios, Carlos. Prime real estate."

"You are testing my patience. How are you getting your information out?"

"I usually send postcards. You got any?"

Lehder picked up his cigarette, but he made no move to smoke it.

"That stuff is bad for your health," said Lenny.

"No, señor. It is bad for yours." Lehder stepped over to Lenny and ripped his shirt open, his amber chest hair glistening with sweat. He held up the cigarette and sucked on it, letting the end glow orange in the dim room. He leaned in close and blew the smoke into Lenny's face, then he slowly crushed out the fiery end on Lenny's chest.

Lenny grimaced as it burned his flesh. Lehder pushed the cigarette into the skin until it was extinguished, then he let it fall to the floor. Lehder leaned in close to Lenny, their noses almost touching. Lenny didn't let out his breath, just looking him in the eyes as the cartel boss grinned out the side of his mouth.

"So, which hand shall we start with?"

"Doesn't matter. I bite my nails. Good luck with that."

Lehder nodded then stepped back and surveyed Lenny, stopping at his boots. "Your feet then." The kerosene lamplight gave his features a devilish look that chilled Lenny.

A knock at the door disturbed Lehder's glare, and he flinched in anger. He pulled the door open and spoke to the solitary guard just outside. Lenny noted the day was brighter. He watched Lehder listen to the guard then step into the threshold of the hut, half lit in sun.

"I have to attend to some business," said Lehder. "I will leave you to my Cuban friends."

He doused the kerosene lamp and looked back at Lenny from the doorway. "Mr. Bruno will be here this afternoon. You will talk to him."

The day moved slowly. Without his vision, Lenny took everything in through his ears and nose. Breakfast was served to the men and then cleaned up. Men marched away. The Jeep drove off then returned. Lenny tried to come up with a plan, but his mind whirred with self-recrimination. The Jeep loading had been a trap, and he had waltzed right into it. Baby birds, indeed. He knew better. It was cocky, and he paid the price. But now Carlos was being cocky. His turn would come. Lenny tested the binds and found them too tight to break, so he waited. Sometimes the other player's move revealed a path forward.

When the door opened again, the sun was fading. Late afternoon. The rhythms of the village told him the boats would be in and the cooking would begin soon. Time was of the essence. Lenny's mind was focused. The knowledge that he had placed an explosive on a timer in the back of the hut, and that he was now positioned on the interior side of that plank wall, helped sharpen his mind.

The door guard lit the kerosene lamp then went back outside.

A man with a long ponytail and a mouth like a pencil line

stepped in, his demeanor darker than Lehder's.

"Mr. Bruno, I presume?"

The man looked at Lenny through dull, colorless eyes. "You are going to tell me everything." He spoke perfect English with a heavy Cuban accent. "And I mean everything. Every question I ask has a purpose, and you will answer to my full satisfaction."

"And if I don't?"

"It is not a matter for debate. When I am done, you will want to reveal the truth."

"So you're gonna kill me. Doesn't sound like much of an incentive to talk."

"No, I will not kill you. My comrades have use of you alive." He dropped a canvas tool bag on the table and unclasped it. "You will just wish you were dead."

"How cliché."

Mr. Bruno nodded but said nothing. He removed a small hammer, like he was going to test Lenny's reflexes. Next, a hacksaw. Then a pair of pliers. He took his time, as if deliberately building tension. Maybe the technique had been perfected on the workers and political prisoners he usually tortured. Lenny's muscles tightened and his breath quickened. Mr. Bruno didn't look like a fun guy to be around.

He placed three blades on the table. The first was long and thin, the second curved like a sickle. The third looked like a standard chef's knife. Mr. Bruno picked up the first blade and held it high, inspecting the quality of the edge. Lenny's mind went back to the drug dealer he had left tied up in the warehouse in Washington. He wondered if he was still there.

Mr. Bruno stepped directly in front of Lenny and came in close, reeking of sweat and stale coffee. The man didn't smile. He just held the knife out. With two flicks he opened the shirt wider where Lehder had already ripped the buttons. Then he put the knife against Lenny's chest and drew it down about three inches. It didn't hurt. Not at first. The blade was sharp. But then the body registered an open wound and the pain rushed in. Lenny clenched his jaw.

Mr. Bruno held the knife up again to see the blood dripping from the tip. "This blade is perfect for filleting fish. And for removing skin."

Lenny didn't want his skin removed, but he said nothing. He focused on controlling his breathing. The panic was setting in at the edges, and he needed to smother it. He needed to focus. He needed this lunatic to not be directly in front of him.

"Let's take a little bit off, hmm?" said Mr. Bruno. He put the knife against Lenny's pectoral muscle again. Then he took a single step to the side to angle the blade.

Lenny smiled.

For the first time, Mr. Bruno offered a facial expression—a frown—but it barely made a ripple on his forehead. "One last smile. I like that."

"Not sure you do," said Lenny.

Lenny kicked out with his right foot and sunk his boot into the side of Mr. Bruno's knee. Mr. Bruno fell like he'd been shot, his legs collapsing under him. As he hit the dirt floor, Lenny stood, still tied to the chair. Mr. Bruno had landed on his shoulder and immediately rolled toward Lenny, lashing out with the blade. The tip sliced a nick in Lenny's thigh and then continued out in an arc. Lenny moved forward as if nothing had happened.

He slammed his right boot into Mr. Bruno's throat. The crack of cartilage told Lenny what he needed to know, but he instantly pivoted and stepped out with his left foot, driving Mr. Bruno's arm into the dirt, where the knife slipped from his hand.

Lenny quick-stepped like a football player and kicked the knife away, then dropped to his knees at Mr. Bruno's side. He was clutching his throat, making low gurgling sounds.

"Sorry, pal. The bad news is your larynx is crushed. The good news is it will stop hurting in a minute or two."

The man snarled as he turned his colorless eyes to Lenny. Even on death's door, the guy offered barely an expression. Certainly not fear. Perhaps a touch of confusion.

"That's what you get for working for cash over ideology. Sloppy work. They never tied my feet, as you can now see. You should have checked. I assume your Cuban army torture goons are a little more professional than Carlos's guys."

Lenny didn't wait for a response. He turned and walked toward the table like a hermit crab with a chair for a shell. He spun around and fell back into the chair, sitting with his back to the table. He bounced twice until his arms hit the table edge, then he stood a little so he could fumble along the table until he reached the chef's knife. He grabbed it and straightened up in a half crouch, his cut leg burning from the effort. Turning the knife slowly in his hands, he began sawing at the ropes holding his wrists to the chair.

The knife slipped from his sweaty grip several times, but that was the point of working over the table. His legs trembled from holding the squat position, but eventually the knife did its job and he was able to pull the bind apart.

The chair fell to the floor, and Lenny again checked on Mr. Bruno. His lifeless eyes stared at the roof. He felt the Cuban's pulse and found nothing.

Lenny stood and grabbed the kerosene lamp. He figured good torture took time and the guard outside was unlikely to disturb him. But he couldn't be sure, so he moved fast, searching every corner of the hut. It was the only solid building in the camp, which made it Lehder's billet. And Lehder's billet would be equipped for any emergency.

Lenny found a brown bag under the cot. Inside were two small pouches. He ripped the first one open: a mirror, some razor blades, and a bag of white powder.

"Carlos, you've been sampling the product. That's bad business."

Lenny tossed the pouch aside and opened the larger one. Jackpot: a field med kit. Lenny had a kit of his own in his pack, but it was yet to be determined if he could reach it, and this wasn't the movies—people didn't get cut or shot and then just romp around the jungle without worry. In this heat and humidity, wounds festered and turned septic fast. And although Lenny wasn't planning on moving here, there was a real chance he might get stuck in this jungle for some time.

He used antiseptic cream on his leg and chest then taped down gauze with Band-Aids. He ran an elastic bandage around his thigh and tossed the kit on the floor. He hung the lamp back on its hook then grabbed the filleting knife and went to the door.

After cracking it open, Lenny softly called to the guard outside: "Amigo." And he moved away.

The door opened a touch more, and the guard stepped halfway into the dark space. Lenny launched from behind the door and plunged the filleting blade deep into the guard's neck, pulled him into the room, and pushed the door closed with his foot.

The guard was dead before he hit the floor. Lenny pulled the rifle strap out from under him and checked it over. It was a short-barreled, selective-fire rifle. Hard to say in the dim light, but Lenny suspected it was an AMD-65, a variant of the Soviet AKM, developed in the sixties by the Hungarian army. A compact design with a pistol grip option. Lenny removed the thirty-round magazine and confirmed it was full. He took the spare mag from the body and readied to leave.

If no one had seen him lure the guard into the hut and no one saw him leave he could sneak into the jungle—that was Plan A. He figured he had a 20 percent chance of success. He gripped the rifle like a pistol and opened the door.

The cook was standing over the fire, looking directly at him. For a long moment they stared at each other, like neighbors out to collect the morning paper in their pajamas. But the cook didn't offer Lenny a nod. Instead he screamed.

"*Americano*!"

CHAPTER TWENTY-NINE

LENNY TOOK THAT AS HIS CUE. AS MEN DASHED IN FROM the perimeter of the camp, Lenny fired several shots toward the fire. He didn't want to hit the cook specifically—that guy likely wasn't armed—but he wanted the enemy to second-guess chasing him.

They didn't. Orders were yelled in Spanish, and men ran across the camp toward Lenny. He headed for the only cover. It was close to dinner time, so most of the men were in camp, and they all headed in his direction. Lenny burst into the trees to the west, firing a shot behind him every few seconds, charging through the jungle and away from camp.

His pursuers were fast and relentless. They didn't worry about stealth. Lenny leaped over fallen logs and crashed through heavy foliage. Branches thwacked him in the face and punched him in the guts.

Then he stopped. He scurried behind a tree and heard the men spreading out behind him. But they were moving forward more rapidly than they were spreading out, and they weren't taking time to do a full sweep. Their quarry was on the run, so they were too.

So the quarry sat tight. Lenny slid between a shrub and the tree trunk, squatting in case he needed to move. He felt the wound in his leg rip, but he ignored it and focused, finger on the trigger. His was breathing hard and his ribs ached like he might have broken something, and he winced as he tried to slow his heart rate in the name of making less noise.

The jungle thrashed around him as the men tore through the foliage in their hunt. A pair of boots landed within two feet of Lenny but kept on moving. Lenny gave the line of men a five-second count. At any moment they might stop to listen and figure out he had stopped running, so he pushed himself up the trunk to stand, eased around it, and headed back toward the camp.

It was counterintuitive but Lenny had his reasons, not the least of which was he had left a trail that he wanted to erase. He also suspected they would assume he'd keep running into the jungle in order to regroup. But Lenny planned on doing that elsewhere.

He went swiftly but quietly around the back of the hut to the far side of the camp. He retrieved his pack, slid it onto his back, and headed for the village.

In the fading light, Lenny made it back to the repair shop. He climbed up to his spotting post on the roof to do a quick reconnaissance. Things were a little different. The men were all out and on the move. Those not searching the jungle were forming a perimeter of sorts around the village, from the camp side around to the road that led to the airstrip. Men were posted along the road and, although he couldn't see them, he suspected some were on the airstrip itself. The villagers had taken the hint and were hidden away in their houses. There was no smell of cooking, no kids on the beach. Lehder's men hadn't found their prisoner, so now they were expecting an attack.

That worked for Lenny. As darkness fell, he checked his watch, then slipped the Zastava M76 over his shoulder and carried the AMD-65 he had taken from the guard at the camp. He crawled down from the rooftop and edged between the village buildings and the camp. After checking he was inside the perimeter of sentries, he dashed down onto the sand near the cut of land that marked the western end of the small bay. Lenny tossed his pack into the farthest boat, put his shoulder into the bow, and pushed. It was hard going, the tide having settled since the boat was brought to shore, but with a deep grunt he felt the hull slide, and then slide again before the stern hit water and the packed sand made the job easier.

As the bow reached the water's edge, Lenny moved to the side and felt the sting of saltwater on his leg wound. He gritted his teeth as he climbed into the boat. That was when he realized the fishermen had taken their oars. There was no engine and no way to paddle. It drifted out on the bay for a moment, but quickly lost any momentum.

Lenny looked around at the options and came up with only one. He pulled out the magazine from the Zastava M76 and removed the cartridge in the tube. Then he used the long stock of the rifle to paddle. It was rudimentary and slow, but the tide helped push him to the outskirts of the bay.

Suddenly he saw the lights in the sky. Plural. A small aircraft banked, and another set of lights followed in its path. Two planes. The engines roared as they hit the kerosene-lit landing strip and stopped fast. One after the other. From his position out on the water, Lenny couldn't see where they stopped, but he caught the headlights on the silver van as it pulled away from the store and headed for the runway.

Lenny kept paddling, although it was technically rowing. He faced the shore and rowed out farther but paused when he saw the flashlight beam from the beach. The signal, followed by a speed-boat starting up offshore. Lenny heard it rumble to life, then the running lights turned on, and a forty-foot white cruiser motored toward the beach. He glanced at his watch.

One man on the cruiser worked the controls from the flybridge. Another stood in the semidarkness of the bow, a silhouette against the running lights. Lenny waited for it to pass and checked the deep transom for a name.

Ballyhoo.

It clicked immediately, and so did the names of the previous boats he had watched from his rooftop perch. Which got his mental gears spinning as he turned his focus to the black horizon out to sea. He flashed his light out into the ether. Morse code. One long, three short. Then one short. Again one short. Then short, long, short.

Then he waited and hoped. That someone was seeing his message and that it was *his* someone. And he hoped they didn't run him over in the dark.

"You order a taxi?" The voice crackled though Lenny's radio, so he snatched it up.

"Aye, aye."

"I see your friends are headed for the beach. I'll stick to running dark, so give us another flash every ten."

"Aye, aye."

Lenny gave a long flash of light then killed it. He waited ten seconds and did it again. And again. He was about to do it once more when he saw the white hull materialize beside him. The boat was sleek and low in the water, built like a bullet, its engine emitting a low throb in neutral. A tie line landed in Lenny's fishing boat. He grabbed the line and pulled it in so the two vessels rafted up side-on.

Lucas's smiling face appeared over the side. "So this is Gilligan's Island."

Lenny tossed Lucas his pack then handed him the long rifle.

"It's wet," said Lucas.

"I needed an oar."

Lenny climbed into the speedboat carrying the AMD-65, and the two men shook hands as if they were off on a fishing trip.

"I appreciate you dropping by," said Lenny.

"No worries, mate. Never been to the West Indies. And this

boat's a hell of a good time." Lenny glanced around the fast boat. The cockpit was tight—the thing was built for speed, not comfort.

He untied the fishing boat and pushed it toward shore. He hoped the tide didn't take it too far out so the fishermen could retrieve it in the morning.

Lucas shut off the engine. They heard the slapping of water on the hull and the rumble of the cruiser as it turned around and backed in toward the beach. Then someone cut the engine and the night fell quiet.

"Like a delivery van," said Lucas, watching through a pair of binoculars.

Lenny took his own glasses from his pack. "Hull's too high to load from the front."

"Looks like a Bertram Forty-Two."

"I didn't know you were a boat guy," said Lenny.

"Sure. You navy knuckleheads aren't the only ones who know boats."

"I'm not navy."

"What's with all that 'aye, aye' rubbish, then?"

"It's what we say in the Marines."

"Sounds like navy to me, mate. The rest of us just say 'okay.'"

"Roger that."

"There you go."

They watched through field glasses as the headlights of the van lit up the grass before the sand. The sliding door opened, and the men formed their human chain across the beach and into the water. The cruiser was too large to get right into shore, so two of the men were chest-deep at the stern. Leaning down from the small swimming platform, the guy who had been on the bow took packages of drugs as they were handed up. From their position, neither Lenny nor Lucas could see this guy on the platform. But they could see the boat's driver above him reaching down to take the keys of cocaine.

"Where's a tidal wave when you need one?" said Lucas.

Lenny smiled but didn't speak. He was moving his binocs along the chain of men back to the van. After the last key was taken from the van, the door was slammed shut, but the driver didn't get in. He was watching something from the west. Lenny shifted his view and saw another set of headlights entering the village, bouncing as the vehicle screamed across the dirt track from the camp.

It was the Jeep. It stopped short, to the right of the van. The passenger got out and ran around to the van's driver side. Lenny framed the man's face in his field glasses.

"Lehder."

That explained the second aircraft. Carlos was either satisfied with his new logistics point or freaked out by an American in the jungle. Lenny put down the binoculars and picked up the long rifle. He pushed home the cartridge and pulled a bullet into the chamber. Then he kneeled on the deck with the rifle braced across a rear-facing seat.

"That's the last brick," whispered Lucas. "The boat's bugging out." He heard no response so he looked down from the field glasses. "What are you doing?"

Lenny didn't answer. He was slowing his breathing and moving the crosshairs onto the target.

"You're taking a potshot?" said Lucas. "It's dark, you're on water, and it's got to be three hundred meters."

"I thought four."

"Give or take, mate, but still. You're gonna give away our position, and you'll be lucky to hit a barn door."

"You'd hit a beer can from here."

"Not from a rolling boat. And the fellas in the Bertram are heading off."

The cruiser accelerated.

"We're gonna lose them," said Lucas.

"One second."

"It's your picnic, mate."

Lenny took in a deep breath and then gently exhaled. The crosshairs rested on the face of Carlos Lehder, lit up by the van lights beside him. He was grinning, pleased with his work. Lenny dropped the sights to the bigger target—Lehder's chest—and thought about Melodie Masters. He saw her father, failure etched across his face from his inability save his daughter, a burden he would never shed.

Lenny pulled the trigger.

As he did, the wake from the cruiser hit their hull, and his eye was knocked away from the scope. He quickly got the crosshairs up again. The beach was chaos. The man standing beside Carlos Lehder had been hit. He was lying on the grass in front of the van.

Lehder had reacted fast—perhaps it was not the first time someone had tried to shoot him—and dashed to the Jeep, which reversed hard, then headed for the airstrip. Men on the beach who had frozen at the sight of their comrade's chest exploding, started running and randomly shooting out into the water. At least one plane started up its engine.

Someone jumped into the van and peeled away. The two light sources tore away so the beach was plunged into darkness. There was nothing more to see.

Almost nothing.

"Time to go, you reckon?" asked Lucas.

Lenny checked his watch. "Five seconds."

"You got a date arriving?"

Lenny shook his head.

His timers clicked over, and the night erupted in pandemonium. The C4 buried on the airstrip exploded underneath one of the planes. The blast caught the aviation fuel in one wing and spewed a ball of fire high into the night sky. Then the barn blew apart.

The van pulled in beside the store, and the driver killed the lights. It was dark for a mere moment. The explosive Lenny had placed in the van blasted the vehicle into a low lunar orbit, flipping it until it landed on its roof. An explosive placed under the radio inside the general store sent the device through the roof, tearing the phone line from the pole and setting the store ablaze. A smaller detonation from the camp told Lenny that the hut was no more.

"You done now?" asked Lucas.

Lenny smiled. "Would you call that trouble?"

Lucas glanced at the fires across the village. "For someone. Hopefully not the locals."

"Their homes are mud brick. Safe as houses."

"In that case—"

Another explosion rocked the village, as the fire from the aircraft had reached the tank in the second wing. It punched the already burning plane sideways into the second aircraft, which burst into flames of its own. Lenny didn't know if Lehder was inside the second aircraft, but he hoped so.

"Let's go," he said.

Lucas started up the speedboat but left the running lights off so they could spot the cruiser's lights in the night.

They saw nothing but black.

CHAPTER THIRTY

"They're running without lights," said Lucas.

"In Cuban waters that's probably the smart move, even if they are working for Carlos."

"Miami's northwest."

"No," said Lenny. "Head due north."

"You know something?"

"You got charts?"

"I put 'em below so they wouldn't blow away."

The two men jumped down the hatch in the cockpit to the lounge in the bow, with a map table where Lucas had a chart held down with cans of spaghetti.

"We're here, right?" asked Lenny, pointing at the eastern end of Cuba.

"Right. So northwest to Miami."

"I don't think they're going to Miami. I think they're afraid of using the Florida Straits because the DEA and Coast Guard are watching it pretty hard."

"So where, then?"

Lenny pointed at a dot on the map that didn't register as land. "I think they're headed through here. Norman's Cay."

"Why? What's there?"

"Not much of anything, barely populated now. But it's a marker. It's a destination if they get into trouble. I think they're headed up north toward Eleuthera and then cutting west from there, around Nassau, and onto the US. They're making it look like they're coming from the Bahamas rather than Cuba, and doing most of the distance out of US waters."

"It's your call, mate, but if you're wrong, you'll never see them again."

"I know. But I saw the name on the boat. *Ballyhoo*. I remembered seeing it on a log a guy on Norman's was keeping. Boats that had no business being there were passing by close enough to be watched through his binocs."

"Using it as a marker buoy?"

"More than that: Carlos Lehder's marker buoy. I'm willing to bet someone else on that island is tracking those boats. One of Lehder's people. Letting him know that the shipment is where it should be."

Lucas used his fingers to measure the distance. "It's gonna take that Bertram twenty hours to reach that point."

"How fast do you think we can do it?"

"In this thing? Eight hours. Six, if we max it out."

"Let's not max it out. Eight will do us."

They checked the chart again to get their heading, then both climbed up to the cockpit. The seats were snug like racing seats, and the boat lived up to its billing—it flew across the water. Lucas pushed a cassette tape into the deck and Stevie Ray Vaughan's "Pride and Joy" filled the cockpit. The warm Caribbean air swooshed across the windshield, so they tucked in low and hoped they didn't hit anything they couldn't see.

They took hour-long shifts, one at the wheel and the other watching for the lights of the cruiser. The first light they saw was a dull glow from Duncan Town on Ragged Island, and by the time they made a wide berth around the shallows off Exuma Island, they figured they were well ahead of the cruiser.

It was predawn when they pulled into the marina at the southern end of Norman's Cay. Lenny had dumped the holster since Lehder had taken the Makarov, so he gripped the AMD-65 in one hand as they tied up.

Lucas suggested a breakfast of canned spaghetti. Lenny suggested he get rid of his remaining MREs instead. They ate rice and chicken and watched the sun rise and turn the dark water turquoise. For a long while, neither man spoke. Sometimes there were no words.

The solace was broken by a man at the end of the dock aiming a shotgun directly at them.

"We've got company," said Lucas.

Lenny waved. "Novak."

"Ventura?" Approaching, Novak lowered the shotgun.

Lucas cocked an eyebrow.

As he stood up to greet their visitor, Lenny winked at Lucas.

"I wasn't sure you'd still be here," Lenny said to Novak.

"I'll be gone in a few days. What the hell are you doing back here?"

"Tracking a boat. You still got that logbook?"

Novak furrowed a brow that was already well wrinkled by the endless sun. "Yeah. Come and get a coffee, then."

Lenny and Lucas disembarked and followed Novak through the debris and burned-out buildings back to his villa.

"Unique fixer-upper opportunity," said Lucas.

Novak eyed him. "Aussie or Kiwi?"

"Aussie, most days."

Novak frowned again, like he didn't get the joke. Lenny didn't blame him for that. Novak put some water on to boil and found three coffee cups. Then he removed his logbook from its hiding spot and gave it to Lenny.

"What are you looking for?"

"Boat called *Ballyhoo*."

"The Bertram? Yeah, it's been by here two or three times."

"You see it go south in the last few days?"

"Nope, but most of the traffic I see is headed north. What's your interest in it?"

"It's full of narcotics."

Novak was shaking some instant coffee into the cups and stopped abruptly. "You don't say."

"We're guessing it's about half a day behind."

"Assuming it's coming this way," said Novak, pouring water in.

"Your log suggests they are. And we think Carlos might have someone else here on the island keeping a similar log and relaying it back to him. You know of anyone else here?"

"Yeah, there are a few who come and go. But the one who'd be doing that? You want Steve. He's a local, used to work for Carlos. Probably still does."

"We don't need Steve. Actually, it would better if he doesn't know we're here."

"He doesn't go down to the marina much."

"Why's that?" asked Lenny.

"Because that's where my boat is, and I don't trust him. I told him I'd shoot him if I saw him down there." Novak handed out the coffee. "What's your plan?"

"Wait here until *Ballyhoo* turns up, and if it does, follow it out to sea."

"And then?"

"Make sure the cargo never gets where it's going."

Novak nodded like this was a reasonable idea.

"They ever pass at night?" Lucas asked.

"Not going north. Always daylight, or at least twilight."

"So your mate Steve can see them."

"He's no mate of mine."

"Yeah, I'm getting that."

Lenny and Lucas finished their coffee. Lenny told Novak they planned to nap under the palm trees for a while.

"Stay near the radio," said Novak. "If I see them, I'll let you know."

"Appreciate it," said Lenny. "And listen, *Ballyhoo* is expected to arrive somewhere in a couple of nights. If it doesn't, Carlos's people are likely to start looking here first."

"I get you. I'll be gone."

Lenny and Lucas thanked Novak and walked back toward the dock. They took the rifle, a radio, and the cushions from below, and set up under the palm trees.

Lucas lay back with his hands behind his head. "Well, ain't this the life."

"Not too shabby," said Lenny as he watched the gentle ripple of blue water.

"I could get used to this." Lucas closed his eyes.

Lenny smiled in agreement and closed his eyes as well.

———

THEY WOKE EARLY IN THE AFTERNOON AND TOOK A swim. After they had air-dried, they checked their weapons and settled in to wait. They hadn't eaten since their early breakfast, but the growing anticipation kept hunger at bay. The sun sunk toward the water, and they checked comms with Novak. He had seen nothing.

They heard it before they saw it. From the tree cover, Lenny looked through his binocs and spotted the Bertram cruiser motoring by. It was close enough to suggest it was going to stop for the night, but it kept its heading to the north.

The radio crackled. "You got that?" asked Novak.

"Loud and clear," said Lenny. "Remember what we said."

"Roger."

Ballyhoo motored onward. Lenny and Lucas wandered down

to the dock and fired up the cigar boat. They were in no hurry. They weren't going to lose the cruiser again.

Lucas took the controls and backed out, then turned to follow. As they passed they saw Novak standing on the shore, watching them. Lenny waved. Novak did not.

Lucas let the cruiser get well ahead. Had the men on *Ballyhoo* looked back, they would have barely seen the sleek, fast boat. Within a half hour, the twilight was gone and the boat ahead was nothing but running lights.

The cruiser was doing about fifteen knots, so Lucas increased his speed to catch up. Ninety minutes after leaving Norman's Cay they did just that. They could see one man in the light of the instrument panel on the flybridge.

"There are two guys," said Lucas.

"The other one might be asleep. They'd have to split shifts. Can't stay alert for two days."

"Ready?"

"Ready."

Lucas hit the throttle and closed in fast. They weren't getting on board a moving boat, so they had to stop it. The first method was to get their attention and ask them to slow down. Lucas pulled alongside and saw the driver on the cruiser do a double take. Lucas picked up his radio and called on VHF channel 16.

"*Ballyhoo*, this is *Open Sesame*. We have an injured crew member and require assistance." The guy on the flybridge had heard the call because he focused on his radio for too long, but when Lucas repeated the call, the guy looked over at them and shook his head.

Lucas pulled in closer, the two boats almost touching. Bumping them was an option, but being in the smaller vessel wouldn't help. Lucas waved. Lenny waved. Then Lenny ducked as the driver fired a handgun at them.

Lucas pulled away and around. "That's not very friendly."

"Plan B," said Lenny.

Lucas hit the throttle and pulled alongside again. The guy fired another shot, and Lucas launched ahead, then cut across the cruiser's path. The cruiser weaved hard, but the bigger boat wasn't designed for high-speed maneuvers, and it lost all momentum as it was engulfed in its own wake. Lucas turned back and punched the throttle, and within a few seconds was upon the cruiser.

Lenny moved fast. As the two hulls butted against each other, he jumped up and grabbed the cruiser's gunwale. Lucas spun away to distract the driver as Lenny used a stanchion to lever himself up onto the forward deck of the cruiser.

The distraction wasn't enough. The driver spotted Lenny and fired two quick shots from the flybridge. Lenny wasn't a fan of having the low ground. He also couldn't hide behind the raised deck that provided headroom for the saloon below, in case the other guy was watching through the portholes.

Lucas played chicken one more time, cutting right in front of the cruiser. The driver eased around him this time, keeping his speed but not his focus. As he turned the wheel, Lenny pulled out the AMD-65 and fired a double tap.

He was better at it than the helmsman. The guy went flying backward and disappeared from Lenny's view. The man was now somewhere in the water. True, he had a bullet wound in his chest, but after falling backward off the flybridge, he had broken his neck as he hit the gunwale, then flipped again off the boat and onto the swimming platform below. His head had settled at an angle that was all wrong, and as the cruiser continued through the cigar boat's wake, the body was jostled off the platform and into the deep.

Lenny didn't wait to say goodbye. *You make your choices and you live with them*. He dashed around the deck to the stern, where a ladder led up to the flybridge. He leaped up to the bridge and shifted the throttle into neutral, then held his gun out front and moved down to the hatch. He swept the space below then walked into the saloon.

It was spacious, with blue shag carpet and a leather sofa. He swept aft and saw a galley tucked in aft on the port side, and access down to the engines on the starboard. Another set of steps led along the starboard side to the forward staterooms. Lenny kept his weapon trained and stepped down. He pushed on the latch to open the door to the first stateroom, then dropped back onto the step to avoid any fire. When none came, he crouched and made his way around the door. The stateroom held a disheveled bed but nothing more.

The main stateroom was at the bow, and the corridor left Lenny nowhere to go, so he opened the door and pressed in hard against the wood paneled wall. A gunshot rang out and a round hit the woodwork opposite Lenny, so he dropped again and spun into the room, firing at the first target he saw.

The second man fell backward as the round hit his shoulder. He was punched back into the cargo—keys of narcotics stacked high—and slumped to the floor.

"Drop the gun," said Lenny.

"You don't know who you're dealing with."

"Carlos Lehder."

The guy frowned and winced at the same time. "You don't steal from Carlos."

"I don't plan on it. Drop the gun."

"He's going to hunt you down. He's going kill you and your family and your dog."

"I don't have a dog, but he's never going to know that."

"He knows everything."

"Not everything. Now I'm not going to say it again. Drop your gun."

"You shot me."

"I did. And I'll do again."

"I don't even know you."

"But I know you. You're the guy who brings in the drugs that kill people I know."

"I don't force them to do anything."

"That seems to be the company line, but it's no excuse. Now either drop the gun, or I'll shoot you again."

"Screw you." He lifted his gun. Only a few inches.

Lenny fired.

"How we doing?" Lucas called out.

"All clear." Lenny stepped back into the saloon, where Lucas waited, long rifle in his arms.

"One guy's fish bait," said Lucas.

"I know. The other one's not doing so great either."

Lucas nodded. "The drugs?"

"In the stateroom."

"What do you want to do now?"

"Get rid of it. Get rid of all of it."

"Burn the boat?"

"No. I want Carlos to know it wasn't an accident."

"Righto."

"Touch as little as you can," said Lenny. "We don't want to leave prints."

"The only thing my fingers have touched is this rifle."

But Lucas's hands then touched the dead man in the stateroom when he dragged him into the saloon. They checked his ID and confirmed he had a US driver's license. Then they touched the drugs. Lenny and Lucas lugged all the parcels up onto the deck. After checking the wind, Lucas pushed the throttle open just a touch, and with the boats rafted together, both vessels moved slowly forward.

They cut open the plastic and tossed kilogram after kilogram of cocaine into the ocean, spreading the keys out across a mile to dilute the poison in the currents.

"Hope a sea turtle doesn't swim into that," said Lucas.

"It's a big ocean and not a lot of coke," said Lenny. "Not in the scheme of things. It'll dilute pretty fast."

I hope.

Next they wiped down the hatches and door latches and frames. Lucas shut off the engine and wiped the controls and then the railings as he climbed back into the fast boat. He didn't wipe down the five thousand dollars in cash they had confiscated from the galley.

"It won't float out here forever, will it?" Lenny asked.

"Chart says we're off Eleuthera to the east and Spanish Wells to the north. Current should see it found in a day or two."

"Roger that. I want to make sure Carlos knows, if he's still alive. Or whoever takes his seat if he's not."

"We could hang around and make sure."

"In this boat? It kind of sticks out."

"Not in Nassau," said Lucas. "Lots of nice boats there. And in this baby, we can be there in an hour."

"Your round."

"No chance, mate. I just went to Cuba for you."

Lenny smiled. "What do you want, a medal?"

"Nah. Just a beer."

CHAPTER THIRTY-ONE

They tied up at a private marina that was closed for the night, and in the morning paid the manager in cash for a couple of nights mooring without the need for paperwork. Then they used the marina facilities to shower before going downtown to get new clothes. Lenny walked out in board shorts and a palm tree–covered shirt, and dropped the khaki uniform at a dry cleaners. Lucas tossed his clothes in the trash and went for a T-shirt that said *Hang Ten* on the front and a pair of blue shorts small enough to be a passing thought.

They spent the day at a bar with no name and no view. The doors were propped open to facilitate the breeze, but the beers were cold and the regulars were anything but. Lenny and Lucas almost bought a business selling conch fritters from a van.

After another night sleeping on the cigar boat, they discussed a plan over morning coffee and toast with marmalade.

"So how do you ask about a dead guy on a missing boat if you're not supposed to know about said boat's existence?" asked Lucas.

"Walking into a police station feels like the wrong choice," said Lenny.

"But the cops would know."

"As likely as anyone."

"The boat was from the US though, right? So would the embassy be told? Or the US Coast Guard?"

"Maybe, but same theory applies—we can't ask about something we don't know about."

"It's a conundrum."

"It is ..."

"What?" asked Lucas.

"Unless someone else does the asking."

"One of your sneaky agency types?"

"Someone better."

Lenny got a pile of change and sat by the pay phone at the back of the cafe.

"Alice Brooks," she answered.

"Ally."

"Oh, my. Lenny, are you all right?"

"Why wouldn't I be?"

"Where've you been?"

He smiled. "Not sure you want to know."

"Just tell me you're not still in the Bahamas."

Lenny nearly choked getting the word out of his mouth: "Why?"

"State and the AG are both in a flap. A US vessel was found in Bahamian waters with a dead man aboard, an American."

"Where was that?"

"A place called Spanish Wells. Apparently someone found the boat, and when the police boarded they found the body. He had a US driver's license, so they called the embassy. Now it's a diplomatic mess."

"Why?"

"We don't like our citizens getting murdered while abroad, Len."

"Just at home?"

"We're not that happy about that either, but that's not the State Department's problem."

"What's all this got to do with you?"

"It's a boat floating in foreign waters. There are legal implications."

"So who was the guy who got killed?"

"I don't have the name, but he's got a record. Possession with intent to distribute, in South Carolina, I think."

"So a dead drug dealer."

For a moment she didn't reply.

"Please tell me you didn't have anything to do with it," Alice said.

He hated lying to her, but her knowing wouldn't just place her in a professional pickle, it would eat her up inside.

"Actually, don't tell me," she said.

"Have you spoken to the DEA?"

"Why?"

"They watch the seas for drug shipments. Maybe they know the boat."

"That's a good idea, but it doesn't excuse murder."

"Not suggesting it does. But in that part of the world, it's likely to be cartel business."

"The locals don't think so."

"What do you mean?"

"According to State, the local police have their eye on two suspects. Local thugs."

"Locals?"

"That's what I hear."

Lenny said nothing.

"So when will you be back?" she asked. "Do you have any clue?"

"Not much of a clue, but I'm hoping sooner rather than later."

"Well, stay in touch. And stay safe."

"You too."

He wanted to say something more, but the dial tone beat him to it. Instead, he fed more coins into the phone and dialed again. He didn't wait for pleasantries.

"Call me back. Here's the number." He recited the number on the pay phone and hung up.

Five minutes later the phone rang.

"Bahamas again?" asked Purchase, without the bar noise.

"Bit of R and R. Where are you?"

"Diner. The bar isn't open yet. So you got out of Dodge, then?"

"I did. And you remember my original orders?"

"Something about trouble. You in it or causing it?"

"Mostly the latter. I tracked a boat out of you-know-where and intercepted it. It was full of you-know-what."

"And?"

"I got rid of it. But the bad guys didn't make it."

"Boo-hoo."

"They were Americans."

"That's a bit thorny."

"I have a source who says they were known dealers. I can give you details of the one guy left on board."

"You left a guy on board?"

"We want the cartel to know this wasn't an accident."

"Okay. Give me his details."

Lenny passed on the details from the dead guy's driver's license. "State has the full details—they're working with local police."

"So what do you need from me?"

"The police are eyeing some locals as suspects."

"But they didn't do it."

"No, they did not. I need you to get in touch with them, or State, or however you do this stuff, and tell them you suspect the boat of trafficking. That you had it under surveillance as far as Norman's Cay."

"And then what? We lost it?"

"You aren't running joint ops in the Bahamas right now, so you can't watch their entire country's waters. You were waiting for it to reappear. Tell them you believe it to be a cartel matter. Maybe you suspect the couriers of stealing some of the haul."

"I don't have any evidence of that."

"You're not taking it to court, Purchase. The guy's dead. It's just a theory."

"It doesn't prove anything to the locals. They can still go after the suspects they have."

"Yeah, you're right. But it will muddy the water."

"Okay, I'll look this guy up. I'll make a call. I can't fabricate anything."

"I don't want you to."

Lenny hung up and returned to the table to outline his calls for Lucas.

"Do you think that will fix it?" asked Lucas.

Lenny sighed. "No."

"Well, we can't let local people go down for something we did."

"I did it, Lucas. Not you. You can walk away. In fact, I'm telling you to walk away."

"Yeah, nah. Let's not get into that rubbish. If we're on an op, we're in it together. And I don't care who pulled the trigger, it's not right that locals get blamed, even if they are thugs."

"Which we don't know."

"So we find out. Spanish Wells isn't far away."

"What are you suggesting?" asked Lenny.

"The direct method."

CHAPTER THIRTY-TWO

Spanish Wells was a township sitting on St. George's Cay off the northwest end of Eleuthera. Lucas pulled the cigar boat around Russell Island to the south until they came to a cut between the two islands, where fishermen were unloading their catch from a line of large lobster boats. The chart they had picked up in Nassau showed a nasty reef north of Spanish Wells called Devil's Backbone, and the water along the northern beaches showed a maze of sandbars they agreed to avoid.

Rather than answering questions at the main ferry terminal farther up the dock, Lucas pulled up behind a lobster boat. As the sun fell into the western horizon, Lenny climbed up onto the dock, once again dressed in khaki drab, carrying a radio and a Hungarian rifle that was all kinds of illegal on Bahamian shores.

Lucas pushed off the dock and motored away to wait offshore.

Lenny marched up the hill that bisected the island, past sun-bleached homes and parched grass. Some of the gardens were decorated with impressive conch shells. The street was quiet until he arrived at the other side. The cay was only a third of a mile wide and a little less than two miles long, but most of the town was settled at the eastern end. Streets cut north-south across the hill, with a main drag running east-west on each long side, one along the beach on the north shore, the other along the docks to the south.

Lenny reached the main street on the north side. The handful of stores he passed looked closed for the day. There was no sidewalk and no traffic other than the occasional golf cart. One zipped by with three white men on board who waved, so Lenny waved back. Everyone he saw was white, which he hadn't expected on a Bahamian island.

Next to a school Lenny found the police station, a dull light glowing inside. He stepped up to the counter, hiding the rifle below it. A fan was circulating the sea breeze blowing in past open shutters.

One officer in a blue uniform sat at a desk.

"Good evening," Lenny said.

The officer looked up with a serious expression. He was the first Black man Lenny had seen so far on the island.

"Can I help you?"

"I'm looking for the officer investigating the boat that was found offshore."

The officer stood and walked to the counter. "That would me. Sergeant Bridges."

The wiry sergeant's shirt hung from his shoulders as if on a hanger.

"Sergeant, I believe you have a suspect or two in mind."

"I can't speak about an investigation with—what was your name, sir?"

"Lenny."

"Lenny. Well, I can't speak about that with you."

"Not even if I have information material to the investigation?"

"In that case, I would appreciate any statement you could make."

"I won't be making any statement, Sergeant. I just came to tell you that no locals did it, thugs or otherwise."

"Thugs?"

"I heard the local suspects had criminal records."

"How did you come about this information?"

"Through back channels."

"I see. I take it you are with the United States government in some capacity."

"You can take it however you like, Sergeant. Bottom line, they didn't do it."

"Do what, sir?"

"You found a body on board."

"You do seem to know a lot, Mr. Lenny."

"It's just Lenny, and yes, I do."

"Well, since you know so much, I will tell you this: I do have two suspects in mind. With the fingerprints we have, I can place one young man on the boat in question, and the other set will match an associate of his, once I obtain prints from him."

"And the other two sets?"

"I didn't say there were any more."

"But I know there are. One matches the dead man. One will match his accomplice, if you're ever able to get them from South Carolina police."

"What accomplice?"

"The guy whose blood was on the deck."

"How is it you know all this, Lenny?"

"I can't get into that, but I need your word that you won't pursue the local boys."

"I have fingerprint evidence."

"That they were on board. Not that they did anything."

"They can't prove they didn't."

"They don't have to. Last I checked, Bahamian law is still based on English law. Innocent until proven guilty."

"If that is what a jury decides. It is not for me to say."

"Except it is, Sergeant. I know a thing about tight little communities like the one you have here. People are resourceful, and they look after each other. But they also know each other's business. I'm willing to bet that despite your reticence to talk about the case, everyone within ten miles of here knows who your suspects are. And if it goes to court, even if they get off, they will have to live with the rumors. Because I also know that you will never actually prove who did it. I can guarantee it. So those boys will live with that stigma. Or worse, the cartel thinks they did it and comes after them and their families. Do they deserve that? Are they really that bad?"

"One of them is. Or at least he will be. He's no good. That's why I already have his prints on file."

"And the other?"

"Not a bad boy." The sergeant flinched. "No, that's not right. He's a good boy. He has aspirations to become a police officer. He hangs around with the wrong types."

"How will that career work out with a court appearance for murder behind him?"

Sergeant Bridges rubbed his chin. It was the first tell the officer had conveyed. "As I say, the evidence is what it is."

"Except when it isn't. Those boys found a boat and got on board. That's all."

"With what intent?"

"Doesn't matter. Thought isn't illegal. Acting on intent is illegal. So maybe the bad kid was going to steal something, maybe not. But he didn't."

"We'll see about that when I search the suspects homes."

"He didn't kill anyone."

"You seem very confident of that."

"I am."

"Why?"

Lenny stood tall. "Because I did it. I shot both those men."

"You did it? Why?"

"Because I was tracking a drug shipment they carried from Norman's Cay."

"Norman's is out of business."

"For air traffic. But Carlos Lehder's still using it for boats."

The sergeant frowned. "Who do you work for?"

"I can't tell you that. But you know I'm telling the truth. I tracked them, we attempted to board their boat, and they fired at us. Both men on board were shot. One fell into the water, the other died below decks. You found him in the saloon, shot in the head, right?"

"Yes."

"But the evidence suggests he was moved, doesn't it? Because he was. I shot him when he attempted to fire on me in the stateroom."

"Why move him?"

"Because he was lying on several million dollars' worth of cocaine."

Sergeant Bridges clenched his jaw. "And what happened to that cocaine?"

"I cut it open and threw it overboard."

"You threw it away? Why?"

"Because the people I work for don't like drugs. And they're sick of the cartel playing by a different set of rules."

"So you're admitting to murder?"

"No. It was self-defense."

"Says you."

"Correct."

"A court might see it differently."

"A court will never hear it. You won't be arresting me today, Sergeant."

"And why is that?"

"For starters, because you don't have a gun, and I do. But mainly because I was never here. Those boys were never on that boat. Two drug dealers got killed moving product that was going to kill thousands more. I can sleep well enough with that knowledge. How will you sleep if you ruin two young men's lives."

"I can't just turn a blind eye."

"I can't either. That's why I'm standing in front of you right now. I have nothing to gain from being here. But I'm sick of these people, and I think you are too. So don't turn a blind eye. Be proactive. Do something to prevent a wrong before it's too late."

The sergeant looked at Lenny with piercing intensity.

"Answer me one question," said Bridges. "Why leave the boat? Why leave the man for us to find?"

"Because I want Carlos and his merry band to know we're prepared to fight on their level. Our police will still prosecute according to the law, and our agencies will still try to the get these criminals extradited, but they need to stop believing they're immune. They're not."

"But if we fight on their level, how are we different?"

"Intent, sir. Intent."

Sergeant Bridges stood back from the counter and sighed. "I can't stop the rumors. Those boys will still have to live with it. And the cartel might come here anyway."

"Then they shouldn't be here to be found."

"It's not that easy."

"When will this boy be eligible to join the police force?"

"Next year. When he finishes school."

"Does police training happen here?"

"No. In Nassau."

Lenny nodded. "I need to know where they are."

"I can't tell you that. This whole thing could be a lie. You could be working for the cartel."

"I've proven I know what happened on the boat and I know they didn't take anything. I'm not with the cartel. My name is Sergeant Lenny Cox, United States Marine Corps. If you want to do something with that information, that's your prerogative. But don't make me go around town knocking on doors."

"That won't do you any good. They don't live in Spanish Wells."

"Not anymore. I'm sorry about that, but it is what it is."

"Come back tomorrow, sir. I need to think on all this."

"Clock's ticking, Sergeant. Once you give the rumor mill credence, you won't be able to take it back."

CHAPTER THIRTY-THREE

LENNY WALKED OUT INTO THE NIGHT AIR. HE HEADED straight up the hill to cross the island, and when he reached the top, he called Lucas on the radio.

"Come on back," he said.

"I'm back. And I've got some news."

Lenny made his way down to the road that ran along the docks, back to the east end where Lucas was waiting beside a lobster boat.

"You talk to the cops?" asked Lucas.

"Yep."

"What's gonna happen?"

"Not sure. The guy was a hard nut, but he needs to process the idea. Why did you come back already?"

"I started thinking about the boat, *Ballyhoo*. Where it was."

"Where is it?"

"They've got it tied up down the other end of the docks. There were some old-timers down there. They seem to know plenty."

"Like what?"

"Like there are two kids who found the boat, but there's no way they killed anyone. The scuttlebutt is that the cartels did it."

"So maybe the boys won't get caught up in it."

"Maybe. But the old-timers say drug movement through here is pretty common. If other bad sorts get the idea these boys took a few keys, they might get a visit."

"I told the police sergeant the boys shouldn't be here if anyone comes looking. I just don't know who they are."

"I do," said Lucas. "I told you. The old-timers know plenty."

Lenny and Lucas climbed down into the cigar boat. It chugged gently out toward Eleuthera. There were channel markers directing boats toward a dock, but Lucas turned south along the coast for about a mile, until they saw a cluster of lights the chart called the Bluff Settlement.

Lenny sat on the bow and directed the boat in toward the shore until the hull ran aground on the sandy bottom in knee-deep water. They jumped out and marched up onto the beach and into the town beyond. There were no signs and streets were more like pathways, but Lucas had been given directions. They agreed that he would hang back since Lenny looked more official in his khaki nonuniform.

The door knock was answered by a petite woman with a hard stare. "He's not here," she said with an accent much thicker than that of Sergeant Bridges.

"Who's not here?" answered Lenny.

"Anybody."

"I wish that were true."

"You have no business here."

"But I'm here anyway, and I want to keep Philip out of trouble."

"He didn't do nothing."

"I know. I was there. He wasn't, not until later. Not until after. But now his name is associated with what happened, and bad people might come looking for him."

The woman's face crinkled like she wasn't sold on Lenny.

"Are you Philip's mother?"

"Yeah."

"My name is Lenny. I know he didn't do anything, but others might not see it that way. I'd like to talk to you about keeping him safe."

The woman pushed the door open, brows still furrowed. Lenny stepped into the one-room home with a section cordoned off with fabric, where Lenny assumed the sleeping quarters were. A lanky man in a buttoned-up shirt stood in the middle, eyeing Lenny with suspicion.

"What are you, GI Joe?" he asked.

"Something like that, sir, yes," said Lenny.

They didn't invite him to sit. He stood at ease and explained what he knew, about Philip and his friend finding the boat, about boarding it, about the body. He told them he knew the boys had done nothing but had no evidence to support that in a court of law, and that a court might be the least of their worries if the cartel got wind of them.

"I told you that Leo was bad news," said Philip's mother. "That's his friend."

"Philip's a good boy," said his father. "He wants to become a policeman, you know that?"

"I do. And I think the best thing for him is to get away from here. I don't think the court thing will amount to anything, but the other thing might. It would be better if he wasn't around."

"You're telling us he should leave his home?" said his mother. "Where do you think he would go?"

"Do you have any family in Nassau?"

"Everybody have family on New Providence," said his father. "But he only got one year to go in school."

"Can he do it in Nassau? That's where the police academy is, right?"

The couple looked at each other.

"We need to ask him," said his father. He stepped out of the house and came back a moment later with a thin young man in tow. He looked like he might be in middle school—the word *man* didn't quite fit him yet.

His father explained who Lenny was and what he was proposing. Philip said he hadn't done anything, and Lenny countered by arguing that he knew that was so, but things could go badly anyway. It would be best to make lemonade out of lemons.

"My sister lives in Nassau," his father said. "But we need to get some money to pay his fare on the ferry."

"Don't worry about that," said Lenny. "I have a boat that can get him there in an hour. But we leave tonight. This rumor needs to end now. He isn't here and he hasn't been for a month, understand?"

"You think I'm going to give some white stranger my son?" said Philip's mother.

"I understand," said Lenny. "And I don't blame you. But we don't have a lot of time to get to know each other."

"I will go with you," said Philip's father.

Lenny was going to argue the point but decided it was pointless. He was some white stranger with a very thin story, and he would do the same in the circumstances.

"As you wish."

"How will you get back?" asked Philip's mother asked her husband.

"I'll get him settled, then I'll find a way. A fishing boat or something."

"I can give you ferry fare," said Lenny.

"I don't want to go," said Philip.

"There's no future here, son," said his father. "You want to be police, you gotta go to Nassau sooner or later."

"Your father will settle you. We'll follow as soon as we can," said his mother.

Lenny said he'd step outside and let them talk, but he needed to find the other boy too.

"He's no good," said Philip's mother.

"We can take him somewhere else, but he should also leave. For both their sakes."

Lenny walked out and listened to the sounds of the night: crickets and a distant television.

When the door opened, Philip stood before Lenny, bag in hand.

"I trust you with my boy," said his mother.

"I understand."

"Do you have a gun?" asked Philip's father.

"I'm unarmed. I have one in the boat."

"How do we know you won't turn it on us once we're on the water?"

Lenny glanced at Philip's mother. He knew where these questions were coming from, but he spoke to her husband.

"I'll give you that gun before we get onboard. You can hold it for the crossing."

Philip's father looked at his wife who nodded. "I'll take you to Leo," he said.

As they moved to leave, his mother came outside. "Why you doing this?"

Lenny wanted to tell her the truth. That his plan, his actions— to leave a boat out on the water in order to upset the cartel—had affected their son in a way he never intended. Maybe it was just the right thing to do. Maybe it was his responsibility. Maybe it was guilt.

"It's my job, ma'am. Your boy got mixed up in this thing by accident. He doesn't deserve to suffer for it."

Philip's father led them to a similar house around the corner. He spoke with a man at the door while Lenny waited in the shadows, then he called Lenny inside.

Leo had a hangdog look, as if he'd been given a talking-to by his mother. He was taller and older than Philip. A man, but barely. His father spoke.

"The police already came," he said.

"Sergeant Bridges," said Lenny. "I know. I've spoken with him."

He regarded Lenny's khakis like he was in full-dress blues. "You think this is the best thing?"

"I do."

"I got a cousin in Nassau. Owns a restaurant. Maybe my son can find some use for idle hands."

"I'll take him there," said Lenny.

"How much will this cost?"

"Nothing. It's on the United States government."

"And how will we know they're safe?" asked Leo's father.

"Philip's father is coming with us. We can squeeze you in, too."

"No. I can't leave here." He looked at Philip's father. "You can go?"

"Yes."

Leo's father nodded at this. "Alright, then."

"Is there a phone nearby?" asked Lenny.

"The general store got one."

"Can you get in this late?"

"Joffra will open it for us."

"We'll call when we get to Nassau." He looked at his watch. "Let's say three hours from now."

"You must have some kind of fast boat."

"It's like a rocket."

Both young men smiled.

"Let's do this," said Lenny.

Leo went to pack a bag, and Lenny saw another boy watching from around a doorway. He looked to be midteens, with Leo's hair but not his body type.

"What's your name, young man?" Lenny asked.

He shied away, but his father prompted him to reply.

"Courtenay," he said.

"Nice to meet you, Courtenay."

"Is this you?" The boy held up a small green army figure holding a field radio. It was the same kind of army man Lenny had played with as a boy on base.

"Yes," said Lenny. "That's me."

Courtenay's eyes widened and he smiled, then he disappeared as his brother swept past him.

Lenny led Philip, Leo, and their fathers to the beach. The boys tossed their bags in the boat and got in. Lenny asked Lucas to hand Philip's father the long gun. The AMD-65 was hidden in the bow and would stay there unless required.

Lenny and Philip's dad got in and Leo's father shoved the bow out into deeper water. As Lucas fired up the boat, Lenny saluted. He didn't know why. Leo's father saluted him back. For some reason, he understood that.

CHAPTER THIRTY-FOUR

They motored back to Spanish Wells. The dock was dark, so Lenny used a flashlight to help Lucas pull into the ferry dock. The island was well and truly closed up for the night.

"I won't be long." Lenny walked down the dock and up the hill. When he got to the police station, a yellow light shone outside but everything was pitch-black within. He took a quick look around then crouched at the door.

It took thirty seconds to pick. He stepped inside, hopped up on the counter, and spun around to drop into the room on the other side. He wasn't sure where print cards from a current investigation would be kept, but he was going to start with the desk where the sergeant had been working.

The lamp on the desk flicked on, revealing the sergeant seated there.

"I thought you'd be back."

Lenny stood up straight but said nothing.

"Looking for this?" He held up a white card with black finger prints on it.

"As it happens."

"You don't care much for due process."

"Actually, I prefer it. I like laws. I abide by them most of the time."

"But not when you're breaking into police stations and destroying evidence."

"I'm not a zealot. I don't believe any system is perfect."

"Except yours."

"Even mine. Especially mine. If my system was perfect, I wouldn't be standing here right now, and those two boys wouldn't have gotten involved. And I'm far from perfect."

"But you're always right?"

"Nope. But about this? Yes, I am. And you know it."

"What makes you think that?"

"Because you're here alone, and you're still unarmed."

Sergeant Bridges stood. "I do believe in due process."

"I hope so."

"I got a call from your Drug Enforcement Agency in Washington DC. They provided me with prints from two felons they had in their files. Drugs, prostitution, racketeering. They are a match for the two sets of prints we found on the boat."

"Two sets of prints?"

"That's right. Just two. The dead man, and I'm sure the other set belongs to his accomplice lost at sea."

"Someone might dust the boat for more prints. Our FBI, for example."

"Your DEA man suggested that wouldn't happen until the boat was back in US custody, and well, that would be too late. I believe a local man hired to maintain boats mistakenly cleaned the wrong vessel. No more prints to be found."

"When did that happen?"

"Sometime tomorrow morning."

Lenny nodded. "And those prints in your hand?"

The sergeant picked a trash can half full of paper off the floor and put it on his desk. He dropped the card into the can and lit the paper. Over the fire, he looked at Lenny.

"Lot of mistakes on this one," Lenny said.

"It seems."

"You're not going to look good."

"And yet, I'll survive."

"People will talk. Lots of police get paid off by the cartel."

"Yes, people will talk. People always talk. Especially on a small island."

The two men looked at each other for a long moment.

"I should let you get home," said Lenny.

"I appreciate that. I'll make my way over to Bluff tomorrow. Let folks know we haven't found anything but to keep their eyes open."

"Sounds good. But not everyone will be there."

"I expect not. There's not a lot of opportunity here."

Lenny jumped onto the counter and swiveled over it again.

"And Sergeant Lenny Cox, United States Marine Corps," said Bridges, "you will become the stuff of legend. People will whisper stories of the military man who passed through the night, but it will be as if you were never here. It would be best if it stayed that way."

"It's a shame," said Lenny. "It's a nice island you've got here. But I agree with you. I was never here."

CHAPTER THIRTY-FIVE

Lenny called the store in the Bluff from a beach hotel and let Philip and his father talk to his mother to confirm they were safe in Nassau. Then they handed the phone to Leo so he could speak with his father. The five of them slept on the boat.

In the morning they delivered each young man to his relatives. The boys were bemused by the sudden change of circumstances but hopeful nonetheless. Lenny gave their relatives five hundred of the confiscated dollars to help set them up, and ferry fare to Philip's father could return home when he was ready.

That afternoon Lenny sat on a barstool under a palapa shade, watching Lucas help a family set up an umbrella on the beach. The bartender carried a phone over to him.

"Your call, Mr. Cox."

"Thanks, Thomas." Lenny took the handset. "Cox."

"Nassau now?" said Purchase. "How do I get your job?"

"It's not for you. I go outside the beltway."

"We've got eyes on the container. Due in San Fran in a few weeks. You sure I shouldn't tell the task force?"

"I guarantee it. The president wants his photo op in the war on drugs, and that will be it. But not everyone in your town wants you to find it."

"I don't want to know, do I?"

"Correct. Thanks for calling the sergeant in Spanish Wells."

"You bet. It wasn't a lie. Those two were dirtbags. You did the world a favor."

"Some of the world."

"Huh?"

"Nothing. It's been good working with you."

"I'll send you a photo of the bust."

"I'm sure I'll read about it in the *Post*."

Lenny hung up and sipped his beer. The phone rang, and he picked it up. "Cox."

"Your orders were to mess with the cartel and get the president a public win," said Caan. "Instead you almost start World War Three."

"You sent me there. And I assure you, the cartel got the message all right."

"Blowback?"

"Nope. I was never there. Nothing to find. Not even a sandwich wrapper. I've done this before."

"What's the win?"

"Let's just call that one a slow burn."

"What does that mean?"

"The president's gonna love it. He's from California, right?"

"What does *that* mean?"

"It means I'll write you a briefing paper one day. You want I should keep going? Ramp up from trouble to chaos?"

"No. For now, stand down. Castro is blaming us for explosions north of Guantanamo. We need to lay low."

"What's the president saying?"

"He's smiling and saying, 'Prove it.' You're back on the Marines' dime, got it?"

"Aye, aye."

Caan hung up.

Lucas wandered up from the beach, slid onto a stool, and sipped the beer Lenny had ordered him. The next call was outgoing.

"Alice Brooks."

"Hey, Ally."

"Let me guess, you're in Manitoba."

"Not this time of year. Sitting at a beachside bar in Nassau."

"Some guys get all the luck."

"You should come down. Take a little break."

"Can't. It's a madhouse here."

"The Spanish Wells thing?"

"No, oddly that's gone quiet. The police are saying they never had a local suspect. All prints match those they got from the feds for two known drug smugglers. They're calling it a cartel dispute."

"So why the madhouse?"

"I suppose you'll hear about it eventually. But not from me, okay?"

"This isn't my first rodeo, Alice."

"I know. The prime minister of Grenada has been assassinated."

"Grenada? As in Spain?"

"No, that's Gran*ada* with a long *a*," said Lucas. "Grenada— sounds like hand grenade—is an island nation in the Caribbean. Former British colony turned socialists."

"Is that Lucas?" asked Alice.

Lucas saluted.

"He says hi."

"Why is Lucas with you in the Bahamas?"

"Long story. I'm telling you, get down here. This Grenada place can look after itself."

"Wish I could. When are you coming back to Quantico?" Alice asked.

"Soon, I think. Just gotta call Lieutenant Colonel Yardley, but it looks like I've outlived my usefulness here."

"Give me a call when you're in town."

"Count on it."

She hung up, and Lenny sipped his beer. "You know Grenada?"

"Not really," said Lucas. "Down near Barbados, I reckon."

"I don't know where that is."

"Yeah, but you don't follow cricket."

"There is that."

Lenny picked up the phone again. "One last work call and I'm done for the day."

He called Quantico and waited to be put through.

"Cox?" said Lieutenant Colonel Yardley.

"Sir."

"You've been having some fun?"

"Some days more than others." He put his hand to the fresh stitches in his chest.

"You're safe?"

"Sitting in Nassau. Should be able to get a flight to Miami tomorrow. Next day at the latest." He said it before he remembered that he had mailed his passport to Alice. "Actually, it might be a little longer."

"Forget that, Cox. Things are happening."

"Don't tell me. Grenada."

"What do you know?"

"The PM's dead."

"The commie army down there killed him."

"I think they're socialists."

"A distinction the president does not care about one little bit, so neither do we. But the wheels are moving. There's a medical school there. Six hundred American students. The administration does not want a repeat of the Iranian hostage crisis."

"So?"

"We've got no eyes, Sergeant. They're commies, so we have no diplomatic mission. We need to know what's going on. Can you get there?"

Lenny glanced at Lucas. "I'll see what I can do."

When Lenny hung up, Lucas was looking at him with a rapidly expanding grin.

"Grenada's a Commonwealth country, you say?" asked Lenny.

"Until seventy-nine, when the socialists took over."

"Australia's a Commonwealth country too, right?"

"It is."

"You guys have, like, operational agreements and such?"

"You bet."

"You like commies?"

"Not much."

"We got a boat."

"Grenada's over a thousand miles from here."

"Oh."

"But I know a bloke with a plane."

"You do, huh?"

"Just need petrol money."

"I've got four grand in cash."

"That'll do it and then some."

"So?"

Lucas smiled. "I better call home and tell them I'm gonna be late for tea."

***

READERS' CREW

Sign up to AJ Stewart's readers' crew for freebies, competitions, updates on new books, and free introductory ebooks to some of AJ's other series.

Visit ajstewart.com/lenny.

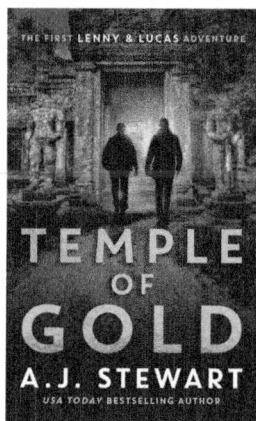

IF YOU ENJOYED THIS BOOK

One of the most powerful things a reader can do is recommend a writer's work to a friend. So if you have friends you think will enjoy Lenny and Lucas's adventures, please tell them, or pass the book on.

Your honest reviews help other readers discover Lenny and Lucas, so if you enjoyed this book and would like to spread the word, just take one minute to leave a short review. I'd be eternally grateful, and I hope new readers will be too.

ALSO BY AJ STEWART

Miami Jones series

Stiff Arm Steal

Offside Trap

High Lie

Dead Fast

Crash Tack

Deep Rough

King Tide

No Right Turn

Cruise Control

Red Shirt

Half Court Press

Past The Post

The Ninth Inning

Big Thaw

Devil's Backbone

Below The Belt

Making The Drop

Three Strikes

John Flynn series

The Compound (novella)

The Final Tour

Burned Bridges

One for One

The Rotten State

Lost Luggage

Lenny & Lucas series

Temple of Gold

Danielle Castle novella

Little Packages

Baskin Island Mysteries

Clearer Waters

* Three Strikes and The Compound are only available to members of AJ Stewart's readers' crew.

ACKNOWLEDGMENTS

Thanks to Lisa Kaitz for seeing the things I don't see, and asking the questions I don't think to ask.

Thanks to all my beta readers who send me feedback. Your keen eyes and support is appreciated more than you know.

This story is based on the real war on drugs but is fictional, so any actions by people real or imaginary is exactly that: fiction.

Any and all errors and omissions—and the bits where I just changed it because reality didn't fit the story—that's on me.

ABOUT THE AUTHOR

A.J. Stewart is the USA Today bestselling author of the Lenny and Lucas adventures, the John Flynn action thriller series and the Miami Jones Florida mystery series.

He currently resides in Los Angeles with his two favorite people, his wife and son.

AJ is working on a screenplay that he never plans to produce, but it gives him something to talk about at parties in LA.

You can find AJ online at
www.ajstewart.com

![f] facebook.com/TheAJStewart

Printed in Great Britain
by Amazon

42825829R00155